Restored

(FAITH UNDER FIRE TRILOGY, BOOK 3)

Gwen Sutton

2017 Gwen Sutton
All rights reserved.

ISBN: 0692858512
ISBN 13: 9780692858516
Library of Congress Control Number: 2017903955
Lift Him Up Productions Inc., Alexandria, VA

Praise for Gwen Sutton's original novel,
All Means All, If You Believe
(Faith Under Fire Trilogy, Book 1)

"I was totally unprepared for the early cliffhanger in the prologue. This reveals the true creativity of Author Gwen Sutton."

"This book is an awesome read."

—Valerie Rouse, Readers' Favorite Reviews

"An exciting read that is sure to keep readers on the edge of their seats."

"I found the novel hard to put down, as I was eager to see what would happen next in this unpredictable and deeply emotional story."

"An incredible and suspenseful fiction novel. Very realistic and compelling."

—Lucinda Weeks, Readers' Favorite Reviews

"Many lessons can be learned from this book."

"Author Gwen Sutton is a strong voice in the Christian fiction field, and I certainly hope she is hard at work on her next novel."

—Chris Fischer, Readers' Favorite Reviews

"A book filled with characters that her readers will connect with, root for, and continue to think about long after the book is finished. If that isn't the hallmark of a great author, I'm not sure what it."

"Author Gwen Sutton is certainly one to keep an eye on."

—Tracy Slowiak, Readers' Favorite Reviews

"The ultimate messages of faith and forgiveness ring clear, providing the novel its most uplifting, thoughtful scenes."

"Readers of faith may revel in these characters, their mistakes and their triumphs."

—*Kirkus Reviews*

Praise for *Endurance*
(Faith Under Fire Trilogy, Book 2)
An International Book Award Winner!

"I don't know the last time a writer has moved me so much."

"Five stars and many, many more for Sutton's great job!"

"Sutton proved it once again that some people are just born with a natural talent that comes to them as easily as breathing."

—Rabia Tanveer, Readers' Favorite Reviews

"I loved this book. Loved. It."

"A heart-wrenching tale of atrocity and redemption."

—Tracy Slowiak, Readers' Favorite Reviews

"Wow…Author Gwen Sutton has provided her readers with an absolutely wonderful piece of work in her new novel."

"Simply a great read."

—Chris Fischer, Readers' Favorite Reviews

"An emotionally charged, and at times heart breaking story…The subject matter of this well-written book…can move you to tears in places."

"There are plenty of surprises and twists to the story too as the battle for good over evil plays itself out."

"A brave story about atrocities that shouldn't happen. But also a story about resourcefulness, hope, courage, and endurance."

—Hillary Hawkes, Readers' Favorite Reviews

"This book reaffirms the need for the world to come together in the fight against human trafficking. Gwen Sutton delivers this message in a very compelling way."

"I was profoundly moved."

—Faridah Nassozi, Readers' Favorite Reviews

Dedications

To my Lord and Savior, Jesus Christ.

To my extraordinary husband, Swindell Sutton. You are my inspiration, my heart, and so much more. Words cannot adequately express what you mean to me.

To my amazing aunt, Ms. Ethel Armstrong. Thanks for always being there for us, even when we did not know that you were. We love you, Aunt Ethel.

To the millions of people with mental illness, and their families, around the world.

Preface

Restored is the final novel in my Faith Under Fire Trilogy regarding the Jones family's tragedies and triumphs. This family's thrilling, emotional, and inspirational saga began in my original novel, *All Means All, If You Believe*, continued in my second novel, *Endurance*, and comes to a dramatic conclusion in *Restored*.

My intent was not to create a trilogy when I wrote my original novel, but God inspired me to continue the story until it was complete. Thus, *Restored* is the final sequel in the Jones family's journey. While not absolutely necessary, I recommend that readers read the previous novels before reading *Restored* for better enjoyment of the complete story.

The Jones family's story, although a work of fiction, is not unlike many of our own stories. It is infused with peaks and valleys, highs and lows, the pleasant and the offensive. Their story covers a wide range of relevant social issues including suicide, child abuse, HIV/AIDS, and human trafficking. Such issues are as pertinent and prevalent in society today as they will be for the foreseeable future.

Restored takes a profound look at mental illness—a devastating disease that affects millions of people around the world. My hope is that *Restored* will create a greater understanding about mental illness and generate more compassion for the millions of people who, through no fault of their own, suffer from this serious disorder.

Prologue

Dereka is running for her life. The ground is cold and wet underneath her bare feet, and her arms are covered with chill bumps due to the night's brisk air. Wearing only a thin nightgown, she races across the front lawn and grabs hold of the tall chain-link fence. She hesitates slightly and looks around nervously to see if anyone has followed her. Then she slowly and painfully slides her toes and fingers through the small openings in the fence and starts climbing upward. The rough wire cuts into her flesh, causing severe pain, but Dereka keeps going. She has to escape from the child sex-slave house where she and other girls are being held captive. She has to get help for them before it's too late.

When Dereka is near the top of the fifteen-foot fence, she hears the sound of a door opening. She looks back and sees three men emerge from the house, one of them carrying an assault rifle and a flashlight. They are her captors, the evil Tavaras brothers, with one of their guards. Dereka knows if she's caught she'll be taken to the shed and tortured nearly to death. Pure adrenaline and fear compels her forward. When she reaches the top of the fence, there are three strands of barbwire mounted there. Dereka doesn't take time to consider the pain her next action will cause. She grabs the barbwire with her bare hands, and climbs over. The sharp wire tears into the flesh of her hands, arms, and legs. Dereka cries out in pain.

Once she's over the barbwire, Dereka drops to the ground, landing heavily on her left side and injuring her leg. She grimaces in pain and lies on the ground for a moment. She thinks about Sun-Yu, Jia, Emma, Gabriela, and her other friends still trapped in the basement of the house. They're depending on her, and she can't let them down. Dereka struggles to her feet and limps as fast as she can into the dense surrounding jungle. She stumbles blindly through the thick brush, barely able to see where she's going, with only the brightness of a nearly full moon to light her path. Thorns pierce her feet and branches scratch her face and body as she staggers forward. She can hear the sound of the men's voices and see the light from their flashlight as they close in on her.

"Help me, Jesus. Please help me, Lord," Dereka prays. Soon she comes to the top of a deep cliff. There's nowhere else for her to run. The men are getting closer and closer, and the light from their flashlight is getting brighter and brighter. Dereka's heart races as she stands there, cold and shivering in her thin nightgown. She hopes against hope that they will not find her. But then suddenly they're there, shining the flashlight full in her face. Dereka looks down the deep cliff and sees nothing but darkness below. She doesn't know what's at the bottom of the cliff. But she's sure it can't be worse than what she's already been through or the pain she'll suffer if they take her back to that place. Even death itself couldn't be worse.

Dereka jumps. Her body tingles with the sinking feeling of weightlessness as she careens faster and faster toward whatever lies below. Dereka braces for impact.

A Lost Soul

Dereka screamed and sat straight up in her bed. Her heart was beating fast and sweat poured down her face. Her eyes darted about wildly as she looked around in fear. Then she breathed a sigh of relief when she realized she was home, safe in her bed.

"It was just another bad dream," she murmured. "Thank God."

Dereka lay back down in her bed and stared up at the ceiling. Although it had been six years since she was rescued from a child sex-slave house, the terror she'd suffered there still haunted her in both daydreams and nightmares. *Will it ever end*, she thought sadly. Her family and friends knew that Dereka had struggled mentally and emotionally when she first returned home after being abducted and sold into child sex slavery, but they thought she was doing fine now. But Dereka knew better.

She sat up, turned on the nightstand lamp, and picked up a pen and her journal. Sleep was impossible now. Writing helped, somewhat. So she wrote.

> *I'm not okay. I do my best to pretend I am. I try to put up a good front for my family. But I'm not okay. Far from it.*
>
> *How could I ever be okay after what happened to me? I was only thirteen when I was kidnapped and taken to that horrible place in Colombia. For five horrific years I was held captive and forced to do despicable, degrading things for the pleasure of sick, perverted men. For five long, miserable years my body was ravished and abused by the scum of the earth. I can still see their beady eyes peeking out from beneath the masks they*

wore to conceal their identities. The masks they wore to hide their faces from the victims of their sick depravities. I can still smell the stench of their sweat and vile semen. I can still feel the pain of their violent, lust-filled thrusts into my body.

There were twelve girls, including me, trapped in the basement of that godforsaken place. A place ironically called La Casa de Placer or the House of Pleasure. The girls became my family, and I'll never forget how kind they were to me. Sun-Yu helped me so much when I first got there. When she died, I wanted to die too. Sometimes I wonder if I would have been better off dying there. At least my torment would be over.

There were times I didn't think I would make it out of that dreadful place. Times that I thought I would die there, be stuffed into a black trash bag, and be buried in the dense jungle like my dear friends Sun-Yu and Crystal. My heart still hurts for them. I think of them every day rotting away in some shallow grave. I can't get it out of my mind. It could have been me. Maybe it should have been me.

As far as I know, only a few of us, including Jia and myself, made it out of there alive. Poor Jia. She was the youngest of us all. Only nine years old when I got there. I'll never forget how her eyes looked back then. Jia had the saddest eyes I'd ever seen on anyone, no less a little girl. And she never said much back then. She'd just look at you with those big sad eyes. If she had something to say, she'd whisper it to her big sister, Sun-Yu, who'd say it for her. Sun-Yu was my best friend there. She really loved Jia and took care of her as best she could. After Sun-Yu died, I did my best to take care of Jia. Now she and I take care of each other. We help each other navigate through the darkness.

Sometimes I wonder if I'm losing my mind. Or if I've already lost it. They tell me that my dear friend Ms. Vee never existed. Ms. Vee, the kind, elderly lady who befriended me in that awful place. She was warm, comforting, and understanding, and frankly I don't know if I would have survived without her. So how can the doctors say that she never existed? That she was just a figment of my imagination—some imaginary person I created to help me endure my ordeal? They say she was just a hypothetical substitute figure for the women in my life I love so much. For my mama, Grandma Ruth, Aunt Kenya, and Auntie Jazz. My family that I thought I would never see again.

They think I don't see Ms. Vee anymore, but I do. Sure, she disappeared for a while when I allowed the doctors and my family to convince me that she wasn't real. But lately, she's been visiting me again. And she's just as real as anybody. Ms. Vee really gets me. She understands what I've been through—the pain and the heartache that will never heal. With Ms. Vee I don't have to pretend that I'm okay. With her I can just be myself, knowing that she'll support me no matter what. But I have to be careful when Ms. Vee visits me. I have to talk to her in hushed tones so Aunt Kenya and Auntie Jazz don't hear us. Sometimes I think they listen outside my door just waiting to catch me doing something wrong. Just waiting for me to slip up.

They think I'm still taking my medication, but I'm not. I just throw one pill away each day to fool them. I don't like taking those pills. They make me feel funny. Like I'm not myself. And I'd rather feel like myself than someone else, no matter how terrible feeling like me can be.

I've finally convinced them that I don't need to go to therapy every week anymore. Now I'm supposed to go every two weeks. But I don't plan to go back. Ever. I hate those therapy sessions. All those doctors trying to get into my head to see what makes me tick or not tick. They don't know. They don't have a clue. How could they? They haven't been through what I've been through. Haven't seen the horrors I've seen. Haven't felt what I've felt. They don't know the damage that's been done to my soul.

What is a soul, anyway? Is it that fuzzy-wuzzy thing that makes us us? Whatever it is I don't think I have one anymore. I think I left it in that dank, dark basement of that awful sex-slave house in Colombia where we were trapped like animals. Perhaps my soul is still floating around in that dark, deserted place—floating around and around in the darkness. A lost soul.

Dereka put down her pen and closed her journal. That was enough writing for tonight. She got out of bed, retrieved a shoebox, and put her journal into the box. Then she stepped up on a stool, and placed the box in the corner on the top shelf of her closet. There it would be safe from prying eyes. Then she went to her nightstand drawer, retrieved a small gold-leaf box, and placed its contents on the bed. These were the things she'd managed to hide from her captors at that house and bring home with her. Esmeralda's rosary beads, Crystal's comb, and an angel figurine made of soap. She considered these her symbols of love in a loveless place—treasures she'd found among ruins.

Esmeralda had been the Tavaras brothers' great-aunt, whom they'd worked like a slave, cooking, cleaning the house, and catering to their every whim. She'd been as much a victim of the brothers' cruelty as the girls they'd held captive there. But she'd treated the girls with kindness and tenderness when she served their meals each day. Crystal, a beautiful, blonde-haired girl, had been taken from Charlotte, North Carolina, and imprisoned there. Crystal hadn't made it though. One day she just gave up and refused to comply with the brothers' demands. Mario, the eviler of the two brothers, had taken Crystal to a wooden shed and attempted to torture her into submission. But he'd gone too far. The next morning they'd found Crystal dead in her bed.

Dereka picked up the angel figurine made from soap. It was the birthday present the girls had given to her on her fourteenth birthday. The angel was symbolic of the nickname, Angel Girl, they had given Dereka. One of the girls, Camila, had used her fingernails to carve it from an extra bar of soap Esmeralda had provided. It was something Dereka knew she'd cherish forever.

Dereka put the items back into the box and returned it to the drawer. She got into bed and reluctantly closed her eyes. Dereka dreaded going to sleep at night. Dreaded the nightmares to come. She squeezed her eyes together tightly hoping to block the ghastly visions from her mind. But she doubted this ploy would work. It never did.

Reflections

Kenya Jones vigorously stirred pancake batter in a large mixing bowl. As was her usual custom on Saturday mornings, she was preparing breakfast for her niece, Dereka, and dear friend, Jasmine. She was making Dereka's favorite breakfast—buttermilk pancakes, grilled smoked sausage, and scrambled cheesy eggs. It was a beautiful sunny day in late March, that time of the year in the Washington, DC area when the weather still fluctuated between winter and spring. Today, it appeared to be more on the wintry side. Kenya, wearing her fuzzy pink robe and slippers, moved efficiently around the spacious, homey kitchen. A tall, regal beauty, Kenya wore her naturally curly hair in a short sassy style that complemented her beautiful ethnic facial features. She had smooth dark-chocolate skin and a slim athletic build. Her high, chiseled cheekbones were every model's dream, and she also had the Jones family trademark—voluptuous, lovely lips.

Kenya softly sung one of her mama's favorite hymns, "We've Come This Far by Faith," as she placed sausages on the grill. While she meditated on the words of the song, she knew without a doubt that's exactly how she'd made it—by faith, leaning on and trusting in the Lord. As Kenya cooked she reflected back on her life, which had definitely had its fair share of trials and tribulations. An especially difficult tragedy was the death of her big brother, Derek, whom she'd dearly loved and idolized. Derek had committed suicide during his senior year in college after he'd contracted the HIV virus and had unknowingly transmitted the disease to Serena, his high-school sweetheart. Serena was pregnant with Derek's baby at the time of his death. The blessing that came from this tragedy was the birth of their daughter, Dereka. Kenya loved her niece with her whole heart.

Derek had not only been Kenya's brother, he'd also been her father figure, champion, best friend, confidante, and protector. It was Derek whom she'd gone to for help when she was a senior in high school and had gotten herself into a scary and embarrassing situation with her substitute teacher, Kevin Curtis. Mr. Curtis, as the students called him, was a sexual predator who had used his job, looks, and cunning to take advantage of Kenya and other young, naïve girls. He'd coerced Kenya into taking and sending him sexually explicit pictures of herself. He'd then extorted money from her, threatening to post the photos on the Internet if she didn't pay up. Eventually Kenya had reluctantly told her parents, BabyRuth and DJ, about her teacher's scandalous behavior, and they'd reported him to the authorities. Kevin was tried, convicted, and sent to prison. He was killed in jail by another inmate.

Kevin's father, Luther Curtis, a.k.a Memphis, was furious that Kenya had snitched on his son and blamed her for Kevin's death. Memphis, a coldhearted criminal, became the Jones family's archenemy and sought revenge at every turn. It was Memphis who had abducted Dereka and sold her into child sex slavery. He'd taken her to Colombia, South America, because he felt they'd never find her there. Memphis kidnapped Dereka because he knew she was Kenya's heart. He knew that making her niece suffer would inflict the worse kind of pain and agony on Kenya and her entire family. And, in that respect, he had been right.

The five years that Dereka was missing were five of the most agonizing years of their lives. And, as if that wasn't bad enough, Dereka's mother, Serena, one of the most compassionate and loving people whom Kenya had ever known, had lost her life trying to protect her child from being abducted. Kenya had not only blamed herself for Dereka's abduction but for Serena's death as well. Consumed with grief, guilt, and shame, Kenya had crawled into her bed with her tail tucked between her legs, humiliated and depressed. But her mama, with love and patience, had propped her up to keep her from falling. BabyRuth had told Kenya that as children of God *we are the head and not the tail*, and *we are more than conquerors* in Christ Jesus.

Unfortunately for Kenya, Memphis's quest for revenge wasn't quelled by his abduction of Dereka. That alone wasn't enough for someone with his appetite for vengeance. He'd also hired an up-and-coming criminal from Detroit named Ryan to infiltrate Kenya's world to deceive and destroy her. Kenya had loved and trusted Ryan and had even become engaged to him. When this imposter and pawn in Memphis's sick, twisted game of revenge betrayed her, she was left brokenhearted, bewildered, and humiliated. But again her mama came to her rescue with unconditional love, tenderness, and patience.

Kenya greatly missed her mama, BabyRuth, who had passed away about two weeks before Dereka came home. It was her mama's strong faith that held the family together during the most difficult and heart-wrenching time of their lives. BabyRuth had always believed that her dear, sweet granddaughter, whom she affectionately called Boogie Boo, would come home someday. And she had stood sturdy in her faith until the Lord called her home. One of her favorite scriptures was *But without faith it is impossible to please him: for he that cometh to God must believe that he is, and that he is a rewarder of them that diligently seek him.*

Memphis was eventually tracked down and arrested in Philadelphia when he disembarked a plane that had arrived from Mexico. Someone had tipped off the authorities that he'd be on that early-morning flight. And, unbeknownst to Kenya, that someone had been Ryan. Memphis was charged and convicted with a smorgasbord of crimes, including kidnapping, sex trafficking, drug trafficking, and money laundering, just to name a few. He got life plus five hundred years, which he was currently serving in a Virginia state prison. For that Kenya was grateful. At least he wouldn't be able to harm her family anymore.

Kenya, Dereka, and their longtime friend, Jasmine, now lived in the family home in Alexandria, Virginia, that BabyRuth left to Kenya. Her father, Derek Sr., a.k.a. DJ, had lost his battle with cancer about seven years after his son's death. Now with BabyRuth gone, it was just Kenya and her niece, Dereka. Thankfully, they had Jasmine in their lives, a friend who had become like family over the years. Kenya considered Jasmine her sister, and Dereka had always known Jasmine as her aunt and affectionately called her Auntie Jazz.

Kenya felt she owed Jasmine a great debt that, in all likelihood, she could never repay. For it was Jasmine who had made the ultimate sacrifice to find Dereka. A successful businesswoman with two health spas in Los Angeles, Jasmine had sold one of her prosperous spas and used the money to support and work with a human-trafficking rescue organization called Operation Undercover. She had traveled far and wide with the organization, performing highly dangerous rescue stings at sleazy sex-slave houses and brothels. She'd put her own life at risk to find Dereka and bring her home. And she'd done it out of great love not only for Dereka but also for her mother, Serena, who years earlier had shown Jasmine a kind of compassion and forgiveness that few humans are capable of demonstrating. Jasmine still worked with Operation Undercover, work that she now considered her life's calling. Although she no longer performed the undercover rescue work, she was one of their most dedicated and well-respected spokespersons and fund raisers.

Kenya reflected on all the progress Dereka had made over the past six years since she'd come home. She'd overcome so much physically, emotionally and, most of all, mentally. Upon her return home, she'd initially been diagnosed with acute psychosis brought on by her traumatic experience as a sex trafficking victim. In addition, Dereka's family history revealed a genetic link to mental illness that was traced to her maternal biological grandmother. Because Dereka's mother, Serena, was adopted as a baby, no one knew much about Serena's biological parents. What they did know was that Serena's biological mother had been a homeless woman living in a shelter. She had been in and out of mental institutions most of her life. She'd died shortly after Serena was adopted.

With the help of antipsychotic medication, cognitive behavioral therapy, support group meetings, and a whole lot of prayer, Dereka seemed to be doing okay. So much so that Kenya and Jasmine had concurred with her decision to reduce her therapy sessions from weekly to bi-weekly. Dereka told them she no longer saw Ms. Vee, which was a major milestone as far as Kenya was concerned. She strongly believed that if Dereka attended biweekly therapy sessions, regularly went to her support group meetings for trafficking victims, and took her medication faithfully, she'd be fine. Dereka had even obtained an online computer science degree from the University of Maryland, and she now worked part-time at Kenya's legal consulting business in Fairfax, Virginia.

Yet, in spite of all the progress Dereka had made, Kenya sometimes got a nagging feeling in her gut that something wasn't right. Perhaps she'd inherited her mother's intuition to sense when something was amiss. Kenya recalled all the times her mother's intuition had gotten her and Derek in a world of trouble. Her mama could always tell when her kids were up to no good. And nine times out of ten BabyRuth had been right.

Is Dereka really okay? Kenya thought as she removed toast from the toaster. *Of course, she is*, she told herself mainly because she so desperately wanted her to be. But she decided to talk to Jasmine about her concerns just for her own peace of mind.

When Kenya finished preparing breakfast, she went to the bottom of the stairs and yelled to Dereka and Jasmine.

"Breakfast ready, lazy bones. Come and get it before it's gone." Kenya laughed to herself at that saying, because it was something she'd heard her mama yell to her and her brother many a morning. She smiled fondly at the memory.

All's Well or Not

Jasmine McKnight sauntered into the kitchen around 9:00 a.m. looking her usual fabulous self. In her mid-forties, Jasmine could easily pass for ten years younger. Fifteen on a really good day, which she had plenty of. She worked out regularly to keep her five-foot-seven-inch frame fit and tight. Her smooth, beautiful vanilla-brown skin always seemed to glow like the sun. And her big sultry hazel eyes had a hypnotic effect. Ms. Jasmine was always well put together. Her toes and nails were always professionally manicured, her makeup applied to perfection, and she dressed to the hilt for every occasion. Jasmine loved experimenting with all types of hair. As a matter of fact, it seemed she had just as many wigs and weaves lined up on shelves in her bedroom as the local beauty supply store. But Jasmine was more than just a pretty face. She had intelligence, business savvy, and street smarts. Most of all she had a huge heart full of love, loyalty, and compassion, especially for her niece, Dereka, and her sister-friend, Kenya.

"Something smells good in here," Jasmine said, peeping over Kenya's shoulder to see what was cooking on the stove.

"Just a little sumpin', sumpin' I threw together," Kenya said laughing.

"Why didn't you wait for me to come down and help you cook? Girl, you know I can really burn when I want to," Jasmine replied.

"Yeah, you can burn all right. You can burn the toast, burn the bacon, burn the grits, the ham, the eggs, and who knows what else. I remember that time you nearly burned the house down making tacos," Kenya said, laughing.

"Now that was a long time ago," Jasmine countered. "And I've improved a lot since then."

Yeah, I know. Where's Dereka?"

"She's just getting in the shower. Said she'd be down in a bit," Jasmine replied. Kenya eyed Jasmine's snazzy attire.

"I like that outfit. Why are you already dressed up so early on a Saturday morning?"

"I got a meeting this morning with AKA sorority sisters in Upper Marlboro. They're working with Operation Undercover to organize a fund raiser for our cause. They've made fighting human trafficking one of their number one priorities. Those sisters are on the ball," Jasmine said as she poured herself a cup of coffee.

"I know that's right," Kenya concurred. "I'm glad you decided to continue your work with Operation Undercover. I so admire what you all are doing."

"Well, somebody has to do something. I just thank the Lord that I'm able to help," Jasmine replied. "Oh, by the way, Percy will be in town next weekend to take me to the Jazz Master's Tribute Concert at the Kennedy Center." Percy Franklin was Jasmine's beau from Los Angeles. They'd met about two years ago when she was in L.A. on a business trip, hit it off from the start, and had kept their long-distance romance going strong ever since. Their dedicated couple's song was none other than Marvin Gaye's classic hit "Distant Lover." Percy knew all about Jasmine's dark past. He knew about her abusive childhood at the hands of her own mother, and the subsequent issues and struggles she'd faced then and still faced. And he accepted her just as she was.

"Percy's cousin, Sean, is driving down from New Jersey to attend the concert with us. Why don't you come along?" Jasmine asked, smiling slyly at Kenya.

"Oh no, you don't," Kenya said, laughing. "I know what you're up to. You're trying to set me up on another blind date."

"Okay, you got me. Guilty as charged. But I think you should go on this one. I've seen a picture of his cousin, and the brother is fine!" Jasmine exclaimed. Kenya looked at Jasmine and shook her head in amusement.

"Well, fine or not, I think I'll pass," she said. Jasmine studied Kenya for a moment. She knew her friend was still hurting from her ex-fiancé,

Ryan's ultimate betrayal. Kenya dated only occasionally, and she had never allowed herself to fully trust another man.

"Kenya, honey. I know the situation with Ryan still bothers you. And I understand. Really, I do. But you've got to give yourself another chance at love. You're only forty, and forty is the new twenty. You still young, girl. You still got a lot of pep in your step. Don't give up on love," Jasmine implored.

"I haven't given up on love, but finding a man is just not a priority for me right now. I'm doing just fine by myself. You don't need a man to be happy," Kenya asserted.

"Yeah, I hear you. I'm not saying you have to marry the guy, but just go on the date to meet Sean and see where things go. If nothing else, I'm sure you'll enjoy the jazz concert. Please, Kenya, please, please, pleeeeease," Jasmine said, putting her hands together in a pleading gesture. Kenya let out a deep breath.

"Oh, okay. I'll go," she relented, more to appease her well-meaning friend. "But he'd better be as fine as you say he is," she said, laughing and pointing a finger at Jasmine.

"He's not only fine, but the brother is 'thank you, Jesus, fine,'" Jasmine exclaimed. Kenya turned serious for a moment.

"Jasmine, I want to talk to you about something before Dereka comes down."

"Sure, sweetie. What's up?"

"It's probably nothing, but do you think Dereka's really all right?"

"Well, she seems fine to me. Thank God she no longer has those hallucinations about Ms. Vee. She's taking her medication, going to therapy, and attending her support group meetings. She seems to be doing well. In fact, I'm thinking about taking her with me when I visit Jia this summer."

"That would be great. I know that they FaceTime and Skype each other often. But it's been a while since they've seen each other. I think the trip would be good for both of them."

"Then I'll definitely plan to take her with me. But why did you ask if she's all right?"

"No reason really. It's just that sometimes I get a funny feeling that something's not right. Maybe I'm just being overly sensitive when it comes to Dereka. It's probably nothing."

"Well, let's keep an eye out for any signs of trouble."

Dereka stood outside the kitchen door listening to her aunts' conversation, her heart beating fast. *Oh my God, Aunt Kenya suspects something*, she thought. *I'll have to try harder to convince them that I really am okay.* Dereka didn't want her aunts to worry about her. They had gone through hell when she was missing and had worked tirelessly to find her and bring her home. These were the two people she loved most in the world, and there was no need for them to suffer anymore because of her. They'd been through enough. Dereka took a deep breath, put on her most dazzling smile, and went into the kitchen.

"Good morning, Aunties," she said, smiling brightly as she gave each of them a quick hug and kiss on the cheek. Kenya's heart soared when she saw Dereka's beaming face. She quickly dismissed any suspicions about Dereka's well-being.

"Good morning, sweetheart. You're awful chipper this morning. I made your favorite pancakes," Kenya said.

"Thanks, Aunt Kenya. You're the best," Dereka replied as she went to the stove and fixed herself a huge plate. Kenya smiled at her niece as she observed her loading her plate to the brim. Still as beautiful as ever, Dereka's full naturally curly hair hung just past her shoulders. She had smooth cinnamon-brown skin, big brown eyes, thick lashes and brows, and an adorable dimpled smile like her mother's. She got her height and athletic build, along with her full shapely lips from her father.

Kenya and Jasmine fixed their own hefty plates and joined Dereka at the kitchen table. After Kenya said grace, the three ladies dove headlong into their food—laughing, joking, gossiping, and just enjoying each other's company. Two of them were under the false impression that all was well. But one of them, unfortunately, knew that it was not.

Criminal Minds

Memphis sat on the concrete stairs and watched as two men hit and kicked another man until he was bloody and battered. The young man under attack tried to curl himself into a fetal position in the corner of the stairway landing as he pleaded with the other men to stop. But the men showed no mercy. Memphis watched carefully because he wanted to be sure they didn't actually kill him. His intent was for them to strike "the fear of Memphis," not God, into the young man's heart to ensure that he never disrespected him again. And by doing so, Memphis would add yet another faithful, albeit frightened, follower to his growing entourage. After what must have seemed like an eternity to the battered man, Memphis stood up.

"Enough," he ordered. The two men immediately ceased their assault, but it was clear that they didn't want to. They still had blood in their eyes. Memphis walked over to the badly beaten man and picked his head up off the floor by his dreadlocks.

"Look at me," Memphis demanded in a low, even tone. The man's eyes were beaten nearly shut, but he did his best to open them as wide as he could. "The next time you disrespect me will be the last day of your pathetic life. Do you understand?" Memphis warned. The man nodded his head. Memphis dropped the man's head which landed hard on the concrete floor. He walked away with the two bloodthirsty assailants close at his heels. They were part of Memphis's team of enforcers, a crew of brutal inmates that Memphis used to rule the prison like he was Attila the Hun.

When Memphis had first entered the Virginia state prison's doors, the prisoners treated him like criminal royalty. His reputation had preceded him, and inmates young and old had literally lined up at the gate to catch a glimpse of the ruthless legendary villain, and pledge their undying allegiance to him. By the way the prisoners had behaved one would have thought the president himself was coming to personally hand out pardons. They had pushed, shoved, and jockeyed for position to be among the first to kiss Memphis's royal ass. Not that they had any great love for the man. They just instinctively knew the benefits of being on his good side and the detriment of being on his bad. And their instincts had been correct. As good as Memphis was to his followers, he was many times as ruthless to his adversaries.

Memphis, being the generous ringleader that he was, ensured his loyal followers enjoyed, as he did, the finer things that incarcerated life had to offer. Memphis afforded them drugs, the best food, extra phone privileges, and, above all, protection. And, of course, sex was plenteous for the charismatic, distinguished, handsome, infamous crook. Although now in his mid-sixties, Memphis was as fit and fine as ever. He had more women admirers and visitors than you could shake a stick at. And a lot of the female guards, and a few male guards (but Memphis didn't swing that way), were ready, willing, and able to accommodate his sexual urges any time of the day or night. Many of the other inmates were satisfied just to feast on the crumbs that fell from Memphis's bountiful table. The crumbs alone were enough to keep many a prisoner as happy as a hog in slop.

Memphis's high jailhouse-rock standard of living was compliments of the many prison guards, staff, and high-level officials that had been deep in his pockets for years. He had so much dirt on them regarding their illegal activities, they were pretty much forced to do as he commanded. They were literally at his beck and call 24-7, knowing that he had information about them that could ruin their careers, marriages, and lives if it was leaked. They probably would have even followed him around with a pooper-scooper to pick on his funky droppings if he so desired.

As it turned out, prison life didn't slow down Memphis's criminal activities one bit. As a matter of fact, it only enhanced them. He still had his extensive external criminal network of gangsters, hoodlums, and mobsters outside the prison walls, which he used to keep his drug and sex trafficking operations up and running. And now he also had an extensive inside network of criminals at his disposal. So being incarcerated gave him access to an abundance of the best criminal minds available, including, but not limited to, the demented minds of mass murderers, serial killers, rapists, racists, pimps, thieves, extortionists, and the like. Memphis often wondered why the authorities-that-be would place criminals together in close proximity in prison, and then expect them to come out as rehabilitated, model citizens. It made absolutely no sense to him. Memphis knew that in reality, although a few prisoners managed to turn their lives around for the better, by far the majority became substantially worse. The minor offenders often became hardened criminals, and the hardened criminals became even harder. Many inmates used their prison time to fine-tune their murderous, sadistic, and devious skills. Thus, to Memphis's delight, he had at his disposal all sorts of perverted, monstrous, warped, twisted, distorted, and depraved criminal minds to pick and probe for the most devilish schemes imaginable or unimaginable to man. And pick and probe those minds he did.

Although incarcerated, money was no problem for Memphis. Even though government authorities had seized or frozen a large portion of the wealth he'd gained through illegal activities, Memphis was still one rich crook. He had accounts and assets in foreign banks that were thoroughly concealed by the use of phony names and companies. The authorities would never be able to uncover all of his wealth. Memphis had always considered himself a savvy businessman. Thus, he'd planned well for the pitfalls of criminal life and that included prison. But although he'd planned for the likelihood of prison, he never thought he would end up there. Yet he had just the same, thanks to Ryan, his once trusted employee.

Albeit it was now six years later, Memphis's blood still boiled every time he thought of Ryan's treachery. And he thought of it often. After all, Memphis had taken Ryan, a two-bit drug dealer from Detroit, under his wing. He'd brought him into his organization and personally taught him the ruthless street culture. He'd given Ryan power, money, and position. Treated that boy like his own son. *And that bastard had the audacity to betray me*, Memphis thought, his eyes narrowed, jaws clenching. Time had done little to defuse the pent up rage inside him. Time had only rooted that rage deep into his heart, where it was pumped into every vein, artery, and fiber of his being.

Memphis knew it was Ryan who had turned him in to the cops. It had to be. Ryan was the only one who knew Memphis would be on that 8:00 a.m. flight to Philly that day. Memphis had trusted Ryan enough to break his own rule about not trusting anyone. He'd made a mistake and told Ryan about his plot to take Kenya out with a bullet between the eyes. And Ryan had used that information to double cross him to save Kenya, a woman whom Memphis had even paid Ryan good money to mislead and deceive. And Ryan had handled that job with flying colors, exercising a cunningness and callousness that had made Memphis proud. So if Ryan had betrayed Kenya for Memphis, why had he turned around and sold Memphis out to save her? Memphis didn't know, nor did he care. He didn't need answers, only revenge. And Memphis knew it wouldn't be too much longer before both Ryan and Kenya were six feet under anyway. He'd used his extensive network of criminal minds to mastermind a fiendish fate for both of them. *Perhaps they can discuss why Ryan betrayed us while they burn together in hell*, Memphis thought with a sadistic smile on his face.

Memphis planned to first take Ryan out in the most vicious and painful way imaginable. But he had to find him. Memphis had already discovered that Ryan had initially fled to Johannesburg, South Africa, where he lived for three years under the assumed name of Motumbo Maharaj. Memphis chuckled at the thought of Ryan living in some South African village. The man was creative, Memphis had to give him that. Memphis liked that about Ryan because he loved a worthy opponent. Ryan had slipped out of South Africa before Memphis could close in on him. Memphis now had a new team of trackers on the outside searching high and low for him. That rat was good at hiding out and concealing his identity. However, Memphis was getting close to finding him again. He could just feel it in his bones. And when he did, there would be hell to pay.

Ms. Ethel's Refuge

Around three thirty Saturday afternoon, Dereka headed to her support group meeting. They met every third Saturday at Ms. Ethel's Refuge. Ethel Mae Graham had started the support group about fourteen years ago when she lost her own daughter, Tiffany, to sex trafficking. Tiffany had been only sixteen when she was murdered by her pimp, who thought she was stealing money from him. Ms. Ethel had tried desperately to save her only child. But try as she may, her daughter was inexplicably drawn to the fast, lurid life of the streets. Tiffany's death shook Ms. Ethel to her core. But Ms. Ethel wasn't one to roll over and wallow in self-pity—that wasn't her style. She quit her job at the hospital, withdrew her retirement savings, and started Ms. Ethel's Refuge—a place where sex trafficking survivors, or those at risk, could come for support, counseling, mentoring, and fellowship. She held several support group meetings throughout the week, including one for young girls aged twelve and below, another for teenagers, and one for adults twenty and above. She even had a group for family members who, like herself, had lost a child to sex trafficking.

Everybody loved Ms. Ethel. It was virtually impossible not to. She was a big, burly, Bible-touting, humorous, Lord-loving woman with a broad smile and a quick wit. She stood about five foot nine and weighed around 325 pounds. Ms. Ethel loved her some good old-fashioned southern cooking. There were no lean cuisines or healthy eating at Ms. Ethel's house. Not a chance. Her kitchen often smelled of ox tails, collard greens with ham hocks, chitterlings, barbeque ribs, fried catfish, and a host of other soul food delights. Everybody in the neighborhood knew you could always get a good home-cooked meal at Ms. Ethel's house.

Ms. Ethel was a big woman in stature, yet her heart was a hundred times bigger. She opened her heart and home to many homeless teens—runaways, drug addicts, and others considered by society to be undesirables. It wasn't unusual for Ms. Ethel to have six to seven youth at a time living in her home, which could be quite a handful. But as loving and spiritual as Ms. Ethel was, everybody knew that Ms. Ethel don't play. Once a teenage boy who was "feeling his oats" riled up at Ms. Ethel as though he wanted to hit her. Ms. Ethel put that poor boy in a headlock, flipped him down on the sofa, and sat her 325 pounds on him until he was squealing like a pig. Ms. Ethel told him, "Your soul may belong to the Lord, but your behind is mine." Needless to say, that young man learned a valuable lesson about messing with her that day. Ms. Ethel insisted that all her live-ins abide by her house rules, respect themselves, and respect one another. That meant no fighting, no cursing, no drugs or alcohol, and no "hanky-panky" under her roof.

When Dereka got to Ms. Ethel's house, her friend, Fatima, pulled into the parking lot at the same time. Fatima was originally from Ghana, West Africa. When she was a young teenage girl, she was often transported from the poor fishing village where she lived, and forced to work as a prostitute in the surrounding urban areas. That was how her family made extra money to supplement their meager income. Fatima's Aunt Zuri, who'd migrated to the United States years earlier, rescued Fatima and brought her to live with her in Woodbridge, Virginia. Her aunt found out about Ms. Ethel's Refuge, and took Fatima there for support group meetings. When Dereka first joined the group, Fatima befriended her and immediately made her feel comfortable. And they'd been good friends ever since. Fatima got out of her car and walked toward Dereka.

"Hey, Ms. Lady. Good to see you," she said in her heavy Ghanaian accent. Dereka gave her a big hug.

"It's good to see you, too. You look pretty," Dereka noted, admiring Fatima's brightly colored African dress and head wrap. Fatima loved to sew, and made many of her own stylish African attire. She'd even made Dereka a couple of fabulous African outfits, which Dereka wore with pride.

"Thanks, sweetie," Fatima replied.

As soon as they entered Ms. Ethel's, the smell of soul food titillated their nostrils. Each of them took a big whiff and tried to guess what Ms. Ethel was cooking up in the kitchen.

"Smells like smothered chicken and gravy to me," Dereka guessed.

"Uh-huh, girl. That's Ms. Ethel's famous neck bones and noodles," Fatima countered. Ms. Ethel came out of the kitchen wiping her hands on a towel.

"Hello, darlings. Y'all sho is a sight for sore eyes," she exclaimed, a broad smile on her face.

"Hi, Ms. Ethel," Dereka replied, giving her a big hug.

"Ms. Ethel. You need to settle something for us. Dereka said you're cooking chicken and gravy. I say it's your neck bones and noodles. Now, which one of us is right?" Fatima asked with a cocky expression on her face as if she knew she was the one.

"Neither," Ms. Ethel cheerfully pointed out to their surprise. "That's salisbury steak with my mushroom-and-onion gravy. It'll be ready by the time we finished our group session. Now y'all go on downstairs. Just about everybody's here. I'm waiting for one other person, so I'll be along in a minute."

"Okay, Ms. Ethel," Dereka and Fatima replied in unison.

When they got downstairs, there were several women of various ethnicities sitting in a semicircle talking among themselves. They greeted Dereka and Fatima warmly with hugs. Over time, these women had become like family. They knew each other's heartbreaking stories and could not only sympathize but also empathize with the terrible plight of being sexually exploited. It was a burden they'd have to live with for the rest of their lives, and being with others who shared that same burden somehow helped to lighten the load a bit. Dereka enjoyed the support group because with them she didn't have to pretend that all was well. And supporting them helped take her mind off her own struggles and issues. It made her feel useful and needed, instead of useless and needy like she sometimes felt at home.

Ms. Ethel soon came downstairs with a young lady they had not seen before. She was a slim, Caucasian female, with brown shoulder-length hair, freckles, and gray eyes.

"This is Julie McMillan. She's joining our group today. Julie, this is Fatima, Dereka, Simone, Melissa, Barbara..." Ms. Ethel announced as she introduced Julie to each lady in the circle. They all greeted Julie with hellos, how are you, nice to have you with us, welcome to the group, and other pleasantries. She smiled shyly, mumbled hello, and quickly took a seat beside Ms. Ethel.

As was her usual custom, Ms. Ethel opened the session with prayer and scripture. Today, she read Psalm 34:8, *O taste and see that the Lord is good: blessed is the man that trusteth in him.* Ms. Ethel then asked if anyone wanted to share any challenges, successes, failures, problems, or experiences with the group.

"This is voluntary only, honey," she said to the newcomer, Julie. "You only have to speak if you want to." Simone, who'd been abducted as a teenager, spoke of an incident that had happened to her at the mall when she thought a man was following her. In a panic, she had run to the security and accused the man of stalking her. But it turned out the poor fellow was only going to his car in the parking garage. Simone felt foolish and terribly guilty for having accused an innocent man. Unfortunately, being fearful of strangers, especially men, was something that several of the women struggled with.

Dereka didn't share anything during the group session but chose to simply listen to and support the others. She carefully watched Julie who appeared to be getting more anxious and emotional with each passing moment. At one point, she looked on the verge of tears. Dereka, a compassionate person at heart, got up and walked over to Julie. She knelt in front of her, took her hands, and looked directly into her eyes.

"It's okay, honey. You're with friends here. You can let go. We got you," Dereka whispered softly. Julie looked at Dereka, big tears brimming in her eyes. And then she broke down and started to cry, placing her arms tightly around Dereka's neck. Ms. Ethel embraced the two of them and began to pray. Soon all the other women surrounded them as if to form a shield of love, compassion, and strength. Many of the women unabashedly shed their own tears as appalling memories of their past resurfaced. The women were there for each other and comforted one another. Because that's the way it was at Ms. Ethel's.

Damaged Goods

After the support group meeting, a few of the ladies accepted Ms. Ethel's offer to stay for dinner. Dereka was emotionally drained and really didn't want to stay, but Fatima talked her into it, saying the fellowship would do them good. Two of the three teenage girls staying at Ms. Ethel's joined them. The ladies sat around the table, on stools at the countertop, or anywhere else they could find to sit in Ms. Ethel's big, cluttered, comfortable kitchen. They chowed down on salisbury steak and gravy, macaroni and cheese, fresh collards, corn pudding, and buttermilk cornbread. Proper decorum fell by the wayside as the ladies licked their fingers and laughed and talked with their mouths full. Fatima noticed that Dereka was quieter than usual.

"Is everything okay?" she asked as she licked gravy from her fingers.

"Yes, everything's fine," Dereka replied. But she was lying. Her heart was heavy and her soul burdened. While she did not yet know Julie's story, she was sure it was a horrible one. A story likely as horrible as her own. And knew that Julie would never be the same again. None of them would. No matter how hard they tried or pretended to be. Dereka felt as though her life was now two separate lives. She had her "before life" when she was happy, carefree, outgoing, and confident. And she had her "after life" which was filled with self-doubt, fear, and pretense.

Dereka's thoughts were interrupted when three rowdy, sweaty teenage boys burst into the kitchen on a mission to get some of Ms. Ethel's good food.

"Aw no y'all don't," Ms. Ethel playfully warned. "Go on upstairs and get cleaned up first. Don't bring that funk in here around these ladies and my food," she ordered, swatting at them with a kitchen towel.

"But I'm ready to get my grub on, Ms. Ethel. I worked up an appetite on the basketball court," one of them said, posturing, poking his chest out, and winking at one of the young teenage girls.

"Boy, don't make me have to hurt you. Now get!" Ms. Ethel commanded, pointing at the door.

"Yes, ma'am," they replied, laughing and galloping up the stairs. Dereka and Fatima got up to leave, both as full as ticks.

"Thanks for the dinner, Ms. Ethel," Dereka said.

"Everything was as tasty as ever," Fatima added, patting her tight belly.

"Well, I'm glad y'all enjoyed it," Ms. Ethel replied, her voice filled with pride. She just loved it when people enjoyed her cooking.

Once they went outside, Dereka noticed a young man standing near her car. It was her friend, Brandon, who lived about a block from where she lived. Brandon helped out at Ms. Ethel's Refuge by mentoring some of the young boys she took in. He had graduated from Howard University last year with a master's degree in computer science. He and Dereka had been friends since first grade when they'd sat together on the yellow school bus. Brandon was the only friend Dereka still had from her "before life." Before she was abducted and forced into sex slavery, she'd had many friends who'd loved and adored her. And to their credit, when she was first rescued they'd rallied around her in a show of support. However, over time those friends had slowly drifted away. But Dereka didn't blame them. They hadn't known how to deal with the new Dereka—the damaged Dereka. She'd made them uncomfortable, so it was easier for them to just move on. All except Brandon.

After saying good-bye to Fatima, Dereka walked over to him.

"Hey there. I didn't know you were here," she said.

"When I dropped the boys off I saw your car and decided to wait for you," Brandon said.

"Why didn't you come in and say hello. You could have gotten yourself a good meal," Dereka replied.

"Well, I'm all sweaty from playing basketball with the young bloods, so I didn't want to come in. Besides, I've seen you and Fatima throw down at the dinner table. So I doubt if there's much of anything left," Brandon said, cracking himself up.

"Oh, you got jokes," Dereka said, laughing along with him. Brandon had proven to be a good friend, and she valued his friendship immensely. There had been times when she'd tried to push him away, mainly due to her own insecurities. But Brandon wasn't having it. He cherished Dereka's friendship. And, if truth be told, he'd had a crush on Dereka ever since she'd sat beside him on the school bus, with her sparkling eyes, fat braids, and that adorable dimpled smile. And his puppy-love crush had grown into a deeper affection over the years. When she was missing, Brandon was afraid he'd never see her again, and had been overjoyed when she was found and came home. He knew Dereka had changed a lot since her tragedy, but that didn't matter to him. How could she not change after what she'd been through? Brandon sometimes wished he had a magic wand, a genie in a bottle, or something that he could use to make all her pain go away.

The two friends talked for about ten minutes before Dereka decided to head home. When she turned to open her car door, Brandon reached out and touched her arm. Dereka jumped in fear and recoiled away from him. Brandon was startled because that had never happened before.

"I'm sorry, Dereka. I didn't mean to scare you," he said, a stunned expression on his face.

"You…didn't…scare me," Dereka stuttered, as surprised by her reaction as he was.

"I just wanted to know if you wanted to go see a movie tomorrow night, that's all."

"Uh, well not tomorrow night. I have something to do. Maybe another time."

"Okay, that's cool," Brandon mumbled. But Dereka saw the confusion, hurt, and disappointment in his eyes. He turned and walked toward his car.

As Dereka drove home, she was confused and mortified by her reaction to Brandon's touch. *He's my friend. Why did I react that way?* she thought. Perhaps it was because of the intimacy she'd felt in Brandon's touch. She sensed that Brandon liked her as more than just a friend. But she didn't understand why he, or any man for that matter, could possibly want her after what she'd been through. For five long years, she'd been used and abused by perverts and deviants. How could any decent man want to be with her now?

When Dereka got home, she sat in her car for a while, deep in thought. If there had only been her "before life," things like intimacy, marriage, and a family of her own would all be highly feasible. But now, stuck in her "after life," those things seemed impossible. Intimacy with a man was something that Dereka just couldn't comprehend. After all, her first sexual encounter had been at La Casa de Placer when she was viciously raped by a sadistic man known as "the Breaker." Thus, in Dereka's mind sex was associated with humiliation, pain, and violence of the worse kind. And because of the damage that had been done to her reproductive system during captivity, she'd been told by doctors she could never bear children.

I'm damaged goods, Dereka thought gloomily. *Damaged beyond repair.*

Lady Marmalade
(Bordeaux, France)

Elliott Tremblay was having the time of his life at his bachelor party in a luxury suite at the Mercure Bordeaux Chateau Hotel. His best man, Zack, had really outdone himself. There was plenty of food, booze, and strippers—the big three for a successful bachelor party. Zack had told Elliott that he wanted him to go out in style because once he got married, it was all downhill from there.

Elliot was born and raised in New Brunswick, Canada. He went to Bordeaux, France, in his junior year of college for the experience of studying abroad in an exciting French city. He spoke fluent English and French, both the official languages of Canada. English was his language of choice since his mother was American-Canadian. His parents, both bilingual, insisted that Elliott maintained his fluency in both English and French, which he did with no problem. His fluency in French was one reason he chose France as the place for his studies abroad. He quickly fell in love with the French culture, cuisine, and, of course, the beautiful women. He moved there permanently after obtaining his Bachelor of Science degree in biomedical engineering. Elliott got a great-paying job at BioScience, LLC, a top pharmaceutical company located in downtown Bordeaux. It was there he met his fiancée, Nicole, a native of Bordeaux, who was as smart as she was beautiful. When some of Elliott's buddies in Canada saw all the success he was having in France, they decided to relocate to Bordeaux hoping their fortunes there would be just as good as their friend's. But try as they may, they could never quite measure up to Elliott.

An extremely handsome man, Elliott stood about six feet three inches, had a muscular build, short blond hair, a dimpled chin, and a pair of the most beautiful Caribbean blue eyes you had ever seen. He had the double good fortune of being both a woman's man and a man's man. His good looks, intelligence, and sex appeal made him an instant hit with the ladies, while his outgoing personality, sense of humor, and love for all things athletic made him extremely popular with the guys. He was the man all women wanted to be with, and all men wanted to be. Zack would often jokingly ask Elliott, "Comment se sent-on vous être l'homme?" which means, "Man, how does it feel to be you?" But Elliot would just laugh it off. He was not arrogant or "stuck on himself" as one would think someone with his considerable attributes might be. And that, too, was part of his charm.

Elliott sat on the huge sofa with some of his boys, drinking beer and watching a couple of the strippers do their thing. He already had quite the buzz from all the booze he'd consumed, and joined his friends in yelling and hooting loudly during the strippers' routine. Somehow, even their hooting and hollering in French sounded suave and sophisticated. Since moving to Bordeaux, Elliott and his buddies all spoke French primarily because most of the people there did not speak English fluently (or would not admit to it). The party boys stuffed money in all the naughty places of the dancers' nearly nude bodies.

After the strippers finished their steamy act, Elliott gave Zack a high five, almost missing his hand entirely because his head was spinning from the booze.

"This is one hell of a party. I knew I had picked the best man to be my best man," Elliott said.

"Man, you should have known I wouldn't let you down. But you ain't seen nothing yet. I got something sweeeeet coming up. I saved the best for last," Zack stated with a wink.

"There's more?" Elliott asked, his eyes wide.

"Yeah, mate. You ready?" Zack yelled.

"I'm ready," Elliott shouted back. Zack hopped up on a table and yelled to the crowd of rowdy men.

"Y'all ready?" he shouted. The men responded with a loud roar of applause, shouts, and hoots.

"I said y'all ready," Zack shouted again. This time the men responded with an even louder roar.

"Well, gentlemen, and Elliott," he joked, causing the men to explode with laughter. "It's my pleasure to present to you one of Bordeaux's most delectable delights. The one and the only Lady Marmalade!"

And as if on cue, someone dimmed the lights and played some smooth jazz saxophone music. The men got suddenly quiet and waited with excited anticipation, salivating at the mouth like dogs waiting for a bone.

And there she was. Elliott's mouth dropped open when he first saw her. She was one of the most beautiful, exotic, sexy young ladies he had ever seen. She danced seductively into the room, her tight, titillating body moving in perfect harmony with the sensual sax sounds. Her eyes were dark pools of loveliness, and her long, jet-black hair hung well past her waist. The men remained quiet, choosing not to shout or hoot as they had with the previous dancers. They watched in silence, some holding their breath as if even breathing would spoil the moment. They were totally captivated by the exotic beauty before them, taking in every curve of her body, every sway of her hips, every swing of her hair, and every glance their way. Everything about her was totally mesmerizing. Near the end of her performance, she moved toward Elliott, straddled him, and gave him a private lap dance while the other men watched with envy. Afterward, she moved away toward one of the bedrooms and seductively gestured to Elliott to follow her. Elliott's eyes widened in surprise as this was something totally expected. He looked at his buddy Zack, who was grinning from ear to ear.

"Go for it, man," Zack urged. By this time the rest of the men, having come out of their trance, began yelling, clapping, and hooting for Elliott to go with the seductive dancer.

"Go for it! Go for it!" they shouted while pumping their fists in the air.

Elliott was temporarily torn as to what to do. After all he did have a fiancée, and he was getting married in about two weeks. But on the other hand, this would be his last opportunity to be with another woman before saying his marriage vows. Still, he would feel like he was cheating on his wife-to-be. But he wasn't married yet. All kinds of thoughts raced through Elliott's mind as he gazed at the young lady waiting patiently for him while she moved seductively to the music. Elliott got up and moved toward the young lady to the shouts of approval by the crowd. It was a combination of booze, male bravado (he didn't want to look like a weakling in front of his buddies), and his fascination with the exotic beauty that swayed his decision.

And once inside the bedroom all his apprehensions quickly disappeared. The young lady took Elliott to heights and depths, and heights again that he'd never experienced before. He'd had sex with quite a few women over the years, but nothing compared to this. It was not only on another level, but a whole 'nother planet. The entire time they were together she never spoke a word. Her body did all the talking for her. Afterward, she got up and quietly began to dress. Elliott watched her every move. He still couldn't take his eyes off her. When she was fully dressed, she smiled slightly at Elliott and headed toward the door.

"Wait a minute," Elliott said while he retrieved his pants off the floor. He took out his wallet and fumbled for his money.

"Everything's taken care of," the young lady stated.

"Well, take this anyway, s'il vous plait," Elliott said, holding some money in his hand. She slowly walked toward Elliott and took the money.

"Merci," she murmured as she moved away.

"Just a moment," Elliott implored. "What is your name?"

"Lady Marma..." she started to say, but Elliott cut her off.

"No, what is *your* name?" he repeated, staring directly into her big, dark eyes. The young lady lowered her eyes for a moment as if in deep thought. When she looked up at Elliott he saw a vulnerability in her eyes that hadn't been there before.

"Jia," she whispered as she turned and quickly left the room.

Jia's Secret Life

When Jia Labossiere got home at 2:00 a.m., she found her grandmother asleep on the living room sofa. Jia kissed her softly on the cheek and shook her gently.

"Nai Nai," she whispered, meaning grandmother in her native Mandarin. "Wake up, Nai Nai. It's time to go to bed." Her grandmother opened her eyes slowly and peeped at Jia.

"Bonjour, ma chère. Il est très tard? (Hello, dear. Is it very late?)"

"Yes, Nai Nai. It's late. Time to go to bed," Jia replied in fluent French.

Jia spoke three languages. She still remembered a lot of her native Mandarin. She also spoke proficient English, which her mother had taught her when she was a very young child in China, and which she had maintained over the years through her relationship with Dereka and her family. And she now spoke fluent French because of living and attending school in Bordeaux. Jia helped her grandmother to her bedroom down the hall. Once Nai Nai was settled in bed, Jia kissed her on her soft, wrinkled cheek.

"Goodnight, Nai Nai. See you in the morning."

"Goodnight, dear," Nai Nai said, closing her eyes and instantly falling back to sleep. Jia smiled at her grandmother and tiptoed out of the room.

Six years ago, shortly after Jia was rescued from the sex-slave house in Colombia, her paternal grandparents had adopted her. They had only learned of their granddaughter's existence several months earlier. They inadvertently found out about Jia and Sun-Yu when they discovered some letters in a toolbox in their garage. Letters that their son, Janvier, had hidden there years before. The letters were from a lady named Lihwa Huang who lived in Beijing, China, and she was pleading with Janvier to return to China to help raise their young daughters. When confronted with the letters, Janvier had admitted to his parents that he indeed had fathered two girls in Beijing when he had lived there during an extended work assignment. His parents were appalled that their son had abandoned his own flesh and blood, and were determined to find their granddaughters. They even solicited the aid of an international investigation firm to find them, spending a huge amount of their retirement savings.

    Jia had only been eight years old when she was kidnapped. She and her sister, Sun-Yu, had been on their way to the United States with their mother. They were looking forward to a better life in the promise land. On a layover in Colombia, their mother had gone to the snack bar to get them something to eat. It was then that two frantic women approached them saying their mother had taken ill and had gone to the hospital. The women told the young girls they'd take them to the hospital to be with their mother. But instead the women had kidnapped the girls and taken them to La Casa de Placer to work as sex slaves. Jia never saw her mother again after that day. And to this day, Jia did not know that their mother had arranged the whole kidnapping scheme. Lihwa had sold her own daughters into child sex slavery.

    Jia was held in captivity at the House of Pleasure for six years. Mario and Diago Tavaras, known as the brothers without souls, managed the place with an iron fist. There she experienced atrocities and vulgarities no child, or person for that matter, should have to endure. When her sister, Sun-Yu, whom she had depended on, loved, and cherished her whole life, died in that place, a piece of Jia's soul died with her. Jia didn't know how Sun-Yu had died. Dereka had only told her one day that she wouldn't see Sun-Yu anymore. That her sister had gone to heaven. Jia had thought then that heaven must be an awful place if it took her sister from her. To this day, she didn't believe in heaven or some God who was supposed to live there.

    When Jia's grandparents adopted her and brought her to live with them in France, she'd been fourteen years old. Her transition to a new life in France was a difficult one. Because she had missed so much of her formal education, her grandparents provided her with private tutoring sessions to get her up to the right grade level. Jia was a fast learner and quickly got up to speed academically. At school she excelled in her studies but struggled socially. Jia always felt like an outcast around the mainly French students. She mostly kept to herself and did not attempt to make friends. The few students who tried to befriend her eventually gave up due to her aloofness. What they didn't know was that Jia was afraid to make friends. She was ashamed of all that had happened to her as a child sex slave, and she carried a heavy burden of guilt and remorse. Jia feared that if the other students found out about her past they would look down on her, pity her, or worse consider her some kind of freak.

Jia's grandfather had passed away two years ago when Jia was a senior in high school. Now it was only her and Nai Nai. Her father, Janvier, chose not to be a part of her life. He was married with his own family and did not want a half-Asian girl around to complicate his life. After high school, Jia's grandmother wanted her to go to college. Jia had done so well academically, Nai Nai just knew she could become a doctor, lawyer, or anything she wanted to be. But Jia knew college wasn't for her. She persuaded Nai Nai to allow her to work for a while and then perhaps continue her education later. Her grandmother reluctantly agreed, but she didn't have a clue about the kind of work Jia had in mind. She didn't know that Jia was an exotic dancer and working lady of the night. Jia told her grandmother that she worked nights as a hostess at an upscale restaurant. Nai Nai, or hardly anyone else, knew about Jia's secret life. And she planned to keep it that way.

The Demon Chaser

Jia hurried upstairs to her bedroom, undressed, and took a long hot shower. Afterward, she sat on the bed in a silk nightgown, her long jet-black hair still wet and glistening from her shower. Jia counted the money she made from the night's job along with the tips she'd received. Jia knew she'd done a great job from the pure, unadulterated lust she'd seen in the men's eyes. She placed the money in an ornate wooden box she kept in the bottom of her nightstand drawer. It had been a profitable night.

Jia demanded and received top dollar for her work as a high end dancer and prostitute. Yet for Jia it was not just about the money. In a weird kind of way, it was her therapy. Where once she'd had no control over men, now she had all the control and power. She wielded her sexual prowess like the medieval samurai wielded his sword in battle. She conquered and tamed all in her path. And where once others had profited from the sale of her body, now she reaped the vast returns.

Jia didn't live lavishly with the money she made. She placed most of her earnings into a savings account which she rarely touched. She preferred to live modestly in the three-bedroom home she shared with her Nai Nai. Jia had offered many times to buy Nai Nai a new, bigger house in the beautiful countryside near Bordeaux. But Nai Nai wouldn't hear of it. She loved the home she'd live in for fifty-plus years with her husband before his passing. Nai Nai wanted to spend her remaining days there. Jia understood her desire to stay put, and was content to spend her time and money making Nai Nai's life cozy, comfortable, and pleasurable in the place that she loved.

Jia had started working as "Lady Marmalade" when she was eighteen. She had got the name from a YouTube video she'd seen of Patti

Labelle singing a song about a street prostitute in New Orleans. She had related to the song because, like the prostitute, Jia believed that her body was her most valuable possession. After all, men had lusted after her body ever since she was a young girl. Her body was what those men held her in captivity six years for. Her body was what customers paid good money for. What men cheated on their wives for. What men lusted after and most likely sold their souls to the devil for. So her body had to be her most valuable possession if men were willing to do all that for it.

So Jia decided to use her most valuable possession to her advantage. She created a website promoting herself as "Lady Marmalade," an exotic dancer with benefits. She practiced her sexy dance routine in front of a mirror until she perfected every move, and posted pictures of herself in sexy poses and attire on her website. Needless to say, it wasn't long before the solicitations for her services came pouring in. Lady Marmalade was in high demand. Jia screened the requests carefully, only considering those she felt were legit and lucrative. Some of the jobs were only for her dancing, while others consisted of both dancing and her "special skills."

Jia both loved and loathed being a sex object. It was confusing even to Jia, for how can you loathe something and love it at the same time? How was it possible to be appalled by something and yet long for it? As a young girl in a sex-slave house, Jia had been treated like a dog or some other animal. She'd been considered mere property and had been passed around from man to man like a wine bottle in a circle of winos. Yet here she was, voluntarily returning to a life of sex, lust, and immorality. The only thing she could compare it to was an old saying she once heard that "a dog returns to its vomit."

Jia lie on her back across the bed, her long, dark hair fanned out around her. She thought about the bachelor party she'd just worked. Her mind wandered to the tall, handsome blond-haired man she'd had sex with. From what she'd been told, he was the guest of honor at the affair. The groom who was getting married shortly. She'd been asked to give him "special attention," which she had. But when he'd asked her name, she'd made the mistake of telling him her real name. A mistake she now regretted for she never gave out authentic information about herself. She preferred to keep her persona as Lady Marmalade totally separate from her identity as Jia Labossiere.

So why did I tell him my name? Jia wondered, her brows furrowed as she pondered the question. She didn't know why except that there seemed to be something about him that was different from any other man she'd been with. Sure she'd seen lust in his eyes like with the others, but there was something else. When he looked at her she felt like he saw *her*—the true her with all her darkness, despair, and lost innocence. It was as if he saw her bare soul.

When Jia glanced at the clock she saw it was almost 3:00 a.m. She thought about FaceTiming Dereka but decided to wait. Jia and Dereka often FaceTimed or Skyped each other late at night. Because they had gone through a living hell together, they were connected in a way that few others could possibly be. They shared everything with each other, dark things they dared not share with anyone else. Jia knew Dereka was no longer taking her antipsychotic medication. And she knew that Dereka still saw and talked to Ms. Vee, who didn't really exist outside Dereka's world. But Jia understood that Ms. Vee was Dereka's way of coping with her demons. And they both had to somehow cope with the demons of their past.

Dereka also knew all about Jia's secret life as Lady Marmalade. Dereka didn't understand how Jia could sell her body considering all they'd been through, but she didn't judge Jia. The two of them simply accepted each other just as they were. They didn't contradict, confront, or try to change each other. And in this way, they became each other's enablers. Unintentional enablers, but enablers just the same.

Jia went into the bathroom and retrieved a plastic pouch from the cabinet beneath the sink. It contained what she called her "demon chaser." Jia carefully laid out the contents on the clean countertop, and went through her nightly routine of preparing her substance. When everything was ready, she tied a tourniquet tightly around her upper arm, and expertly injected the substance into her vein. She moaned softly as the familiar euphoric rush radiated throughout her body and a feeling of total peace and bliss overtook her. There would be no demons in her dreams tonight or any other night. Jia had discovered her perfect demon chaser. Heroin.

Hand in the Cookie Jar

Elliott arrived home around four in the morning, fully saturated with wine, woman, song, and sex. It had been one helluva bachelor party. He tiptoed into the bedroom and found his fiancée snoring softly in their antique, mahogany four-poster king-size bed. Once they became engaged, Nicole had moved in with Elliott since she was already spending the majority of her time there anyway.

Elliott quietly went into the adjoining master bath, stripped off his clothes, and stepped into the large Italian marble double shower. While he washed away all external traces of his unfaithfulness to his fiancée, he thought about Jia, the petite, sexy lady who was the cause of his disloyalty. As a matter of fact, Jia was practically all he had thought about since their sexual rendezvous. The rest of his bachelor party was a mere blur. That she was an exquisite, exotic beauty was undeniable. But Elliott instinctively knew there was much more to the young woman who called herself "Lady Marmalade" than met the eye. There was something very intriguing and alluring about her. Elliott sensed that the young lady had endured a tragic life. There was a passionate desperation in the way she'd made love to him. It was as if she was releasing some inner burden. Elliott didn't understand why he felt a deep connection with and empathy for her. She'd told him her name was Jia. To Elliott, it was a fitting name, almost as beautiful as the lady herself. He closed his eyes and whispered her name, *Jia*. He could almost still feel the touch of her hands on his body, and could see the passion and vulnerability in her beautiful, alluring eyes. The saying that "eyes are the windows to the soul" was certainly true of Jia.

Elliott mentally scolded himself for thinking so deeply about another woman. After all, his fiancée was right in the next room. He finished his shower and quietly got into bed trying not to awake Nicole. She opened her eyes and smiled at him.

"How was your party?" she questioned, looking at him intensely as if daring him to tell her the truth.

"It was very tame. Quite boring actually," Elliott replied, trying unsuccessfully not to smile.

"Liar," Nicole said, giggling and wrapping her arms around Elliott. She smelled of Nina Ricci, her favorite French perfume. Elliott playfully snuggled his nose into her neck causing her to burst into high-pitched, girlish laughter. Elliott did love his fiancée. Nicole was what most men considered the total package. She was beautiful, smart, sexy, and fun. But although Elliott loved her, there were some things, in all honesty, that he didn't like about Nicole. She was spoiled, materialistic, and a bit of a snob.

Nicole was from a well-respected, wealthy, scholarly family of old and new money. Her highbrow, prim-and-proper parents doted on their only daughter. Nicole was born with a gold, not silver, spoon in her mouth, and was provided the best nannies, education, vacations, clothes, cars, and such that money could buy. It was no wonder she grew up with a strong sense of entitlement. Nicole had little regard or tolerance for those not fortunate enough to have enjoyed the same highbred life she'd had. Elliott tried to overlook her character flaws, chalking it up to her family's influence. He was by no means perfect himself, which was evidenced by his unscrupulous behavior at his bachelor party. It had not been his intent to allow things to go as far as they had. But intent or not, the result was the same.

All the next day while at work, Elliott continued to think about Jia. Later that night, he sat at his big mahogany desk in his home office. It was after midnight, and he was dressed for bed, wearing his boxers and a robe. Elliott turned on his computer and pulled up the website for Lady Marmalade. He looked at the sexy pictures of the enticing temptress.

Elliott used his fingers to enlarge her face on his touch-screen computer so he could look into her captivating eyes. Even on the computer screen, her eyes had a hypnotic effect on him. And Elliott knew without a doubt he had to see her again.

Nicole's voice behind him made Elliott nearly jump out of his skin.

"Why are you working so late, darling?" she asked as she placed her arms around his neck. Elliott had been so engrossed with Jia's photos he hadn't even heard Nicole come into the room. He quickly slammed his computer shut, barely missing closing the lid on a couple of his fingers in the process.

"Just catching up on some paperwork. I'm all done now," he replied smiling.

"Good. Come to bed, baby. It's lonely without you," Nicole purred sexily, taking Elliott's hand and leading him toward their bedroom. As Elliott followed Nicole, he breathed a sigh of relief. Glad that he'd not gotten caught with his hand in the cookie jar.

Things Are Looking Up

It was Friday night, and Kenya and Jasmine were on their way to meet Percy and Sean at the Kennedy Center for the jazz concert. It was Kenya's idea to meet them there instead of having the guys pick them up. That way, if she didn't like her blind date she could make up an excuse, and they could duck out early. Kenya hated blind dates and was getting more nervous with each passing mile.

"I don't know why I let you talk me into this. I'm not feeling this at all," Kenya said truthfully.

"Girl, just relax and try to have a good time," Jasmine encouraged as she took the exit for the Key Bridge into DC.

"I can't relax. I'm a nervous wreck. I shouldn't have come. What if I don't like him? What if he doesn't like me? What if…"

"I'll tell you what," Jasmine interjected, cutting Kenya off in midstream. She could tell Kenya was really antsy about the date. "We can leave anytime you want. Just give me a signal, and we're out. I got your back," Jasmine assured, trying to calm her down.

"Deal," Kenya stated, sticking her pinky finger toward Jasmine for a handshake to seal the deal.

Jasmine parked in the underground parking, and they took the elevator up to the lobby. The men were already there, standing near the bar area. Their backs were turned so Kenya couldn't get a good look at Sean. Her legs were trembling slightly as she and Jasmine approached them. When Sean turned around Kenya's eyes widened and her mouth fell open. The brother was "thank you, Jesus," "hallelujah," and "great googly moogly" fine. He stood at least six foot three, had a sexy bald head, neatly trimmed mustache and goatee, and chiseled facial features. He reminded Kenya of actor Boris Kodjoe, only better looking, and that was saying a lot. Percy greeted Jasmine and Kenya with hugs and kisses, and Jasmine proudly introduced Kenya.

"Sean, this is Kenya, my sister-friend, my BFF, and much more," she announced with pride as if she was introducing the Princess of Wales. Sean gave Kenya a warm, engaging smile that accelerated her heartbeat.

"It's a pleasure to meet you, Kenya," he said, taking one of her hands into his while covering it with his other.

"Pleasure to meet you as well," Kenya replied, giving him an equally engaging smile. Jasmine and Percy exchanged knowing looks because they sensed the instant chemistry between Kenya and Sean.

"Jasmine has told me a lot of great things about you. And I have a strong suspicion she didn't exaggerate one bit," Sean said.

"Thanks," Kenya replied, blushing like a schoolgirl.

The blinking of the lobby lights signaled that the concert was about to start. As the foursome entered the theater, Sean moved close to Percy and gave him a secret fist bump to indicate his satisfaction with the situation. He too had been leery of a blind date. But his misgivings quickly vanished the minute he laid eyes on the beautiful, classy, sexy Kenya. During the concert, Sean and Kenya moved and grooved in their seats to the music and whispered to each other about this song or that musician. It seemed the vibe between the two of them was as smooth and sensual as the mellow jazz tunes. Kenya could feel him checking her out during the concert, and she felt herself getting warm all over. *Either he's getting to me or I'm having a hot flash*, she thought, smiling to herself. But she knew that Sean was the cause of her temperature rising.

During intermission, Jasmine and Kenya excused themselves to freshen up in the ladies' room. Jasmine could hardly wait to tease Kenya.

"I can tell you two are not hitting it off, so let's duck out of here while we have a chance," Jasmine said with a mischievous smirk on her face.

"Girl, don't play. Wild horses couldn't drag me away right now," Kenya stated, laughing.

"I knew you two would hit it off," Jasmine excitedly proclaimed as she reapplied her lipstick.

"Slow your roll, girlfriend. I've only known the man about an hour. The jury's still out. But I must say, I like what I've seen so far," Kenya admitted.

"Honey, that's great," Jasmine replied. "Now let's get back to our handsome men before the vultures start circling."

The rest of the evening could not have gone better. After the concert, they went to the special "invitation only" after party with music and dancing on the Roof Terrace. To please the diverse crowd, the band played a variety of music including jazz, country, pop, and soul. Around midnight, a DJ took over and played the latest hip-hop tunes for the new schoolers. But he took things up a notch when he catered to the old schoolers with classics from the Temptations, Chuck Berry, Stevie Wonder, and the Isley Brothers. And when the DJ put on Chubby Checker's 1960 hit, "Let's Do the Twist," the whole crowd went into a twisting frenzy. Chubby Checker's booming voice filled the air with a nostalgic aura.

> Come on baby,
> Let's do the twist.
> Come on baaaaaaaaby,
> Let's do the twist.
> Take me by my little hand,
> And go like this.

Young and old were twisting the night away like there was no tomorrow. The old folks really showed out because they were in their comfort zone. A few of them were twisting so fiercely it looked as if they were having an epileptic fit. Jasmine laughed until she cried because she thought there was nothing more ridiculous looking than a bunch of old geezers doing the twist. But it was Kenya and Sean who stole the show. They twisted to the left, to the right, sideways, and every which way they could. Kenya was going for it, and Sean matched her twist for twist. Jasmine, Percy, and others in the crowd watched and cheered them on. Jasmine was thrilled to see her friend relax and enjoy herself.

After the party, Kenya and Sean held hands while they walked to the parking garage. Jasmine and Percy walked in front of them all hugged up. When they got to Jasmine's car, Sean wasn't ready to say goodbye to Kenya.

"Say, Kenya. Let's give these two lovebirds a break. They're probably anxious to get rid of us. Why don't I take you home?" Sean inquired.

"You sure you don't mind?"

"Positive."

"Okay with you, Jasmine?"

"Honey, you know it is," Jasmine affirmed, not taking her eyes off Percy. After they said their goodbyes, Sean escorted Kenya to his car and opened the door for her. *A gentlemen*, Kenya thought. She hated it when guys got into the car first, and then popped the door open from the inside for their lady. In Kenya's book that one small gesture spoke volumes about a man's character.

When they arrived at Kenya's, Sean got out and opened the door for her. They strolled slowly to the front door.

"Thanks, Sean. I really enjoyed myself," Kenya stated sincerely.

"Thank you, Ms. Lady. I hope I can see you again soon," Sean said.

"Well, I don't see a problem with that," Kenya said, smiling flirtatiously. Then came that awkward moment typical of most first dates when the man must decide how to end the night. *Should I go in for a kiss on the lips, a kiss on the cheek, or a handshake*, Sean pondered as he looked at Kenya for a sign of what she preferred. Kenya could see he was struggling, so she took him off the hook by kissing him gently on his cheek.

"Goodnight, Sean. Thanks again," she whispered.

"Goodnight, Kenya. I'll be in touch soon," Sean said before leaving.

Kenya was on cloud nine as she floated up the stairs to her room. *Dereka's doing fine, and I've just met a wonderful man who's definitely peaked my interest,* she thought. *And it's been a while since a man has done that. Things are looking up.*

Saved for a Reason

Dereka sat at the desk in her bedroom writing in her journal as was her usual custom before going to bed.

> *What if none of it had happened? What if I had celebrated my thirteenth birthday at home with my family and friends?*
>
> *What if I had gone to high school like a normal girl? Who would I have gone to the senior prom with? Brandon? What color dress would I have worn?*
>
> *What if my mama was still alive? What if she had not died trying to save me? What if Grandma Ruth was still alive? What if she hadn't died of a heart attack probably because of me?*
>
> *What if I wasn't afraid to be touched by a man? What if I could look forward to getting married and having children someday?*
>
> *What If I could sleep at night without nightmares?*
>
> *What if I was a normal person with a normal life?*
>
> *What if? What if? What if?*

Dereka finished writing and glanced at the clock. It was 3:15 a.m. She knew Jia had a job tonight but figured she'd be home by now. She usually got home between 2:00 and 3:00 a.m. She FaceTimed her, and was relieved to see Jia's beautiful face appear on her screen.

"Hi Dereka, I was just thinking about you."

"Hi, sweetie. Everything go okay tonight?" Dereka asked. She worried about Jia because of the type of work she did. Her profession was far from safe, and Dereka feared that Jia would end up back in the same or an even worse situation than before.

"Everything went well. I worked a corporate party a law firm hosted for some businessmen from Dubai," Jia replied.

"Well you just be careful out there," Dereka cautioned. "You know I worry about you."

"Yes, I know. And I love you for it," Jia said smiling. Then her face turned somber. "You've always looked out me. Especially after my sister died. I wouldn't have made it without you. I don't know if you'll ever understand how much you meant and still mean to me," Jia said, her voice choked with emotion and eyes welling with tears.

"Taking care of you was my salvation. You helped me more than I could ever have helped you," Dereka confessed, her own eyes tearing.

"I'm so glad we have each other," Jia said.

"So am I. And we always will," Dereka assured her.

Jia and Dereka spent the next hour or so talking about anything and everything. Jia told Dereka about the bachelor party she'd worked recently, and how she'd made a mistake and told a customer her real name.

"I've never done that before. I hope he doesn't find out who I am or where I live. Suppose he does and tells others. I'd hate for Nai Nai, Auntie Jazz, or Aunt Kenya to find out what I do. I don't want them to be disappointed in me," Jia stated sounding worried. She took great care to protect her private life and had never had a problem being identified as Lady Marmalade. It was as though they were two totally different people. There was the reserved, sophisticated everyday Jia, and then there was her sultry, sexy alter ego as Lady Marmalade.

"Well, I wouldn't worry about it too much. Men can get pretty drunk at bachelor parties. Let's hope he doesn't remember what you told him," Dereka replied. Then Dereka told Jia how she'd overreacted when her friend, Brandon, touched her.

"I could tell he was shocked and hurt by my response. I don't know why I reacted that way," Dereka said. Jia could see the dismay on Dereka's face.

"It's understandable. I think we'll always struggle with certain things because of what we went through. I'm sure your friend knows that," Jia asserted. She and Dereka were silent for a moment.

"Do you ever think about what our lives would be like if it hadn't happened?" Dereka asked, a dreamy look on her face. "I think about it all the time. What if?"

"Same here," Jia replied honestly. "I often think about what would have happened if my mother had not left us alone at the airport for a few moments to get us a snack? What if she'd come back in time to save us? What if we all had just gone to the States, as my mother had planned, for a better life? You know, I never saw my mother again after that day. I can barely recall her face in my mind now. I just remember that she was very beautiful and always wore red. I remember her bright-red lipstick. I wonder if she's out there somewhere looking for me. I wonder if I'll ever see her again."

Dereka was quiet because she knew the god-awful truth of what had happened at the airport in Colombia. But she'd promised Sun-Yu that she would never tell anyone. And she planned to keep that promise.

"You know another thing I think about a lot?" Dereka asked rhetorically. "Why did I survive, while Sun-Yu, Crystal, and others didn't? Why me and not them? Sometimes I wish I would have just died there," Dereka confessed. Jia's ears perked up when she heard Dereka's last statement. She'd never heard Dereka say something like that before. But Jia had noticed that Dereka was becoming more depressed and despondent, especially since she'd stopped taking her medication. Jia wanted to persuade Dereka to start taking it again because she needed it. But she didn't want to push Dereka away. They needed each other.

"Dereka, please don't talk like that. If you had died there, I would have died there too. I don't know why, but perhaps we were saved for a reason," Jia replied. She decided to change the subject to lighten things up.

"Auntie Jazz told me you were coming with her to visit this summer. It will be great to see you and…"

"I think they spy on me," Dereka interjected, cutting Jia off. Jia was taken aback for a moment.

"Spy? Who? What makes you say that?" she asked.

"Well the other night I was talking to Ms. Vee, and I think I heard Aunt Kenya listening outside my door. But when I opened the door there was no one there."

"I don't think they would spy on you. They just love you and want to make sure you're all right."

"I know they love me. But their love is suffocating me. I feel trapped. I can't be myself around them. I'm tired of pretending, Jia. With them I'm always on guard. But it's not like that with Ms. Vee. She understands me, like you do. I thank God for Ms. Vee," Dereka stated gratefully.

"Yes, thank God," was the only thing Jia could think of saying.

After ending their call, Jia sat on her bed for a while thinking of all the things Dereka had said. She was concerned about her friend but didn't know what to do. She didn't know how to help Dereka. She didn't even know how to help herself. She'd told Dereka that perhaps they were saved for a reason. But Jia herself wondered if there really was a legitimate reason why they were spared. *What if?* she thought wearily as she made her way to the bathroom to take her nightly heroin hit. Afterward, she lay across the bed, and let the potent drug wash all her worries away.

In the Ring with the Devil

Early Sunday morning, Kenya and Jasmine were on their way to the nine o'clock service at Mt. Lebanon Baptist Church. Dereka had decided not to go with them, saying her stomach was a bit upset from some Chinese food she'd eaten. Attending church faithfully on Sunday mornings was a tradition in the Jones family household as far back as Kenya could remember. Kenya's parents had dragged her and Derek out of bed to attend Sunday school many Sunday mornings. Kenya recalled one time she and Derek were sitting in the back seat with their faces frowned up and lips poked out, grumbling about why they had to get up and go to church every Sunday when a lot of their friends didn't. Their mama had a ready response.

"Well, God never sleeps in on us so I don't see no reason why we should sleep in on him. Now straighten those faces out before I straighten them out for you," she'd said in her no-nonsense tone while winking at her husband. Now, Kenya was glad that her parents had raised her in the church. As an adult, she appreciated the spiritual foundation her mother especially had provided her.

Jasmine sat on the passenger side singing along to a gospel song on the radio. Kenya's ears cringed a bit because Jasmine couldn't sing a lick. Kenya tried to keep from laughing, but when Jasmine hit a particularly sour note she couldn't hold it any longer and burst into laughter.

"What are you laughing at? You know God don't like ugly," Jasmine admonished, laughing herself.

"Well, if God don't like ugly I guess that means he don't like your singing very much," Kenya countered, cracking herself up.

"The Lord knows I'm singing from my heart. He doesn't care how I sound," Jasmine replied.

"Obviously," Kenya jokingly affirmed. She took Exit 2A toward National Harbor and merged into traffic on Oxon Hill Road.

"By the way, how are things going with Sean? Has he been in touch?" Jasmine inquired.

"He called yesterday and asked when we could get together again. We're having dinner Friday night at that new restaurant on K Street in DC," Kenya said nonchalantly, trying not to show her excitement.

"I see," Jasmine responded, trying to sound just as cool and casual as Kenya. Then they started giggling like two schoolgirls.

About five minutes later, Kenya pulled into the already crowded church parking lot and squeezed into a rear parking space. They happily greeted other parishioners who were also hurriedly making their way to the early-morning service. When they entered the church, the choir was already in full swing, singing a rousing rendition of the hymn, "We'll Understand It Better By and By." The male usher, who had a crush on Jasmine, escorted them to their usual place on the right side of the church, third pew. After the songs, prayer, scripture reading, announcements, and offering, Reverend Robert Edwards, fondly called Pastor Bobby by the church members, stood in the pulpit to deliver the sermon. The congregation could tell by the glint in his eyes it was going to be a good one.

"Have you ever had to box with the devil?" Pastor Bobby asked with a sly grin on his face. "I mean, have you ever had to get in the ring and throw down with the devil?" Shouts of "Yes, Lord" and "Preach, Pastor" arose from the congregation.

"Well, I have," Pastor Bobby admitted. "And if you haven't just keep living, and I guarantee there'll come a time when you'll have to fight with that rascal. Because my Bible tells me that *the devil walks about like a roaring lion, seeking whom he may devour*. And that scoundrel don't fight fair. I mean the devil will hit you with some sucker punches that you'll never see coming. His plan is to knock you out for the count. But I'm here to tell you this morning that God has a battle strategy of how to win when you get into the ring with the devil. God has a surefire strategy for his children that will knock the devil out."

Pastor Bobby then directed the church to turn to Ephesians 6:11, *Put on the whole armour of God, that ye may be able to stand against the wiles of the devil*. Pastor Bobby went on to preach about the faithful men and women of God in the Bible that the devil had tried to destroy. People like Job, Daniel, Esther, Joseph, Peter, Paul, and John.

"But these mighty warriors for the Lord were able to withstand the devil's vicious attacks because they knew about the whole armor of God. And if you want to win when you get in the ring to box with the devil, here's seven things you got to do."

Pastor Bobby then moved from behind the pulpit podium and got into a boxer's stance.

"First thing I want you to do is hit the devil with a straight right punch of the truth," Pastor Bobby said, demonstrating a straight right boxer's punch. "Because the *devil is a liar*, and one thing I know is that he can't handle the truth." The congregation praised and cheered the pastor on.

"Next thing I want you to do is to catch that rascal with a straight left of righteousness. You can't fight evil with evil, you have to fight evil with good. Hit the devil with righteousness," Pastor Bobby proclaimed. The crowd jumped and shouted.

"Then what I want you to do is jab the devil with the gospel of peace. The devil likes confusion and discord. He can't stand peace. He won't know what to do with peace. Jab him with some peace," Pastor Bobby declared. The congregation hooped and hollered.

"Next, I want you to catch him with an uppercut of faith. Tell the devil you can't make me doubt him 'cause I know too much about him. *For we walk by faith, not by sight*."

Pastor Bobby threw an uppercut and pranced around like a boxer for a few seconds.

"Aw, we got the devil on the ropes now," he proclaimed. The crowd agreed wholeheartedly as they clapped and praised God.

"Now church, it's time for a good combination punch," Pastor Bobby announced. "I want you to hit the devil with a left hook of salvation and follow that up with a right hook of the Spirit, which is the Word of God. Now that's a winning combination right there. That combination stunned the devil. Can't you see him stumbling around, wobbly and bewildered? He's going down," Pastor Bobby yelled. People shouted in the aisles, choir stand, vestibule, and even the overflow rooms.

"Hold up, hold up," Pastor Bobby cautioned, wiping sweat from his face with a towel. "The devil might be down but he's not out yet. Now there's one more thing you need to do. And this here is the clincher. I want you to sock that sucker with a knockout punch of prayer! Because my Bible tells me that *the effectual fervent prayer of a righteous man availeth much*. If you don't believe me, just ask Elijah. He prayed, and fire rained down from heaven. If you don't believe me, just ask Joshua. Joshua prayed, and the sun and the moon stood still. If you don't believe me, why don't you ask Paul and Silas? When they prayed prison doors flew open and chains fell off. And if you still don't believe me, I dare you to ask Elisha. He prayed and the blind started seeing, and the seeing went blind. There is power in prayer. Enough power to knock the devil out…for…the…count," Pastor Bobby exclaimed, concluding his soul-stirring sermon and sending the whole congregation into a hallelujah frenzy.

After church, Kenya and Jasmine talked about how powerful the sermon was.

"Pastor preached today, didn't he?" Jasmine asserted.

"Yes, he did," Kenya agreed. They went to brunch and continued discussing various points of the sermon. However, neither of them fully realized just how much they would need to put on the whole armor of God in their battle ahead with the devil for the souls of the ones they loved.

Between Now and Hell

They're spying on me. I just know it, Dereka thought as she relentlessly searched the house for hidden cameras and microphones. Since she'd stopped taking her antipsychotic medication, she was getting more and more paranoid. Dereka had only pretended to be ill to get out of going to church with her aunts so she could do a thorough search of the house. She'd also wanted time to have a long conversation with Ms. Vee without fear of discovery. Just this morning she'd had the most wonderful talk with her dear friend, telling Ms. Vee about her suspicions that her aunts were spying of her. Ms. Vee had listened patiently, and comforted her just as she'd done many times in Colombia.

    Dereka had already searched all the rooms upstairs. Now she was in the kitchen looking in the cabinets, underneath the kitchen sink, behind the refrigerator, in all the drawers, under the toaster, in the canisters, pantry, and so on. After searching the kitchen, Dereka went into the living room and looked in the big flowerpots, vases, bookcases, underneath the lampshades, and anywhere she thought a small camera or microphone could be hidden. *Something's here. I just have to find it*, she thought as she frantically searched.

Exhausted and frustrated from hours of searching, Dereka flopped down on the sofa. It was now half past noon, and her search had been fruitless. To Dereka that didn't mean nothing was there, she just hadn't found it yet. The ringing of the doorbell made Dereka jump. *Who could that be?* she wondered as she tiptoed to the door and looked out of the peephole. Dereka gasped as her mouth fell open in surprise. She opened the door quickly and stared in disbelief at the young lady standing there. It was Regine, a girl who'd been held captive at the same sex house in Colombia as Dereka was. Regine had been brought to the house several months after Dereka arrived, and she'd come in fighting, kicking, cussing, and screaming at her captors. The girls had nicknamed her "Scrappy" because of her fiery, feisty attitude.

"Scrappy!" Dereka screamed once she recovered from her initial shock. She threw her arms around Scrappy's neck and hugged her as tight as she could.

"Angel Girl!" Scrappy exclaimed, using the nickname the girls had given Dereka because of her kind, compassionate spirit. Dereka took Scrappy's arm and pulled her into the house.

"Come on in. My aunts went to church and brunch, so we have the house all to ourselves," Dereka said excitedly. She was thrilled beyond belief to see her friend. Thrilled that she'd also made it out of Colombia alive. "Oh my God, I'm so glad to see you, Scrappy. I can't believe you're here. I thought you were dead. I thought they'd killed you when they took you away."

"Not a chance, honey. You all didn't call me Scrappy for nothing," she replied sassily, her hands on her hips.

Originally from the Bronx, New York, Regine had traveled to Colombia with two male members of a Dominican American street-gang she belonged to. They'd gone there to buy cocaine to smuggle back into the Bronx and sell. However, the drug deal had gone bad, and the two male members of her gang were killed in a shoot-out with Colombian drug dealers. She'd been kidnapped, raped repeatedly, and eventually sold to Mario and Diago Tavaras.

"How did you find me?" Dereka asked, still in a state of shock.

"Well, my father still runs drugs from Colombia from time to time. On one of his runs he heard about a big raid at a child sex-slave house near Cartagena. When he told me about it, I just knew it was the same place where we were held. I tried to get information about the girls who were rescued, but for privacy and security reasons everything was fairly hush-hush. I remembered you told me that you were from Alexandria, Virginia. I have an uncle who lives in DC, so whenever I come to visit, I always try to find you. For some reason, I just knew you'd made it out of there, so I kept looking for you. And I guess I must be a good detective because here I am," Scrappy proudly proclaimed.

"But how did you get away? How did you escape from Mario and Diago?" Dereka questioned, curious as to how she'd pulled that off.

"Honey, them m'fers did everything they could to kill me that day? They drove me deep into the jungle, beat me, kicked me, spat on me, stomped me, and did whatever else they could think of. But you know me, I was time enough for them. I fought, scratched, bit, kicked, and did whatever I could to those assholes. And I got off a really hard kick to Mario's balls that had him screaming like a punk-ass bitch," Scrappy exclaimed, throwing her head back and laughing at the memory of Mario clutching his crotch in pain. "I guess that's when they figured that enough was enough. Mario put his hands around my neck and started choking me. I must have passed out because the next thing I remember was waking up in a ravine at the bottom of a deep cliff they'd thrown my ass into. I was covered in blood, dirt, bugs, and weeds. They must have assumed I was dead," Scrappy said, pausing for a moment to take a deep breath before continuing. Tears welled in Dereka's eyes as she listened to her story and learned what she'd gone through.

"It took me two days but I was able to claw and crawl my way up that steep cliff. Sometimes I'd get close to the top and then slip and fall back down to the bottom. But I kept trying, and I made my way out of that hole," Scrappy said, smiling broadly at her accomplishment. "I walked through the jungle for two days, drinking rain water and sleeping in trees at night. Finally, I found my way to a small road where I must have collapsed. Woke up in a hospital two days later. They told me an elderly couple found me and brought me there. I told the hospital staff what had happened to me, and that other girls were being held captive at a house in the jungle and needed help. They called the police, but those prick Colombian cops didn't believe me. And even if they did believe me they didn't care. They joked about me being crazy or on drugs."

Dereka shook her head sadly. If the police had only believed Scrappy perhaps they could have been rescued much earlier. And maybe Sun-Yu would still be alive.

"How did you get back home," Dereka asked.

"I contacted my father, and he and my uncle traveled to Colombia to get me," Regine replied. She paused and took Dereka's hands into her own. "But I never forgot about you and the others. There wasn't a day that went by that I didn't think about you all and wondered if you had gotten help or escaped. I wished I could have done more to help," Regine said, her face etched with anguish.

"Don't feel bad or blame yourself. You were just a child like we were. Blame the devils who held us captive and forced us to do those disgusting things," Dereka said with a shudder.

"Yeah, I hate those bastards," Scrappy stated adamantly, her eyes smoldering with a red-hot hatred. They were both silent for a moment as feelings of anger, resentment, and exasperation enveloped them like a heavy fog.

"But you know who I blame the most?" Dereka asked. "I blame the perverts who came to that place day after day, night after night to rape us. I still have nightmares of those men on top of me. I can still see their eyes and smell their funk," Dereka divulged.

"And what's sad is that those sons of bitches got away with it," Scrappy stated.

"Yeah, for now. But my grandma Ruth always said, 'every dog has his day.' They'll burn in hell someday for what they did to us," Dereka assured her. Scrappy was silent for a long moment deep in thought. Dereka could practically see the wheels turning in her head.

"But hell may be a long ways off. And freaks like them need to pay for their sins before they get to hell," Scrappy said, looking at Dereka intently. "What if there is something we can do now to make them sick m'fers suffer before then? Something we can do to them between now and hell." Dereka looked confused.

"I don't understand. What could we do?"

"Give me some time to think about it. I'm sure I can come up with something fitting. It's time to get even with them sick bastards," Scrappy responded with a smirk on her face and a glint of evil in her eyes.

Chance Encounter

Elliott, Nicole, and Nicole's BFF Brianna sat on the patio of a small bistro on Rue Ste Catherine Street, a bustling street filled with shops and restaurants, located in the heart of Bordeaux. Elliott loved the bistro because it was a great place to relax, eat, and best of all, people watch—one of his favorite past times. Elliott enjoyed watching the faces of the tourists who came from all over the world. He enjoyed listening to their various languages and accents, and observing their different styles of dress and mannerisms. In Elliott's observation, the Americans were usually the liveliest and loudest; the Asians, fairly quiet and reserved; the Italians, relaxed and easygoing; the Latinos, friendly and family oriented; and the Middle Easterners, serious and restrained.

Dining on the outside patio at the bistro also gave Elliott the opportunity to personally interact with many of the tourists. Most foreigners who traveled to Bordeaux didn't speak French at all—or perhaps just a bit that they'd learned on the fly from the *French for Dummies* handbook. Tourists would often boldly or timidly approach Elliott's table and ask, with a glimmer of hope in their eyes, "Do you speak English?" While Elliott took pleasure in helping the mainly English-speaking tourists with directions, the menu or anything else they needed, Nicole was an entirely different story. She exemplified the stereotypical snobbish attitude that French people are justly or unjustly said to possess. She absolutely resented the tourists' intrusion into her private space and had little compassion for visitors to France who didn't speak French.

"How dare they come to our country and ask us if we speak their language," she'd say. "I don't go to their countries and ask them if they speak French. They're a bunch of idiots."

Thus, when tourists approached Nicole she would either pretend she didn't speak English, which she did speak well, or simply ignore the tourists. Sometimes she'd even curse them in French, finding great amusement in the fact that they didn't understand the derogatory names she called them. Elliott was offended by her behavior and had scolded her for it several times, but all to no avail. So he learned to just accept her attitude, heeding his mother's advice that in life sometimes you have to "take the bitter with the sweet."

While Nicole and Brianna chatted happily about the upcoming wedding, Elliott sat back and watched the people pass by. One young lady in particular caught his eye as she moved with purpose among the leisurely, mainly tourist crowd. Elliott didn't know why, but there was something familiar about her. She was slim and petite, dressed conservatively in a crisp white blouse and black slacks. Her dark hair was twisted upward into a tight bun. Elliott watched her intently as she walked pass his table and entered the bistro.

Hmmm, where do I know her from? he pondered. *Could it possibly be…Jia? No, not likely. But perhaps. Nah, it couldn't be. But what if it is?* Elliott knew he had to find out. He excused himself from the ladies saying he needed another cup of espresso. When he entered the bistro, the young lady was standing in the carryout line to order. There was only one other person in line behind her, so Elliott quickly took a place in line. He watched the young lady intently from behind, still wondering if it could possibly be her.

Once she ordered, she moved to the side to wait for her items. After a few moments, she must have sensed someone staring at her because she turned and looked directly at Elliott. When he stared into those dark, beautiful, vulnerable eyes, he knew without a doubt it was Jia. The one who called herself "Lady Marmalade." He could still remember like it was yesterday the way she had smelled, the way she'd tasted, and the way she'd felt in his arms that night. He hadn't been able to get her out of his mind. She must have recognized him also because she immediately averted her eyes. She also became very flustered and rushed out of the restaurant without her items.

"Mademoiselle, votre commande," a server yelled after her to remind her of her order. But the young lady quickly disappeared into the bustling crowd.

Second Time's a Charm

Kenya and Sean walked hand in hand down K Street toward the public parking garage. It was their second date, and they'd just finished dinner at a new, much raved about restaurant in DC, which had definitely lived up to its hype. During dinner Sean had been everything Kenya could have hoped for. He was interesting, charming, funny, and attentive. She learned that he'd gotten married shortly after graduating from college, divorced about five years later, and had a twenty-year-old son attending Brown University. It was clear that Sean cared deeply for his son and was very involved in his life. A trait that Kenya found endearing. With so many fathers missing in action, it was refreshing to see there were some men who knew being a father was a whole lot more than just being a sperm dispenser. Men who knew it takes accountability, commitment, strength, discipline, patience, and a whole lot of love.

"It hasn't been easy raising a son with so many distractions like drugs, drinking, gangs, violence, peer pressure, and such pulling him in the wrong direction," Sean acknowledged. "Keeping that boy out of trouble during his teenage years was a full-time job. I had to jack him up by his collar a few times. But, he turned out okay," Sean asserted, blushing with pride.

More points for Sean, Kenya mentally tallied. So far this evening he had accumulated quite a few points on her "good man pedometer," including one for leaving the waitress a sizable tip. She hated dating what her mother used to call "cheapskates." Once Kenya had dated a guy wearing raggedy, dusty shoes, and he'd had the nerve to leave the waitress a two-dollar tip on a fifty-dollar tab. Then, he'd even had the audacity to ask Kenya for money to put gas in his car.

"Say, baby, I'm running a little short on cash," he'd said. "Can you help a brother out and fill up the tank for me on the way back to your place?" Kenya had politely excused herself from the table, slipped the waitress some extra bucks, exited by a side door, and taken a cab home. Needless to say, she never saw that dusty-shoes-wearing, no-gas-having, broke-butt brother again.

When Sean and Kenya got to her house, she decided to invite him in for a while. Jasmine was in L.A. on business, and Dereka was spending the night with her friend, Fatima.

"Would you like to come in for a cup of coffee or something" she asked.

"Yes, I would love a cup of coffee or something," Sean replied, putting extra emphasis on the words "or something." Kenya just smiled. Once inside she went into the kitchen to make coffee. Sean busied himself in the living room looking through what seemed like hundreds of CDs, neatly stacked and sorted by artists, in a huge wooden storage cabinet.

"I see somebody loves music," he yelled to Kenya. She entered the living room with two steaming cups of coffee.

"That's my father's old-school CD collection. That collection was his pride and joy. I grew up listening to music by the Temptations, Smokey Robinson and the Miracles, Ray Charles, Stevie Wonder, and the Supremes. On Sundays we'd listen to Mahalia Jackson, Shirley Caesar, the Five Blind Boys, the Dixie Hummingbirds, James Cleveland, and other gospel greats. That's why I love old-school music to this day," Kenya stated.

"Yeah, me too. My love for oldies came from my favorite uncle, Ezelle. He has passed on now, but he was a good man and quite a character. He started every other sentence with 'And, I'll tell you another thang,'" Sean said, smiling at the memory.

"Sounds like an interesting fellow," Kenya replied. She browsed through the CDs. "What would you like to hear?" she asked. Sean looked thoughtful for a moment.

"How about some Marvin Gaye or Luther?" he asked with a sly smile on his face. *Umm huh, I know what you're up to*, Kenya thought. She figured that Sean wanted to hear some mellow, sexy love songs so they could get all kissy-huggy. But this was only their second date, and Kenya wasn't ready for all that yet. After her fiasco with Ryan, she was guarding her heart more carefully. She chose an upbeat tune, "Lonely Teardrops," by the late, great Jackie Wilson. Sean chuckled softly when he heard it.

"My grandma Leona was crazy about Jackie Wilson," Kenya stated. "The story goes that whenever Jackie Wilson came on TV, housewives everywhere stopped dusting, cooking, ironing, sewing, moping, or doing whatever they were doing to see the smooth, sexy singer strut his stuff on the stage."

"Yeah, 'Mr. Excitement' was a masterful performer," Sean acknowledged. He and Kenya talked for the next two hours about anything and everything. Although she hadn't meant to, Kenya found herself opening up to Sean in ways that she hadn't opened up to a man in years. She told him all about her brother, Derek, father, DJ, and the love of her life, her mama, BabyRuth. She even told him about Dereka's kidnapping and captivity at a sex-slave house in Colombia.

"Dereka's gone through so much. Especially mentally. It's been a struggle. But with therapy and medication, thank God, she's doing okay. I promised my mama on her deathbed that I'd look out for her. And I plan to do it until my dying day," Kenya said wholeheartedly.

"She's lucky to have you," Sean said, looking admiringly at Kenya. He respected her love of family and her commitment to her niece. He'd known there was something special about her from the moment they'd met. Around midnight, Kenya walked Sean to the door and stood outside with him on the front porch. This time there was no hesitation as they simultaneously moved in for a slow, lingering kiss.

Neither of them were aware of the dark-colored car parked a few houses away on the opposite side of the street. The person inside watched the entire exchange between Sean and Kenya. The person kept watching while Sean got into his car and drove away. The person watched Kenya go back into the house and close the door. Then, the person slowly pulled the car away from the curb and drove away.

The Lady Is a Tramp

For three days Elliott hung out at the bistro hoping to see Jia again. But so far, she'd never shown up. Elliott, knowing she had recognized him also, suspected that she would avoid coming to the bistro, at least for a while. Yet, here he was, hoping against hope that she'd return. Today, he sat outside at the same table he'd been at when he saw her. This time he'd asked his friend Zack to join him, but he hadn't told him what he was really up to. Deep down he felt guilty about even trying to see Jia again. After all, his big wedding day was only a couple of days away. Soon he'd be standing at the altar marrying Nicole, a woman any man would be lucky to have. So why was he so entranced by another woman? A lady he'd only spent one night with. A lady he didn't even know. A lady of the night.

"Did you hear anything I just said?" Zack asked, looking at his friend curiously.

"I'm sorry, what did you say?" Elliott replied absently.

"What's up with you, dude? You invited me down here for lunch, and you've hardly said two words to me since I got here."

"I'm sorry. I just got a lot on my mind."

"Well you're getting married in two days. You should have a lot on your mind. You're about to take the big plunge into the abyss. Jump off the cliff. Go off the deep end. Give up your freedom, privacy, and good sex," Zack joked, laughing hysterically. Elliott didn't crack a smile. Zack turned serious because he could tell something was weighing heavily on his friend's mind. "You getting nervous?" Zack asked.

"No. Well, yes. Perhaps a little. I don't know."

"Listen, Elliott. It's okay to be a little nervous. But I don't think you have anything to worry about. Nicole's a great girl. You two were made for each other," Zack stated. Elliott decided to confide in Zack about his fascination with Jia.

"Zack, you remember that dancer, Lady Marmalade. The one that you hired for my bachelor party?" he asked.

"Remember her?" Zack exclaimed. "Dude, she's hard to forget. She's actually shown up in a couple of my wet dreams since then," Zack confessed. Elliott cringed a bit at his response.

"Well, I can't get her out of my mind. I think about her day and night," he admitted.

"She really put something on you that night, didn't she? Man, I heard she was good at what she does. That's why I hired her. But she didn't come cheap. I paid good money for your night of wild, hot sex. And that's why I'm the best man you could have picked," Zack replied, patting himself on the back.

"But it was more than just the sex. I think I really feel something for her. I can't explain it. But if I feel like this, maybe I'm not ready to get married," Elliott said. Zack got up and placed his hand on Elliott's forehead.

"Buddy, are you feeling okay?" he asked comically.

"I feel fine," Elliott replied, slightly annoyed by Zack's antics.

"Then you must be crazy! Loco! Stone out of your mind," Zack proclaimed.

"I'm not crazy, loco, or anything. But there's something special about that lady. Something very intriguing. Something…"

"The lady is a tramp," Zack interrupted. "She's a tramp. She's a piece of ass," Zack callously declared. Elliott felt his anger rising.

"Now hold up, mate. You're my friend and all, but I'm not going to sit here and allow you to disrespect her like that," Elliott warned. He didn't get angry often but when he did Zack knew to back off.

"You're right. But didn't you disrespect her yourself when you slept with her for money?" Zack accused. Elliott was silent because he knew Zack made a good point.

"Elliott, you and I go back a long way, and I'm telling you what you are thinking doesn't make sense," Zack continued. "You're sitting here doubting whether to marry a great girl because of a prostitute you met at your bachelor party. That's crazy. I think you've just got a bad case of pre-wedding jitters, that's all."

Elliott thought about all his friend had just said. Of course, Zack was right. That had to be it. What else could it be?

♦ ♦ ♦

Two days later, Elliott stood at the altar of the La Chapelle Cathedral looking handsome in his tailor-made black-and-white tuxedo. He gasped when his fiancée appeared in the grand archway, looking like a dream in a beautiful Vera Wang designer wedding gown. She seemed to float down the aisle toward him as a grand symphony orchestra played a beautiful wedding song. Her eyes sparkled as bright as the diamond necklace she wore, and her smile was as bright as the rays of the sun shining through the cathedral's majestic stained glass windows. As Elliott watched his stunningly beautiful bride march down the aisle, he thought to himself, *Zack is right. We are made for each other.* And when the priest recited the traditional wedding vows, Elliott hesitated only slightly before saying, "I do."

Them

Dereka sat in her car in a small neighborhood park near Old Town Alexandria. It was the same park her mother used to bring her to when she was a little girl. It didn't have much back then—just a couple of swings, a sliding board, a monkey bar, and a plastic stationary pony. Now it was expanded to a full recreational facility with several large colorful play stations.

Back in the day, the small park was always packed to the brim with kids running, screaming, laughing, jumping, and having the time of their lives. Dereka recalled the times when her mother would push her in the swing while she yelled, "Higher, Mama, I want to go higher." Sometimes her mama would swing along beside her, and they would compete to see who could swing the highest. Their laughter would fill the air as they pumped their legs and pulled back on the swing chains to propel themselves forward. Of course, unbeknownst to Dereka at the time, Serena always let her win. Her mama took great joy in seeing her daughter's wide, gap-toothed smile as she shouted, "I won. I beat you again, Mama." Dereka smiled at the memory. That's when life had been good and innocent.

Dereka watched several children playing in the park while their parents or babysitters sat on a park bench nearby, chatting among themselves. Because it was Monday morning, there were only a few preschool-aged kids at the park. Dereka was supposed to be at her biweekly therapy session. Kenya had reminded her about the appointment before she'd headed to the office. But Dereka wasn't going to this session or any other sessions. Her plan was to just stay at the park for an appropriate amount of time, and then go to the office and work the remainder of the day.

Dereka felt that her therapist, Dr. Bedford, didn't understand her. Dr. Bedford had not been through what she'd gone through. Dr. Bedford had not been held captive and treated worse than an animal. Dr. Bedford had not been sexually violated by demented men night after night. Dr. Bedford had not been taken to a shed and tortured nearly to death. Dr. Bedford had not watched her friends' bodies be unceremoniously dumped in black trash bags and lugged up basement stairs. So what was the point of continuing to see Dr. Bedford?

She can't help me. No one can, Dereka thought sadly as she blinked back tears. She felt like a lost cause, beyond the reach of recovery. She earnestly believed she'd never be a normal human being again. And it was all because of them. The repugnant pedophiles who hid behind their masks while they assaulted and degraded their victims. And afterward, in all likelihood, they'd returned to their wives and children without any thought of the damaged souls they'd left behind. Dereka blamed them even more than the men who sold her to them. Without them there would be no sale. Without the demand, there would be no supply.

Dereka despised them, but despise didn't begin to capture how she felt. She downright hated them. Deep in her heart she knew it was wrong. She'd been taught in her home and church that it was wrong to hate anyone. She knew the Bible verse that said, *Love your enemies, bless them that curse you, do good to them that hate you, and pray for them which despitefully use you.* But at this point, Dereka could neither love, bless, or pray for those men who used her like some filthy sex object. She loathed them. Resented them. Detested and absolutely abhorred them.

♦ ♦ ♦

Around noon, Dereka left the park and drove to the office. When she got there, Kenya's assistant, Trevon, was in the front lobby talking with Cyndy, the receptionist.

"What's up, Boogie Boo," Trevon teased, calling Dereka by the nickname he'd learned her grandma called her.

"Watch yourself," Dereka replied playfully. *He's not one of them*, she thought. *He's one of the good ones.* She thought of him as a big brother, and he treated her like his baby sister.

"I'm headed out to lunch. Want to join me?" he offered.

"Sure, just let me tell Aunt Kenya I'm here," Dereka replied.

"She's at a meeting and will likely be gone most of the day. You know what they say, 'When the cat's away the mice will play,'" Trevon said with a twinkle in his eyes. "Let's go to that sandwich shop in Fair Oaks Mall. I've got a taste for a philly cheesesteak."

Trevon and Dereka had a very enjoyable lunch at the mall. Trevon was easy for Dereka to be around. After the depressing morning she'd had, he was just what she needed. When Dereka returned to her office, she noticed the blinking red light on her phone indicating she had several messages. She listened and discovered one of the messages was from Dr. Bedford's office inquiring about Dereka missing her therapy session, and asking her to call the office as soon as possible to reschedule. Dereka knew she had to cover her tracks so her aunts would not find out. At least not yet. Her hope was that eventually she'd be able to convince them that she no longer needed therapy. But until that time, she intended to cover her tracks.

Dereka picked up the phone and nervously dialed the doctor's office. She hated lying but felt it was a necessary evil in her current situation.

"Dr. Bedford's office. How may I help you?" the chipper receptionist said.

"Hi, Mindy. This is Dereka."

"Oh, hi, Dereka. How are you?

"I'm fine. I got your message. And I am so sorry about missing my session this morning. I forgot to let you know that I won't be coming back. Aunt Kenya and I found another doctor at our church that I'm going to start seeing. She's really good at dealing with sex trafficking victims. She's a survivor herself, so she really understands what I'm going through."

"Well, okay. I'll let Dr. Bedford know. We'll miss seeing you. Please keep in touch, and let us know how you're doing."

"I will. Have a great day!"

"Thanks. You too. Bye." As soon as Dereka hung up the phone Kenya knocked on the door and peeped in.

"Hey you," she said. "How was your session?"

"It was great," Dereka lied.

"Are you sure? You look a little flustered," Kenya stated, coming into her office.

"No, no, no. I just got off the phone with a sales rep promoting some new antivirus software. You know how pushy those sales people can be."

"Tell me about it," Kenya concurred. "Jasmine will be back in town this evening. Perhaps the three of us can eat out tonight."

"No thanks. I had a big lunch with Trevon," Dereka replied. At least that was true. "I'll just eat a light meal at home."

"Okay, sweetie," Kenya said as she started out the door. Before leaving, she turned around with a smile on her face. "We're so proud of you, sweetie. You're doing everything you need to do to take care of yourself."

"Thanks, Aunt Kenya," Dereka replied, forcing a smile on her face.

When Kenya left, Dereka exhaled a deep breath. Her head was aching, no doubt from tension and stress. She let out a soft whimpering sound like that of a wounded puppy. She felt so sad inside. Sad that her life had come down to nothing but lies and pretense. And it was all because of them. She thought about what Scrappy had said about getting even with them, and slowly but surely the idea began to take hold in her mind and heart. *Scrappy's right*, she thought. *Somebody has to do something to make them pay.*

♦ ♦ ♦

Later that evening when Dereka got home, she noticed a message on the home phone answering machine. She hit the play button and heard Dr. Bedford's voice.

"Hi Kenya. This is Dr. Bedford. Mindy told me that you all found another doctor for Dereka. Someone at your church. I'm sorry to hear that. I know sometimes it may have seemed that the progress was slow, but in cases such as Dereka's, it does take time. I can certainly understand if you all prefer for her to see another doctor more suitable for her particular issues. The main thing is that she remains consistent with her therapy and medication so she won't relapse. Anyway, have her doctor get in touch with me so we can talk, and I can send over my records and notes. Thanks so much. Take care."

Dereka deleted the message.

The Supreme Hunter

Memphis walked across the prison yard toward a security guard. As they casually passed each other, the guard secretly slipped Memphis a cell phone which Memphis quickly put into the waistband of his prison uniform pants. He then went into a gray stone building nearby and sat in one of several wooden chairs in a small room. This was Memphis's unofficial business office that he'd confiscated for his use shortly upon his arrival. He dialed the number of one of his trackers that he had looking for Ryan. *This fool better have some good news for the money I'm paying*, Memphis thought. The person on the other end picked up immediately.

"Talk to me," Memphis demanded. He listened intently for about five minutes to the tracker's report. Afterward, he dialed another number and relayed the information he'd just received. When Memphis hung up the phone, a smile slowly crept across his face.

Memphis loved the hunt. He thrived on it. In his mind, he was the supreme hunter—unparalleled in skills, wit, and determination. He loved the artistry of the hunt, the devious and devilish imaginings of the mind as it roamed free to plan and set a trap for the prey. He'd known it was just a matter of time before he'd hunt Ryan down like the rabid dog he was, and make him pay with his life for his treacherous betrayal.

Memphis went to the door and signaled for three men sitting in the prison yard to join him in his office. These were the top three men in Memphis's entourage. They had proven they were willing to do anything and everything Memphis directed them to do. He considered them his pseudo–board of directors. The men hurried in and took their respective places on Memphis's right and left.

"You got some good news," one of them asked.

"Yeah, my top tracker got a hot tip on Ryan. He thinks that fool is back in the States, living in Denver, Colorado."

"Denver?" another asked. "What he doing there?"

"Supposedly, his new identity is Lyle Kinston, and he's pretending to be a plumber of all things," Memphis informed him.

"Lyle the f——king plumber! What he gone be next? A butcher or some s——t like that," the third man said, laughing so hard he nearly fell out of his chair.

"There'll be no next," Memphis stated. "If it turns out to be true I've already given word to one of my enforcers to execute Ryan's death sentence. And, just for the hell of it, I requested that Ryan, or should I say Lyle the plumber, be cut into tiny pieces and flushed down the toilet. How's that for irony?" Memphis said with a smirk on his face. He'd gotten that idea from one of the criminal minds at his disposal. An inmate called Daddy Mack, who swore up and down that he had actually disposed of a body that way. "Now all I have to do is sit back and wait for word that the job has been done," Memphis stated.

After Ryan ended up floating through Denver's sewer system, Memphis planned to turn his full attention to Kenya, and the rest of the Jones family clan. This included Dereka, who had defied all odds by surviving for five years in the sex-slave house in Colombia he'd sold her to. And what was even more mind-boggling to Memphis was that she'd even survived her last two weeks at a place in Brazil known as The Last Stop. Memphis also planned to take out Kenya's hussy friend, Jasmine, who had ridden in like a happy harlot on a white horse to save the day and had rescued Dereka.

It's time to get rid of those thorns in my side once and for all. And this time failure is not an option, Memphis thought menacingly.

Game On, Doc

Ryan was living the good life, but not in Denver as Lyle the plumber like Memphis thought. Ryan was in Miami, Florida, under the alias of Lamar Green. He was working for Hector Rebello, the kingpin of a major cocaine smuggling operation, and making good money doing so. He'd been hiding out for over six years and had lived in four different countries. He was counting his lucky stars that he'd left South Africa just in the nick of time.

Ryan knew his betrayal of Memphis had propelled him into the top ten of Memphis's most-wanted list. And he also knew that Memphis would not rest day or night until he paid him back with deadly interest. So that tidbit of information kept Ryan on his toes. He was always looking over his shoulder, around corners, under beds, and such, just waiting for his retribution from Memphis to come. And he knew it was coming. Men like Memphis didn't let things go. Especially when that thing had caused him to be locked up in a prison cell.

Memphis was one of the coldest men that Ryan had ever met, and he'd met plenty. Memphis was an expert in all things evil and malevolent. Ryan shuddered to think of all the ways that Memphis could make him suffer if he caught him. But Ryan had no regrets about selling Memphis out to save Kenya's life. He'd spent a lot of time with her, albeit as part of Memphis's ploy to deceive and destroy her. But what Ryan had thought would be just another con job had somehow turned into something else. He'd developed deep feelings for Kenya. This was surprising to him because, for the most part, he didn't care much about anything or anybody.

Thus, when Memphis had told Ryan about his plan to kill Kenya, he'd turned him in to the authorities. Perhaps he'd done it for love or perhaps he'd done it for his own ego to prove that he could take out one of the most revered criminals alive. For whatever reason, Ryan was well aware that Memphis would not rest until he had tracked him down and taken his life in the most horrific way imaginable. So Ryan's major goal in life was to not get caught.

Ryan was good at hiding out. Extremely good. To throw Memphis off his scent, he'd created a phony story about him being some guy named Lyle Kinston, a plumber living in Denver. Oh, there was a Lyle Kinston living in Denver, and he was a plumber. But he just wasn't Ryan. Ryan had stolen the guy's identity and used it to set up a fake identity for himself. He'd intentionally leaked the phony information about his new identity to Memphis via his cousin, Michael. Michael just happened to be cellmates with a man named Louie, who was a member of Memphis's so-called board of directors. According to Michael, Louie was always bragging about being one of Memphis's top dogs. The man just couldn't keep his big mouth shut. Ryan and his cousin had nicknamed him "Blabbermouth."

And, lucky for Ryan, Blabbermouth often shared critical information with Michael, which was subsequently passed on to Ryan. That is for a fee. Michael had told Ryan, "You my blood and all, but I want to get paid for helping save your ass from Memphis's wrath. And it's coming, blood. I'm just helping you put if off as long as possible. And that's worth something right there." So Ryan paid Michael to pass on Blabbermouth's vital information. That's how he'd discovered that Memphis was hot on his trail in South Africa and managed to escape perhaps moments before his time on earth ended.

But Ryan was getting tired of running from Memphis and decided that he'd turn the tables and play offense rather than continue to play defense. He'd use his brains, wit, and cunningness to beat the master at his own game. After all, he'd been one of Memphis's most trusted confidantes for years and had learned all the tricks of the criminal trade from one of the best crooks in the devil's den. Ryan called Memphis Doc, because he considered him to be at the top of his game, an expert in his chosen criminal profession. And Memphis had been a good teacher too, perhaps a little too good if you asked him now. He'd schooled Ryan well in the laws of thug criminology. He'd taken a young hooligan from the streets of Detroit and turned him into a seasoned, legitimate con artist who could match wits with the best of them. Ryan had already outmaneuvered Memphis once by stopping him from the cold-blooded murder of Kenya. And he was positive he could outwit him again. Especially if it meant saving his own neck. Ryan likened himself to the biblical David. He was getting ready to take Goliath down.

Ryan knew the misleading information that he was living in Denver as a plumber named Lyle Kinston would surely get back to Memphis. As it happened, the real Lyle the plumber was actually a middle-aged, pot-bellied divorced white man. Ryan knew, from personal experience, that when Memphis got a hot lead on someone, the first thing he did was send one of his employees to conduct surveillance on the target to verify the lead before executing the sentence. Ryan figured that the real Lyle Kinston was in no real danger. But even if something did happen to him, Ryan could have cared less. Under Memphis's tutorage, he'd learned a lot about the necessity of "collateral damage." Sometimes the innocent had to suffer to get things done. That's just the way it was. There was little room for a heart or conscience in the ruthless criminal world.

Ryan was looking forward to matching wits with Memphis. Ryan was cocky, callous, crafty, and conniving. And he was confident in his ability to stay one step ahead of his one-time idol. Ryan smiled to himself as he pictured the look on Memphis's face once he found out that the lead he'd received was phony, and that the real Ryan was nowhere to be found. Creating the false identity as Lyle the plumber was just one of the tricks Ryan had up his sleeve. He had many more tricks and moves to make in his deadly cat-and-mouse game with Memphis.

Game on, Doc, Ryan thought cockily, rubbing his hands together in anticipation of the battle of wits to come.

The Twilight Zone

Dereka waited anxiously for Scrappy to arrive. It had been over two weeks since she'd seen her. Dereka was glad Scrappy was coming tonight, because Jasmine was on a fund-raising trip for Operation Undercover, and Kenya was out on a date. Dereka was excited and nervous to see Scrappy again, and hear her plan of how to make sadistic men suffer for their sins. She'd thought about it a lot, and had even become obsessed with the idea. She convinced herself it was why she had survived her ordeal in Colombia. It was her purpose. Her special mission from God. She hadn't had much hope lately, but now she felt hopeful again.

Dereka looked at her watch and saw it was 9:00 p.m. Scrappy should be there any minute. Dereka paced back and forth anxiously, hardly able to contain herself. She had a surprise to share with Scrappy, something she'd not shared with anyone for a long time. When the doorbell rang, Dereka yanked the door open, grabbed Scrappy's hand, and pulled her into the house.

"Come on in. Let's go upstairs," Dereka said excitedly.

"Well, hello to you too. What's the rush?" Scrappy responded, pausing to remove her jacket and sit on the sofa.

"No, we can't talk here. There may be microphones or hidden cameras around so I don't want to take any chances. Besides I have a surprise for you," Dereka stated, pulling Scrappy to her feet. Scrappy looked confused for a moment, shrugged her shoulders, and followed Dereka upstairs to her room. Dereka closed her bedroom door and strolled over to a Queen Anne chair in the corner of the room.

"Scrappy, this is my very good friend, Ms. Vee," she announced proudly. "I met her at that house in Colombia after you left and after Sun-Yu died. She's been like a grandmother to me ever since. I don't think I would have made it without her. Ms. Vee, this is Regine, but we call her Scrappy," Dereka said, her face beaming with joy at introducing the two of them. Scrappy's eyes widened in shock and disbelief. She looked from Dereka to the empty chair and back to Dereka again.

"Dereka, what the hell are you talking about," she proclaimed loudly.

"What do you mean?" Dereka asked, confused.

"There's no one there!" Scrappy stated bluntly.

"Scrappy, how can you say that? Ms. Vee's right here. I thought for sure you would be able to see her. Everybody else has been trying to convince me she's not real. But I thought…I just knew…" Dereka stammered.

Damn, Dereka's losing it, Scrappy thought. She sighed deeply and shook her head sadly as she realized that Dereka was mentally unstable. She walked over to Dereka and placed her hand on her shoulder.

"Dereka, you know I'm a straight shooter. And I ain't gonna bulls——t you. There ain't no little old lady sitting in that chair. You're imagining things," Scrappy pointed out.

"Why are you saying that? This was a bad idea. I'm sorry I brought you up here," Dereka replied, frustrated. Scrappy exhaled sharply. She felt like she was caught in a bad episode of *The Twilight Zone*.

"Okay, I guess I'll just have to prove it to you," she asserted. Then Scrappy moved to the chair and plopped down into it.

"Scrappy, noooooooo!" Dereka yelled as she closed her eyes and covered them with her hands. She didn't want to see the spectacle of Scrappy sitting on top of poor Ms. Vee.

"Open your eyes, Dereka. See for yourself," Scrappy challenged. Dereka peeped through her fingers before slowly removing her hands away from her eyes. Her mouth dropped open in bewilderment. There was no one there except Scrappy.

"How did you do that? What happened to Ms. Vee?" Dereka asked in a total state of shock. Her mind was spinning, and she was breathing rapidly as if in a panic. It was really confusing to her. Scrappy moved quickly to Dereka's side and put her arms around her.

"Honey, you're okay. Don't let it get you down. Them bastards over there just screwed up your mind, that's all," Scrappy said. Dereka walked to her bed as if in a trance and sat down.

"They were right all along. Ms. Vee's not real. She never was," Dereka admitted, looking totally deflated and disillusioned. Scrappy joined her on the bed. It was time for some tough love—the only kind that Scrappy knew about.

"No, she's not real. But it's just as well. The last thing you need is some kind old lady spirit hanging around. The hell with ghosts. It's time to take matters into our own hands. I've got a plan. But you've got to be strong if you want to do this with me. If you don't, I'll understand. So, what's it gonna be, Dereka? Do you want to hear my plan or do you want me to leave?" Scrappy asked.

Dereka looked at the empty chair. *They did this to me*, she thought. *They broke me. Screwed up my mind. They can't keep doing this. Somebody has to do something.* Dereka turned to face Scrappy, the dismay that was in her eyes earlier was now replaced with resolve.

"No, don't leave. Stay, and tell me your plan," she said calmly.

Shybirdie

The steely look in Dereka's eyes and the conviction in her voice assured Scrappy that Dereka was up for the task ahead.

"Okay, here's the deal," Scrappy said, leaning back against the headboard and crossing her long legs. She told Dereka about her plan to bait, lure, and punish vile men who prey on young girls. She'd gotten the idea from the TV show, *To Catch a Predator*, hosted by Chris Hansen, which aired between 2004 and 2007. The gist of the show was to lure sexual predators to specific locations by pretending to be underage girls. When the men arrived, expecting to have a sexual encounter with a minor, Chris Hansen would suddenly appear from behind closed doors with cameramen in tow. The looks of absolute dismay, shock, and fear on the men's faces when they realized they were caught were priceless. Chris Hansen would politely ask the stunned pervert to have a seat, and attempt to interview him by asking questions such as "What was your intention for coming here?" and "Did you expect to have sex with a minor?" Sometimes he'd even show them a printed copy of the often-lurid sexual language they'd used to chat with the person who they'd thought was a child. Some of the men would attempt to lie or con their way through the interview, while others just made a quick exit. The majority of the men were apprehended by the police and arrested at the scene.

"The big difference with my plan is that there'll be no police involved, but there will be justice. Street justice. That's the only kind I know about," Scrappy said, looking at Dereka intently to gauge her reaction.

"Street justice? What do you mean? You're not talking about killing anybody, are you?" Dereka asked worriedly. She was thinking about Scrappy's connection with a violent Dominican-American street gang in the Bronx. She knew such gangs thought little of killing a foe.

"No, I'm not talking about killing them although them m'fers deserve to die. But we're gonna make them wish they were dead. We're gonna make them suffer like we suffered. You remember the shed?" Scrappy asked, referring to a wooden shed their captives had used to torture the girls who misbehaved. Dereka cringed just at the mere mention of the shed. She'd been taken there once, and once was enough. She had barely survived. The memory of the excruciating pain inflicted on her brought tears to her eyes.

"Yes, I remember," she replied, wrapping her arms around herself and rocking back and forth as if she could still feel the pain. "I wish I could forget, but I know I never will."

"Yeah, they almost killed my ass in that place," Scrappy conceded. "I've been through some pain in my life, but nothing like that. Yet it did teach me a thing or two about inflicting pain. Lessons we'll use on them. I might even do a Lorena Bobbitt on them," Scrappy joked, referring to the infamous woman who'd gained world fame in 1993 by cutting off her cheating husband's penis. Scrappy jumped off the bed, retrieved her well-worn leather satchel, and removed some papers.

"I've done some research on sexual predators that will help us lure them into our trap. A lot of these assholes use Internet chat rooms and instant messaging to find girls. Ain't that something? They even pose as teens. They get a lot of information from the user profiles, stuff like age, school, favorite music or food, sports interests, likes, dislikes, or anything they can use to help them relate to the girls, or in some cases, boys."

"That's really scary. There's so much you can learn from someone's profile," Dereka replied, thinking about the personal information she had so innocently included on her own profile as a young girl.

"I know. And that's how we're going to trap them. We'll create a profile pretending to be a thirteen-year-old girl."

"I'd just turned thirteen when I was taken."

"I know," Scrappy replied, looking at Dereka with sympathy in her eyes. "Most of the perverts surfing the Internet prefer children right around puberty because at this age they're generally curious about sex, but also clueless. One sick bastard they interviewed said..." Scrappy paused and rummaged through her papers looking for the exact quote. "Oh, here it is. He said, 'Give me a kid who knows nothing about sex, and you've given me my next victim.' That's messed up. I can't wait to get my hands on one of these lowlifes. Once we make a user profile, we'll post some enticing comments in several chat rooms and see what happens. Where's your computer?" Scrappy asked looking around.

"There on the desk in the corner. I'm already logged in so you should be good to go."

While Scrappy worked on the computer, Dereka reviewed the information on sexual predators that Scrappy had downloaded from the Internet. She was surprised to see that in a recent survey one out of five children between ten and seventeen who use the Internet said they'd received "unwanted sexual solicitations online, ranging from sexually suggestive comments to strangers asking them to meet in the real world for sex." And, surprisingly, often the children went willingly to a meeting with the person they met online. This is because sexual predators are extremely savvy at singling out and befriending young vulnerable children. They look for posts that signal the child is having problems at home, is unhappy at school, or is feeling lonely and misunderstood. They befriend the child and may spend weeks, months, or sometimes years "grooming" the child by showering him or her with affection, flattery, kindness, attention, and even gifts. These "master manipulators" are highly skilled at breaking down the child's emotional barriers and gaining their trust. And the ambiguity of the Internet is the perfect disguise for them to spin their web of entrapment. *Wow*, Dereka thought as she read.

"Hey, Angel Girl," Scrappy said. "Come take a look at this profile I made, and tell me what you think." Dereka pulled up a chair and joined Scrappy at the computer. "I chose the username LonelyBirdie because it sounds like someone with low self-esteem. What do you think?" Scrappy asked.

"Hmmmm, how about Shybirdie? That does the same thing without being too obvious."

"Hey, good point. I see you're going to be good at this," Scrappy replied. Dereka looked over the rest of the information. Their pseudo-Shybirdie was born May 3, 2004. She liked playing video games, finger painting, making homemade pizza, and spray dying her hair different colors. The profile listed other mundane things typical of a teenager's profile, like favorite food, favorite movie or TV show, best place to shop, and so on. The clincher, which Scrappy hoped would be the chum for the shark, was that Shybirdie's biggest fear was "fitting in."

"I like it," Dereka said. "I think you say all the right things based on the research of what sexual predators look for. What's the next step?"

"Let's post something and see what happens," Scrappy replied. She sat at the computer in deep thought for a moment, tapping her fingers on the desk. "How about this?" she said. Scrappy started typing on the computer, talking as she typed. "Nobody gets me. 4COL. Feeling misunderstood ☹."

"What does 4COL mean?" Dereka quizzed. She knew a lot of Internet acronyms but was unfamiliar with that one.

"It means 'for crying out loud,'" Scrappy revealed. "Teens use a lot of shortcuts and symbols to chat with each other. It also helps them hide certain information from their folks. For example, PAW stands for parents are watching. Did you know that?"

"No, I didn't," Dereka said. Since most of her teen years were spent in captivity, she'd missed out on the teen Internet culture. Just one more thing they'd robbed her of.

Scrappy sat back in her chair, yawned, and stretched her full five-foot-eight-inch frame.

"Well, that's it for tonight. Dereka, you know you can't tell anyone about what we're planning to do. Not even your aunts. They won't understand. They haven't walked in our shoes."

"I know. I won't tell."

"I'm heading back to New York in the morning. I want you to monitor the chat rooms while I'm away, and let me know if Shybirdie gets any suspicious posts."

"But how will I know the difference between a regular boy chatting who's just being a typical teenager and a sexual predator? How will I know if it's one of...*them*?" Dereka asked.

"Oh, I got a feeling you'll know," Scrappy assured her.

Private Dancer

Jia drove across the Pont Saint-Jean Bridge toward downtown Bordeaux. It was a beautiful spring evening in late May. She was on her way to perform a private dance for a client. Jia was paid top dollar for the intimate experience of her sensual, erotic lap dances. But Jia was nervous, which was unusual for her because she was rarely nervous before a job. However, it was not the job per se that was making her anxious, but the person who'd requested it. His name was Elliott Tremblay, and she'd learned he was the tall blond-haired man from the bachelor party. The one to whom she'd inadvertently told her real name. The one she'd seen a few weeks ago at a bistro and who'd made her flee from the restaurant in a panic. The one whose intense stare seemed to caress her soul. She knew he was now a married man but that didn't matter to her. Most of her clients were married.

His friend, Zack, had setup the job. And while Jia pretended that she was only performing the job as a favor to her loyal client, she knew that was not the real reason. In truth, she wanted to see this mysterious man again who was having such an unusual effect on her. Out of all the men she'd been with, and there'd been plenty, he was the only one who'd made her feel like...a person. All the rest only made her feel like an object of their desire. None had made her feel like *she* mattered. But then again, she'd only spent one night with the man so perhaps it was all in her imagination. Perhaps he was no different from the rest. Perhaps he wanted her for one thing and one thing only like all the others. To satisfy his sexual cravings and fantasies. *Why should he be any different?* Jia thought.

And in a defective, sad kind of way Jia hoped that he wasn't any different. She inexplicably wanted him to fit into her long-held belief that men wanted her for one reason and one reason only—sexual gratification.

Jia didn't mind that men lusted for her. That's how she preferred it. It made her feel special—like she was noteworthy. As "Lady Marmalade" she knew she was the best at what she did. After all, she'd been pleasuring men since she was eight years old. Experience made her the best. And it felt good to be the best at something. So there was no need for complications at this point in her life. No need to change her way of thinking about men. If Elliott turned out to be like all the others, she could go along her merry way with her concept of the world intact.

♦ ♦ ♦

Elliott waited anxiously in the penthouse suite of the Mercure Bordeaux Ville Hotel for Jia to arrive. It had taken some doing, but he'd finally arranged a private session with her. He'd placed multiple requests on her website to no avail. Finally, his friend Zack reluctantly agreed to setup a private session with her even though he'd felt Elliott was headed for trouble and heartache.

"It's your funeral, buddy," Zack had said.

Elliott checked his watch. Jia was due to arrive in about five minutes. He ran his fingers through his hair nervously. He and Nicole had now been married for about a month. He'd chosen this night knowing she'd be in London attending a girlfriend's wedding. But what if his wife found out? She would never understand. In earnest, he'd tried to forget about Jia but couldn't. Choosing to see her again had not been an easy choice. He'd justified it in his mind by telling himself it was just a private dance, and since no sex would be involved it really wasn't cheating. But deep in his gut he knew it was wrong. *It's not too late to back out. I could just leave before she gets here*, he thought. But for some reason, leaving didn't seem to be an option.

At 10:00 p.m. promptly there was a soft knock on the door. When he opened the door and saw Jia, he was glad he'd decided to stay.

"Hello, Mr. Tremblay," she murmured, her eyes looking directly into his.

"Hello, Jia. Please come in. And do call me Elliott," he requested. When she walked past him, Elliott inhaled her scent which was as intoxicating as she was.

"Would you like a drink?" Elliott offered.

"No, thank you," she replied. "I'd like to get started if that's okay with you." Jia was a professional and was ready to get right down to business.

"Sure," Elliott said, taking a seat on the plush sofa. Jia removed a small digital music player from her bag and placed it on the center table. She pushed a button, and the sound of smooth sax jazz music filled the air. She began to move in sensual sync to the music. She slowly untied her black silk dress and let it fall slowly to the floor. Elliott inhaled slowly and tried to keep himself from panting with his tongue hanging out like a thirsty dog. Jia performed for a solid hour without interruption, and Elliott was totally enthralled the entire time. Her routine included a series of lap dances in which her eyes were locked with his eyes and never wavered. Elliott had never experienced anything as seductive in his life and doubted he ever would again. Afterward, although Jia had done all the work, he was drenched with sweat.

"Are you pleased with your service?" Jia asked demurely as she slowly put on her dress.

"Very much so," Elliott assured her. He reached into his wallet, retrieved a hefty tip, and held it toward her.

"Merci," Jia said as she took the money, placed it in her purse, and walked toward the door.

"Wait," Elliott heard himself saying although he hadn't intended to say anything. He'd intended to let her walk out of the door. He'd intended to go home. He'd intended to let this one incredible night with Jia be enough to last him a lifetime. Jia turned to face him with a puzzled expression on her face.

"Is there something else you want?" she asked quizzically. Elliott moved toward her until he stood mere inches away. He looked down into her lovely, vulnerable eyes.

Yes, Jia. There is something else I want. I want…you," he said.

His last three words made Jia's eyes involuntarily water. Why did they make her feel like crying? She unsuccessfully tried to blink back the tears, but they defied her and slowly slid down her face. Elliott tenderly kissed her tears away. Jia wrapped her arms around his neck and began to cry uncontrollably as if some invisible dam had been breached. *What could have happened to this beautiful lady that has wounded her so deeply*, Elliott wondered. While he wanted to know, he was hesitant to ask. After all, he was relatively a stranger and didn't know if she'd be willing to talk about it. But he gathered his courage and decided to ask anyway. He felt compelled to know everything about her. He waited patiently until her crying subsided, and looked directly into her dark, lovely eyes.

"Tell me your story," he said.

"My story? There's really not much to tell," Jia replied. Elliott gently lifted her chin so he could look directly into her eyes.

"I think there is," he said. Jia cast down her eyes and took a deep breath. She had never told anyone her real story before. Not even Dereka knew all the horrors she'd experienced. Dereka had an idea, but she didn't know everything. Dark things, abominable things, repugnant and reprehensible things. Things she'd buried deep within the impenetrable walls of her heart. Things she never thought she'd be able to share with another soul. That is until now.

"Are you sure you want to know?"

"Yes, I want to know. I need to know," Elliott admitted. So Jia told Elliott her story, in all its deplorable and heartrending details. She talked as if she'd been waiting a long time to tell her story to someone—the right someone. As if by telling it she could cleanse herself from the wretchedness of it all. She left nothing out, no fact obscured, as she painfully recounted the events that had shaped, or better yet, misshaped her life. She told it all—the good, the bad, and the ugly. The good was Dereka and the other girls she'd met at that place. The rest was just the bad and the ugly.

Elliott listened intently without interruption, rubbing Jia's back to comfort her as tears slid down her cheeks. Why this stranger seemed to care so much was a mystery to Jia. She knew what she was. Men didn't care about her, they only lusted for her. That's how it had always been. But here she was, in the arms of a man she barely knew, feeling things she'd never felt before. She wrapped her arms around his neck and covered his face with soft kisses. They made passionate love until the crack of dawn.

Dodged Another Bullet

Elliott got home around 7:00 a.m. When he opened the door, he got the surprise of his life. There was Nicole, sitting on the living room sofa, arms crossed, lips poked out, and eyes smoldering.

"Where in the hell have you been all night," she yelled.

"Nicole, sweetheart. What are you doing here?" Elliott asked, his eyes wide in surprise at seeing his wife. Although he really was surprised to see her, his question was really a defense tactic to buy him some time to think of a really good lie.

"I live here remember and so do you. Or did you forget where you live. Like I said, where the hell have you been all night?" Nicole asked again, jumping to her feet and moving toward Elliott. He had to think fast.

"I went out to a bar with some friends and stayed at Zack's place last night. Drunk a little too much and didn't want to drive home. I crashed on Zack's couch, and he took me to pick up my car this morning," Elliott stated, making a mental note to text Zack as soon as possible to verify his alibi if need be. "I knew you wouldn't be home," Elliott continued his tall tale. "So I didn't see a need to rush home. You know how lonely I get when you're not here," he said, smiling charmingly and reaching for his wife. But Nicole was not convinced.

"But why didn't you answer your phone? I called you several times to let you know I was home," she countered, looking at Elliott through narrowed, suspicious eyes. Elliott had turned his phone off, not wanting to be disturbed while he was with Jia.

"I don't know, baby. It was pretty noisy in the bar. I didn't even hear my phone ring. You know how it is when I get together with the boys. You know how wild and crazy things can get."

Nicole had been out with Elliott and his friends several times, and she knew they were a boisterous bunch that could get very rowdy at times. Perhaps she was overreacting.

"Yes, I know. I'm sorry, baby. But when you didn't come home last night, and I couldn't reach you my mind begin to think all kinds of crazy thoughts. Forgive me?" she asked, placing her arms around Elliott's waist and smiling up at him coyly.

"Of course, I forgive you," Elliott replied, feeling guilty for deceiving his wife, and at the same time relieved that he had dodged yet another bullet. He decided to quickly change the subject before she renewed her inquisition regarding his whereabouts.

"So why are you home early? I thought the wedding was today?"

"Well, it was supposed to be but Melissa and Eric had a big fight, and she called off the wedding. She found out that he had a love child by a girl he dated in college. He said he'd planned to tell her all about it after they were married. Can you believe that?" Nicole asked incredulously. And while Elliott could believe it, he knew better than to sympathize with the man.

"No, I can't," he replied smartly.

"Well, Melissa was livid. Not so much that he had a child but that he'd hid it from her. She called off the wedding because she said she couldn't trust him anymore. And I don't blame her. Because without trust there is no marriage. Of course, you have to love your mate. But trusting is a big part of marriage, don't you think?"

"Yes, it is," Elliott said, feeling guiltier about his own infidelity and deception.

That night as Elliott lay in bed with Nicole in his arms, he was torn up inside. He knew that Nicole would be devastated if she ever found out. So he secretly vowed in his heart that he would not see Jia again. But even as he made that vow, he sensed it was a vow that would in all likelihood be broken.

Warning Sign!

Things were going well for Kenya and Sean. After seeing each other regularly for nearly two months, they were in a good place. Kenya had even met Sean's son, Terrence, when he was home from college during spring break. He was an outgoing, smart, handsome, and humorous young man, and reminded Kenya a lot of his father. She liked him right away and she could tell, to Sean's delight, Terrence liked her too.

Although things were going smoothly, Kenya had not yet introduced Sean to Dereka. She'd wanted to be sure he was someone she could at least envision a long-term relationship with before introducing him to the niece she'd come to consider more as her daughter. Such an introduction would be a big step forward in her relationship with Sean, and she didn't take it lightly. And, if truth be told, Kenya's heart was still guarded. She had made the mistake of giving her heart to Ryan too soon, a mistake she'd paid dearly for.

When they pulled up in front of Kenya's house at 3:00 p.m., she decided it was time for Sean to meet Dereka.

"Sweetheart, would you come in for a moment? There's someone I want you to meet," Kenya stated with a big smile on her face.

"Sure, baby. Who?"

"My niece, Dereka." Sean was a bit surprised. He'd heard a lot about Dereka and had even wondered why he'd not met her yet. He hadn't pressed the matter because he knew Kenya was a very private person and was very protective of her niece. He was relieved that she felt comfortable enough with him now to introduce him to Dereka.

"I would love to meet your niece," he replied sincerely. Once inside Kenya went to the bottom of the stairs and yelled.

"Dereka, would you come down for a moment? There's someone I want you to meet."

"Okay, be right there," Dereka shouted. When Dereka came out of her room she saw her aunt standing at the bottom of the stairs grinning from ear to ear.

"Hey, Aunt Kenya," she said smiling brightly, figuring her aunt wanted her to meet a girlfriend or one of her sorority sisters. But Dereka stopped in her tracks when she saw a strange man standing behind Kenya and smiling up at her. She felt her heartbeat quicken. *What is Aunt Kenya doing with this strange man in our house? He could be one of them?* she thought, frantically looking wildly from Kenya to Sean. But Kenya was so excited to have the two of them meet she barely noticed Dereka's reaction. She hurried up the stairs, grabbed Dereka's hand, and led her down to Sean.

"Dereka, this is my friend, Sean. Sean, this is my beautiful niece, Dereka, whom I've told you about," Kenya announced, beaming with pride.

"It is so nice to finally meet you, Dereka. Your aunt brags about you all the time," Sean said, extending his hand toward Dereka for a handshake. Dereka looked at Sean's hand and backed away.

"Are you one of them?" she blurted out. Sean was taken aback and looked in puzzlement from Kenya to Dereka.

"I beg your pardon," he said quizzically.

"Are you one of them?" Dereka repeated, louder this time. Kenya decided to intervene.

"Dereka, honey. This is a good friend of mine. We've been seeing each other for a while. I told you about Sean, remember?" she prompted. Dereka moved closer to Sean and looked directly into his face as if she was inspecting him. Sean was smiling on the outside, but inside he was thinking, *Aww shigady. What is this all about?* Kenya had told him about Dereka's abduction and captivity, and her subsequent mental and emotional problems. But she'd also told him that her niece was doing great, and everything was fine. But it sure didn't look that way to him. After scrutinizing him thoroughly, Dereka visibly relaxed and smiled.

"Of course, you're not one of them. Aunt Kenya wouldn't bring one of them home. It's nice to meet you," Dereka said, extending her hand to Sean. Sean, still kind of caught off guard by Dereka's odd behavior, hesitated slightly before shaking her hand heartily. The three of them spent a few minutes engaged in idle chatter before Dereka excused herself and went back to her room. Sean exhaled deeply.

"Whew—what was that all about?" he asked, looking perplexed.

"I'm not sure. I don't have any idea why she asked you that question. I think I better go check on her to see if everything's okay. See you tomorrow after church?"

"Sure, sweetheart."

Kenya walked him to the door, gave him a quick kiss, and watched him drive away. That's when she noticed a dark-colored Honda parked near the house that had not been there when they arrived. A young lady wearing long braids, who appeared to be in her early twenties, was sitting in the passenger seat talking on her cell phone. Kenya had seen her parked at the curb several times over the past months. And to Kenya it appeared as if the young lady was watching her. *Hmmm*, Kenya thought. *I wonder who she is. I guess I'll find out.* When Kenya approached the car, the young lady hurriedly drove away. *That's strange*, Kenya thought, looking at the car as it sped down the street.

But her thoughts quickly shifted to Dereka. She went back into the house, rushed upstairs, and knocked on Dereka's door.

"Come in," Dereka called. When Kenya entered, Dereka promptly closed the lid of her computer.

"Is your friend gone already?" she asked.

"Yes, he's gone," Kenya replied, taking a seat on the bed.

"Dereka, honey, why did you ask Sean if he was one of them? Who's them?"

"You know. Them. Men like those customers who came to that place. I love you Aunt Kenya, and I just want to be sure that you, or anyone else, will never go through what I went through."

Kenya relaxed a bit after learning that Dereka was just concerned about her well-being. She'd always cared deeply for others. It was just a part of her nature. Kenya went to Dereka and hugged her tight.

"Honey, I appreciate your concern for me. But all men are not like those men. You understand that, don't you?"

"Yes, I know. And don't worry, Sean is not one of them. I can tell," Dereka said with confidence.

"Well, thank God for that 'cause I really kinda like him," Kenya replied laughing and getting up to leave, her mind now at ease. Unfortunately, Kenya had just missed a vital warning sign that all was not right with Dereka.

One-Way Ticket

Ryan was on the move in Miami. He'd learned from his cousin that Memphis had gone ballistic when he'd discovered that the tip about Ryan being Lyle the plumber was phony. Ryan would have liked to be a fly on the wall when Memphis got that news. Ryan had seen firsthand how furious Memphis could become when things didn't go his way. Memphis absolutely hated being played, and right now Ryan was playing him like a fiddler on the roof. But Ryan also knew that Memphis's fury only fueled his ruthlessness and determination to take out his enemy. Thus, Ryan was already planning his next move in their dangerous chess match.

Ryan likened his battle of wits with Memphis to one of his favorite TV series, *Game of Thrones*, where power hungry kings, queens, knights, and lowlifes battled each other to rule the seven kingdoms and sit on the iron throne. And Ryan, being the cocky, confident fellow that he was, knew for sure he'd be the last man standing to take his rightful place of glory on the throne. And what he had planned next for Memphis was pure genius. *I'm getting too good at this*, Ryan thought conceitedly as he cruised his new luxury jaguar sports coupé down Lincoln Road in South Beach.

Although Ryan liked South Beach, a place renowned for its great shopping, restaurants, and high-energy, music-thumping, booty-popping nightclubs, he preferred the grittier areas of Miami such as Opa Locka, Overtown, Miami Gardens, and Liberty City. Grit was in his blood. It ran through every fiber of his being. He'd used that grit to survive growing up in one of the toughest neighborhoods in Detroit. And Ryan planned to use that same grit to outwit, outlast, and outplay his archnemesis, Memphis.

Having learned, also from Memphis, not to stay in one place too long, Ryan was planning to leave Miami soon. He was on his way to Liberty

Gardens to do one last drug deal for his boss, Hector, before leaving. He'd made this particular drug run lots of times, and it had become rather routine. He'd drop off the drugs, pick up the cash, and that was that. He was meeting with Malique Clark and Ashani Edwards, two Jamaican immigrants who were now the top drug dealers in the Liberty Gardens area. Ryan really liked these dudes because they were good at their trade. The two friends had used their drug money to open a restaurant called Best of Jamaica Grill in Liberty Gardens. They served the best jerk chicken and rum punch this side of heaven. Ryan frequented the place often and was always treated like royalty by the owners, who depended on him to keep delivering them high-quality cocaine at a fair price. The restaurant had an authentic Jamaican atmosphere, and it was one of the few places where you could get a good meal upstairs and a good high downstairs. In Ryan's opinion, the only thing missing was good sex. He'd even suggested that the owners expand into the sex trade, but they'd decided against it, preferring to stick with what they knew.

When Ryan arrived at the meeting location, which was a huge parking lot behind some vacant warehouses, Malique and Ashani were already there. Both were leaning against their car smoking joints. In addition to selling cocaine, the two also imported and sold homegrown Jamaican marijuana, known as ganja in Jamaica. It was some of the best weed Ryan had ever smoked. Ryan got out of his car and took a deep whiff of the pungent, sweet aroma of ganja. He walked to the back of his car and retrieved two duffel bags from the trunk.

"My brothers, my brothers. The sweet smell of ganja is in the air," Ryan joked as he walked over and gave each of them a half-man hug.

"Yeah, mon. Just got this in today. Fresh off the boat," Malique replied, taking several joints from his shirt pocket and handing them to Ryan.

"This what I'm talking about," Ryan said, immediately putting one joint in his mouth, lighting it, inhaling deeply, and exhaling slowly.

"Ou ah everyting guh?" Ashani asked. Although he'd lived in Miami for a while, he still talked mostly in the native Jamaican lingo, unlike his friend Malique.

"Everything's great, man. Life's good. But I'm sorry to say that this will be my last run with you all, at least for a while. I'm moving on," Ryan revealed.

"Say what? Where you going to?" Malique asked, surprised.

"Can't say for sure. But I'll be back through here from time to time. My boss is going to look after y'all while I'm away."

"Well, I've enjoyed doing business with you, Mon," Malique stated.

"Yeah, mon. Wi gwine miss yuh," Ashani said.

"I'm going to miss y'all asses too. But you know what I'm really going to miss. That jerk chicken. If you all could mail it, I'd have y'all send me some special delivery," Ryan kidded. The three men engaged in friendly banter for a few minutes.

"Well, gentlemen," Ryan said after checking his watch. "It's about time to get down to business." He bent down and unzipped both duffel bags. "Care to check out the merchandise?" he inquired. Ashani looked briefly in the two bags.

"It's aal gud. Wi trust yuh," he said. Malique reached into the back seat of his car and retrieved a black briefcase. He placed it on the hood and snapped it open. When Malique turned around, he was aiming a Glock 42 semiautomatic handgun directly at Ryan's chest.

"This is compliments of Memphis, mon. Your one-way ticket to hell," he said coldly. Ryan looked like a deer caught in the headlights.

"Is this some kind of a joke," he shouted, his eyes like saucers. The last thing he saw was two rapid flashes of fire from the tip of the gun when Malique pulled the trigger.

Game, Set, Match

Memphis waited anxiously for news of Ryan's demise. Although it had taken him longer than expected, he'd finally outmaneuvered Ryan. Sure Ryan had bested him with that false lead about being Lyle the plumber. Memphis was still kicking himself in the butt for falling for that con. Over time, he'd come to realize that someone was passing inside information to Ryan. How else could Ryan have been able to sneak out of South Africa just when Memphis was closing in on him? There had to be a mole in Memphis's operation. That was the only logical explanation he could think of as to why Ryan had managed to stay one step ahead of him.

Memphis had methodically smoked out the mole, which, to his surprise, turned out to be Louie, one of his top three. Enraged, Memphis had threatened to cut the poor guy's tongue out unless he told him who he'd been sharing information about Ryan with. Louie told him that the only person he'd been talking to about Ryan was his cellmate, Michael. Memphis went ahead and cut Louie's tongue out anyway, just to send a message to anyone else who dared defy him by not having sense enough to keep his mouth shut. Blabbermouth would not be blabbering anymore.

Memphis decided not to harm Ryan's cousin, at least temporarily, but to use him to get to Ryan. Michael, being in fear of his life, quickly turned on Ryan. He'd told Memphis that Ryan was in Miami and working for Hector Rebello. Memphis knew Hector from back in the day and had done a few drug deals with him. So Memphis solicited his help to set Ryan up. Hector was more than glad to oblige, and had come up with the idea of using Malique and Ashani because he knew Ryan trusted them.

Around 9:00 a.m. Memphis got the word, via one of the guards, that Ryan was a done deal.

"I won't believe it until I see evidence that he's dead with my own eyes," Memphis stated. The guard took out this cell phone and showed him a picture.

"Is this evidence enough?" he asked with a smirk. Memphis grabbed the phone and looked at the image. A devious grin spread across his face. There in living color was a picture of a blood-soaked suitcase full of body parts. Ryan's head was sitting prominently in the top right corner of the suitcase.

"Game...set...match," Memphis said as he gazed at the photo. "I finally got that two-bit bastard."

"I'll say, and then some. I ain't never seen no s——t like that before," the guard said, cringing as he looked down at the gruesome image.

"Figures," Memphis replied, annoyed by the guard's behavior. Memphis immediately sized him up as a wannabe crook who only measured about 2.5 on the criminal Richter scale. He handed the cell phone back to the guard.

"Have they disposed of the body?" Memphis asked.

"Yeah, man. Took it to a secluded area about one hundred miles north of Miami Beach. Threw the body parts into the water in an area known to be infested with sharks. It will never be found," the guard assured him.

"Good. Stand by for further instructions," Memphis directed. He then walked across the prison yard to his office where he knew his top three were waiting for him, including Louie who was now notoriously known throughout the prison as "No-tongue Louie." The man who once had the gift of gab could now only making gurgling, grunting, or squawking sounds with his mouth. Memphis kept No-tongue Louie around only because he believed in keeping his enemies close.

As Memphis strutted across the yard he had a little more pep in his step, a little more dip in his hip, and a little more glide in his stride. He was thrilled that he had finally closed Ryan's chapter for good. And with an exclamation point at that. And now that Ryan was shark chow, Memphis could completely focus his vindictive criminal mind on whom he considered his public enemies number one, two, and three—Kenya Jones and her two partners in crime, Dereka and Jasmine. Memphis already had something in mind for them. And it was a doozy.

Need a Friend?

It was a quarter past midnight, and Dereka was at her computer monitoring the chat room and instant messages for the pseudo-thirteen-year-old Shybirdie that she and Scrappy had created. Monitoring the chat room to trap a predator had become an obsession for her because she was convinced it was her mission from God. Other than going to work, she spent practically all her time in her room in front of her computer. When Jasmine and Kenya had questioned Dereka about it, she'd told them that she was helping Brandon with a software development project. In reality, Dereka hadn't seen Brandon in weeks, and had only spoken with him by phone a couple of times. And she'd seen Fatima only twice during the past month, including at their last support group meeting. The only person, other than her aunts, that she was in regular contact with was Jia.

Jia was the only one that Dereka had told about what she and Scrappy were planning to do. Jia remembered Scrappy as the wild woman who'd cursed and fought the guards frantically when they'd dragged her into the basement of La Casa de Placer. She'd spent most of her time there ranting and raving. Jia had never seen a girl like her before. And, if truth be told, she'd been intimidated by the one called Scrappy, and would often hide behind her sister when Scrappy went on one of her tantrums. Of course, Jia fiercely tried to talk Dereka out of getting involved with Scrappy in something she'd regret. But Dereka's mind was made up.

A few days ago Dereka had successfully intercepted another phone message from Dr. Bedford to Kenya, stating that she was just checking to see how things were going, and curious as to why the new doctor had not yet requested Dereka's medical records. Dereka had deleted the message, annoyed with Dr. Bedford's persistent, busybody behavior. *Maybe she's working with them*, she'd thought, referring to sexual predators.

Over the past month, Dereka had chatted with numerous people and had even engaged in one-on-one conversations with a few via instant messaging. But so far, outside of the typical teenage banter, crudeness, and silliness, nothing of note had occurred. She was beginning to wonder if she and Scrappy were barking up the wrong tree—if their ploy to catch a predator online would really work. Scrappy had phoned Dereka a couple of times to see how things were going. Dereka was discouraged that she'd had nothing to report.

"Just hang in there," Scrappy had said. "This may take some time. Just keeping posting stuff. One of them is bound to take the bait. And like I said you'll know when it's one of them."

And Dereka did. The instant message came at 2:00 a.m. from someone named Bat007. He posted only three small seemingly innocent words, but they sent chills up and down Dereka's spine, and made the hair on her arms and neck stand on end. It was one of them.

> *Need a friend?* he asked.
> *Yes. R u a friend?*
> *I'd like to be. Can I be your friend?*
> *Sure.*
> *What r u doing up so late?*
> *Bored. Can't sleep.*
> *Something bothering u?*
> *Feeling blue. My folks don't let me do much. I just get lonely.*
> *IKWUM*

IKWUM was the teen Internet slang for (I know what you mean). Dereka knew he was trying to be empathetic.

> *U do? OMG* (oh my God), she replied.
> *Sure I do. I get lonely 2. We can keep each other company.*
> *I'd like that.*

> *I bet URAQT (you are a cutie)*
> *No, stop.*
> *Do you have a BF (boyfriend)?*
> *No. Boys don't like me.*
> *I like u.*
> *Y2K (you're too kind)*
> *Send me a pic.*
> *MB (maybe) later.*
> *K*

Dereka spent the next hour or so chatting with Bat007. He called himself Bat007 because of his fondness for Batman and James Bond movies. He told her he was a senior at Clinton High School in Bethesda, Maryland. They chatted about all the routine things teens talk about including music, school, parents, and such. Bat007 was sympathetic, supportive, kind, and understanding. He flattered Shybirdie whenever he could, no doubt to make her think she was the best thing since sliced bread. He told her that she had him GFETE (grinning from ear to ear). After Dereka had taken all she could stand for one night, she decided to bring their chat to an end.

> *Getting tired. G2B (going to bed).*
> *Nice chatting with u. YMMD (you made my day).*
> *THX (thanks).*
> *CWYL (chat with you later).*
> *K. GN (good night).*
> *GN. Sweet dreams, luv.*

Dereka shut down her computer and exhaled. She felt as if she had been holding her breath during their entire chat. She was both relieved and repulsed that one of them had taken the bait. Relieved that her efforts over the past month had not been in vain, and repulsed by the very fact that such sexual predators existed. When Dereka thought about the millions of innocent children at risk everyday simply by chatting online, she felt nauseous. Those children could end up being raped and brutalized like she'd been. They could end up hanging themselves like Sun-Yu or being tortured to death like Crystal. Dereka rushed to the bathroom and vomited into the toilet.

Time to Face the Music

Elliott tried to stay away from Jia but failed miserably. He'd seen her regularly for the past two months, ever since his private dance. They met at least two or three times a week in the same penthouse suite at the Mercure Bordeaux Hotel. Sometimes they met before her jobs, sometimes after. He'd tried to persuade Jia to stop working as Lady Marmalade, saying that he would gladly just give her the money she made if she quit. But she refused his offer. While Elliott wasn't happy about Jia's desire to continue her work, he didn't pressure her to stop. After all, what right did he have to complain—he'd met her while she was working his bachelor party. If it had not been for her line of work, it was highly likely they wouldn't have met at all. He'd even gotten into the habit of taking Jia to some of her jobs. He'd wait outside in his car, sometimes for hours, until she was done. It calmed his fears to be nearby just in case something went wrong. They never talked about what she did on any particular job. He didn't ask, and she didn't tell. Elliott also knew about Jia's heroin addiction, which he also accepted as just a part of who she was.

So far, he'd been able to keep Nicole in the dark regarding his relationship with Jia, making up one excuse after another regarding his absences. But he knew she was growing more and more suspicious and impatient as time went by. Elliott hoped he would never have to choose between the two women because, as of now, he really didn't know if the choice would be his wife. As crazy as it sounded even to him, he knew he could not give Jia up.

Elliott sat in his car outside a luxury high-rise apartment building located in Caudéran, a posh neighborhood in western Bordeaux. It was

Saturday afternoon, and he was waiting for Jia who had gone inside to buy heroin from her dealer. Jia's dealer, a guy named Enzo, was no ordinary run-of-the-mill street dealer. He sold the purest form of "china white" heroin on the market. It was expensive, costing around $400 to $500 per gram. Enzo's wealthy clientele spent hundreds of dollars a day to support their habit.

Elliott was jolted when someone knocked sharply on his car window. To say that he was shocked to see Nicole standing there was an understatement. He nervously rolled down the window.

"Honey, what are you doing here?" he sputtered out.

"Going shopping with Brianna. We stopped by here to pick up her sister who lives in the next building. What are you doing here? I thought you said you were going to the office for a while?" Nicole questioned. Elliott had to think of something fast.

"Well, I am. I mean, I did already. You know my business partner, Mathis. I brought him down here to…uhh…pick up…uhh…a proposal. We're heading back to the office as soon as he comes down."

"We're in no hurry," Nicole said, motioning to Brianna to get out of her car and join them. "We'll keep you company while you wait. You've been so busy lately, I rarely get to see you anymore."

No, no, no, this can't be happening, Elliott thought as sweat beaded on his forehead. Brianna and Nicole leaned up against the car, chitchatting about one thing or another. Elliott kept looking anxiously toward the front door of the apartment building, hoping that Jia wouldn't come down while they were there.

"Uhh…it looks like Mathis is going to be longer than I thought. Why don't you ladies go ahead and do your shopping? I don't want to hold you all up," Elliott said.

"Yeah, let's go," Brianna said. Nicole hesitated for a moment but agreed to leave.

"Okay. I'll see you at home, baby," she said, giving Elliott a quick kiss before leaving. Elliott breathed a sigh of relief as soon as they drove away.

And not a moment too soon. Within a couple of minutes, Jia came out and got into the car.

"Are you all right?" she asked, noticing that Elliott looked a bit flustered.

"Yes, I'm fine."

"I saw the women," Jia revealed.

"You did?"

"I saw them through the window and decided to wait in the lobby until they left."

"Thank you for that."

"The woman with the long dark hair, she's your wife?"

"Yes, that's Nicole."

"She's very beautiful," Jia acknowledged. They were both quiet for a moment.

"Jia. I'm sorry…"

"Elliott don't," Jia replied, cutting him off. "You don't have to apologize to me because of her. She's your wife. If anything, you should apologize to her because of me. I'm the outsider," Jia conceded, her face somber.

"Not to me," Elliott replied.

Elliott knew he was playing with fire. And he was relieved that he'd escaped yet another close call with Nicole in regard to discovery. But Elliott wondered just how many more close calls he'd be granted. However, he didn't have to wait long before he knew exactly how many. The answer was zero.

♦ ♦ ♦

As soon as Elliott arrived home after dropping Jia off, Nicole and Brianna drove up. Nicole jumped out of the car. She was visibly shaking as she marched toward Elliott.

"Who is she?" she shouted angrily.

"Who is who?" Elliott replied, trying to look as innocent and clueless as he possibly could.

"Don't play with me, Elliott. You know exactly who I'm talking about. Who was that Asian bitch who got into your car?"

Elliott just hung his head, knowing that he had been caught red-handed. It was time to face the music. He'd always known this time would come. Nicole got right up into Elliott's face.

"When you seemed so anxious to get rid of us, I had a feeling that something wasn't right. So I told Brianna to drive around the block and circle back around so we could watch you. I saw that Jap slut get into your car," Nicole exclaimed, revealing her subliminal prejudice against Asians.

"She's actually Chinese, not Japanese," Elliott corrected, simply trying to buy some time.

"Who in the hell cares if she's a chink or a Jap?" Nicole yelled indignantly. Elliott heard a car door open and saw Brianna standing near her car, glaring at him with fire in her eyes.

"Nicole, sweetheart, can we go inside and talk about this?" Elliott pleaded.

"Don't sweetheart me," Nicole replied. She asked Brianna to wait for her before going inside and resuming her tirade.

"Now tell me who she is and what you were doing with her?" she demanded. Elliott decided to tell the truth, the whole truth, and nothing but the truth.

"Her name is Jia, and I've been seeing her for several months. I met her at my bachelor party. She's one of the ladies Zack hired. We slept together that night. We've been seeing each other since."

"You mean she's a stripper? A prostitute?" Nicole asked incredulously. Elliott nodded. "Are you telling me that you've been having an affair with a goddamned whore, and coming home and making love to me?"

"Yes. But we always practice safe sex."

"You practice safe sex! And that's supposed to make it all right?" Nicole yelled. Elliott had to admit that the whole thing sounded sordid and shameful, even to his own ears. Nicole sat on the floor suddenly as if she could no longer stand on her own two legs. Her anger and hostility were now replaced by shock and disappointment. She pulled her legs up against her chest like a small child and began to sob deeply. She looked up at Elliott, her face stained with tears.

"Why?" she asked. "Why, Elliott? Why would you do such a thing? I trusted you. I just don't understand," she cried. Elliott's heart was breaking too because he still loved Nicole. He went to hold her, but she quickly scooted into a corner out of his reach. Elliott sat on the sofa, his own eyes filled with tears.

"I'm sorry, Nicole. I didn't mean for this to happen. It's all my fault, and it has nothing to do with you. I still love you. I know that sounds crazy, but I do. And the last thing I wanted to do was hurt you, sweetheart," he stated earnestly. Nicole stayed couched in the corner, sobbing so hard her body shook. Brianna knocked on the door and poked her head in.

"Is everything all right in here?" she asked looking around. She gasped when she saw Nicole crying in the corner of the room. She ran and knelt beside her friend. Nicole tried to talk, but she was crying so hard no words came out. Brianna struggled to help Nicole to her feet. Elliott moved toward them to assist.

"Stay away!" Brianna shouted. "I'm taking her home with me." Elliott stood by helplessly and stared at his wife, who looked broken and dejected. Brianna helped Nicole get into her car and drove away.

Elliott slammed his fist into the hardwood door several times, bruising his knuckles badly and drawing blood. It was his weak attempt to hurt himself as badly as he'd just hurt his wife.

"Damn," he murmured over and over in frustration. Yet even then Elliott didn't regret his affair with Jia. He only regretted that his affair had deeply wounded his wife. He'd tried to have it all, even though he'd known all along that he couldn't.

Three Birds with One Stone

"And you're sure this is going to work?" Memphis asked an inmate, Vinny, who was sitting with him in the prison cafeteria.

"Yeah, man, it's gonna work. It worked for my brother. He wiped out a whole family, and no one suspected nuthin. The cops didn't suspect nuthin. The relatives didn't suspect nuthin. Everybody thought it was just some freak accident. It's a foolproof plan, man. You can't miss with this," Vinny replied confidently. Memphis looked at him through narrowed eyes.

"I'll tell you what. Your brother better be as good as you say he is for the money I'm putting out for this job," Memphis warned.

"Oh, he's good, awright. My brother done some mean, crazy s——t in his life. And he ain't never been to prison. He too smart to get caught. Locks, bars, security systems, and whatnot, don't mean nuthin to him. We call him the Houdini of the hood. He's like some kind of magician when it comes to breaking and entering. Man, he the best at what he do," Vinny assured.

"Well, he'd better be," Memphis cautioned. "Let me know when the job is done."

"Awright, man. Chill out. My brother gonna take care of it."

Memphis got up and headed to his office. *Finally*, he thought. *Finally, I'm going to get my revenge. If all goes well, I can easily wipeout Kenya, her stubborn, refuse-to-die niece, Dereka, and that slut, Jasmine.* Memphis was feeling pretty good about the plan he'd come up with to take out the Jones family trio. He'd likely never would have thought of it on his own, but thanks to the vast smorgasbord of criminal minds at his beck and call, he had the perfect plan. He would not only be able to kill two birds with one stone, but three. And no one would suspect that he was involved. Not that he really gave a damn what others thought. But Memphis had a real good thing going in prison as far as favor and privileges, and he didn't want any suspicions about him being involved in a triple murder to louse it up. He chuckled to himself as he considered what was about to go down. Vengeance had been a long time coming.

"It's payback time, bitches," he murmured under this breath.

◆ ◆ ◆

Kenya, Jasmine, and Dereka were awakened in the middle of the night by the loud sound of fire truck sirens and banging on their front door. The three of them had gone to bed relatively early that night complaining of flu-like symptoms including headache, fatigue, and nausea. Kenya stumbled out of bed, pulled on her robe, and went into the hall where she found Dereka and Jasmine in their nightgowns, looking perplexed.

"What's happening?" Dereka asked anxiously.

"I don't know, sweetie. But you stay up here. Jasmine and I will go down and see what's going on," Kenya instructed.

Kenya and Jasmine carefully made their way down the stairs, both feeling a bit woozy and light headed. The bright red and white flashing lights of a fire truck outside illuminated the living room. Kenya peered through the peephole and saw two firemen dressed in full gear. She nervously cracked the door open.

"Ma'am, we got a 911 call of a fire at this location," one of the firemen stated. Kenya opened the door wide.

"Fire! But there's no fire here as far as we know," she said, looking around and sniffing the air for the smell of smoke.

"And our fire alarms haven't gone off," Jasmine added.

"We need to come in and take a look around," the other firemen said.

"Yes, yes, of course. Please do," Kenya responded, moving back to let the firemen in. There were at least two other firemen walking around outside inspecting the property.

"Is everything all right?" Dereka called from upstairs.

"Yes, honey. Come on down," Jasmine replied. The three of them huddled close together as the firemen checked the house. When they were done, Fireman Roberson, a tall good-looking brother, approached the ladies.

"Everything seems to be in order. It was probably just a false alarm. The 911 call came from someone passing through the neighborhood who thought they saw smoke. It happens. No big deal. In these situations it's best to be safe than sorry," he informed them.

"Yes, I agree," Kenya replied.

Jasmine involuntarily let out a wide, loud yawn. "Excuse me," she said, feeling slightly embarrassed. "I don't know why I'm so tired."

"We've been feeling out of it today. I think there's some flu bug going around," Kenya said sitting down, suddenly fatigued. Fireman Roberson looked at Kenya and Jasmine curiously.

"Are you ladies sure you're all right?" he asked, concerned.

"Aunt Kenya, you don't look so good," Dereka said, sitting beside her.

"I'm feeling a little achy and tired. I took some cold medicine before I went to bed," Kenya replied.

"You know, I'm feeling a little nauseous myself," Dereka revealed.

"Hmmm," the fireman uttered. "Would you ladies mind waiting outside while we check something out?"

Fireman Roberson escorted them outside, where they were provided light blankets to put around them. He instructed another fireman to get the air-monitoring instrument and check the air for carbon monoxide. The fireman moved slowly through the house, giving the instrument time to register a reading or alarm. Sure enough, there was a relatively high concentration of carbon monoxide found in the basement, and lower amounts were found on the main and upper levels of the house. The symptoms that the ladies had initially thought were just a flu bug turned out to be something far worse. They were provided oxygen on the spot and transported by ambulance to the emergency room for further diagnoses and care.

♦ ♦ ♦

When Memphis found out what went down at the Jones residence on the night that was supposed to be their final night on earth, he was pissed. Everything had been planned to a tee. Vinny's brother, a plumber, electrician, locksmith, and all-around jack-of-all-trades, had expertly maneuvered his way through two locks on the Joneses' basement door, including a dead bolt. He'd detached the flue pipe on their hot-water heater so the toxic carbon monoxide would leak into the house instead of being vented outside. He'd then left the premises without a trace of his ever being there. The Jones females were supposed to go to sleep that night and "wake up dead."

But, somehow, they'd managed to escape death. Somebody had made that 911 call that spared their lives. Someone was looking out for them. And since Memphis didn't believe in a higher power, he knew it had to be some lowlife. Perhaps he had another mole in his posse of thugs. *Damn*, Memphis thought, pacing back and forth in his prison cell like a caged panther. His face was set in a vicious scowl, and he breathed heavily as he paced. He sat down on his cot and took a deep breath.

"Get control of yourself," he murmured. He knew he couldn't think clearly when his emotions were raging. And now was the time for a cool head to go along with his cold heart. Memphis was tired of fooling around with the Joneses. *There's only one way to deal with this*, he thought. *I've got to get out of here and exterminate them personally. I've got to handle this s——t myself.*

Charge over Thee

For he shall give his angels charge over thee, to keep thee in all thy ways. That was the scripture on Kenya's heart as she and Jasmine sat outside on their patio a week after the carbon monoxide incident. Thankfully, they had only been exposed to very low levels of the toxic gas. After spending one night in the emergency room, they'd gone to stay at Uncle Isaac's place for a few days, celebrating the Fourth of July there instead of home as planned. The utility company had determined that a defective hot-water heater in the basement was the source of the carbon monoxide leak. They had the defective appliance replaced and received an all clear to move back into their home. While before they didn't have a carbon monoxide monitor in the house, they now had not one, not two, but three monitors in their home—one on each level.

The doctor at the emergency room had schooled them on the dangers of carbon monoxide poisoning and the importance of having a monitor.

"While most families have fire alarms in their homes, for some reason many do not have carbon monoxide monitors," he'd said. "I don't think many people take seriously the dangers of this gas. It's odorless, tasteless, and colorless yet extremely toxic. In the United States alone, it's estimated that exposure to carbon monoxide accounts for about fifteen thousand emergency room incidents and five hundred accidental deaths per year. Did you all know that?" he'd quizzed. They had stared at each other and shaken their heads.

"And with our dependence on so many fuel-burning devices, the death rate is likely to go higher. You see, once carbon monoxide is inhaled, it enters your bloodstream and attaches to the hemoglobin molecules," the doctor lectured, getting all technical. "Well, to make a long story short, the carbon monoxide inhibits the blood's ability to carry oxygen, and without enough oxygen, the cells suffocate and die," he'd concluded. Kenya and Jasmine were still counting their blessings in regard to their close encounter with the toxic gas.

"Ain't God good," Jasmine said, shaking her head in wonder.

"Yes, he is!" Kenya concurred. "Girl, when I think about what could have happened to us that night, I can't help but say, thank you Jesus," Kenya proclaimed, raising her hands up in praise.

"It's a miracle that someone made that 911 call. If not for that call, who knows what would have happened to us. God had a special angel watching over us that night."

"He surely did. I wish we knew who made that call. I would like to personally thank him or her. The 911 operator said it came from an unknown number. You know, I've seen a young lady in a dark blue Honda either parked near the house or driving by several times. Have you seen her?" Kenya asked.

"No, can't say that I have."

"Well, I have a feeling that she's been watching the house for some reason. Once I tried to approach her, and she drove away. I wonder if she had something to do with that 911 call," Kenya pondered.

"But why would someone be watching our house?"

"I don't know. That's the mystery."

"Well, don't worry about it too much. As Mama Ruth use to say, 'It will all come out in the wash.'"

Kenya decided not to dwell too much on who made the call and why. She believed with all her heart that the 911 call that saved their lives was no coincidence. It was by God's divine intervention. For that she was extremely grateful.

But Dereka was truly unnerved by the carbon monoxide incident. In her weakened state of mind, she was convinced that one of them was responsible for the whole thing. She believed a sexual predator had somehow found out what she and Scrappy were planning to do and had tried to kill her. But she also believed that God had intervened and kept her safe so that she could go forth with the mission he'd assigned her.

"Thank you, Jesus," she prayed. "I'll do whatever you want me to do. I won't let you down."

Revelations

It was dress-down Friday, and Kenya and Jasmine had both taken off work early to enjoy a relaxing afternoon of shopping at Tyson's Corner Center. In Kenya's estimation, none of her employees seemed to accomplish much on Fridays anyway. It seemed that her office staff, probably like many others, thought casual Friday meant coming to work late, taking longer than usual lunch breaks, and leaving early. As the dress code slackened on Fridays, so did productivity as folks saw Fridays as a free for all. But Kenya didn't mind because her staff more than made up for it during the rest of the weekdays.

While they strolled casually through the mall, Kenya noticed that Jasmine kept flinging her hand around dramatically in the air as she talked. And when Kenya saw the big, beautiful French-cut pavé diamond ring on Jasmine's finger, she let out a shrill shriek of joy.

"Oh my God! Jasmine, is that an engagement ring?" Kenya exclaimed, grabbing Jasmine's hand for a closer look.

"Yes, it is. Percy popped the question last night, and I said yes," Jasmine proclaimed. The two friends screamed, embraced each other, and jumped around in a circle of pure joy, their laughter filling the air.

"It's absolutely beautiful. How many carats is it?" Kenya asked boldly.

"A little over three, but who's counting," Jasmine replied.

"I am," Kenya responded, causing them to crack up laughing. "When did Percy propose? How did he propose? Did he get down on one knee? Were you surprised? Did you say yes right away or make him sweat? Have you set a date? Where will you all live?" she asked, firing off one question after another.

"Slow your roll, girlfriend," Jasmine said, trying to settle Kenya down. She answered as many of her questions as she could, informing her that no date had been set and they had yet to decide about their living situation.

Jasmine and Kenya continued their shopping, now on cloud nine about Jasmine's engagement. After they left Neiman Marcus, Jasmine's favorite place to shop, they headed to Macy's, Kenya's choice place to bargain shop and use her 20 percent off coupons.

"I don't see the sense in paying two hundred dollars for the same top you can get at Macy's for thirty dollars," Kenya said.

"It's all about the quality. I'd rather pay top dollar for clothes that will last rather than bargain shop for clothes that may come apart at the seams after a few wears," Jasmine replied, laughing.

"I'll have you know my clothes do not come apart at the seams, thank you very much," Kenya pointed out, spinning around for effect to show off a snazzy outfit she'd gotten at a Macy's sale several weeks ago. Kenya wasn't cheap, but she loved a good bargain.

After shopping well into the evening, the ladies made their way to an Italian restaurant for dinner. They sipped lemonade while they waited for their entrée.

"I sure wish Dereka could have come shopping with us," Kenya stated. "I asked her, but she wanted to go home to do some work. She's helping Brandon with some software development project. She's certainly dedicated, I'll give her that."

"Yeah, I know. That's why I think the trip to France to see Jia will do her good. I'm really looking forward to seeing Jia. You know she's like a daughter to me."

"Just think, you came very close to adopting her before her grandparents found her. She could very well have been your daughter."

"I think about that a lot," Jasmine said dreamily. "But all in all, I'm glad she's with Nai Nai. She's the only blood relative Jia has in her life."

While they enjoyed their delicious meal, the young Italian waiter flirted shamelessly with the two ladies, no doubt hoping to increase the size of his tip. Kenya and Jasmine found the waiter's behavior rather amusing, and they flirted back. After dinner, they left the restaurant and headed toward the parking garage. Kenya heard someone calling her name. She looked around and saw Dr. Bedford walking toward them.

"Kenya, Jasmine, it's great to see you all," Dr. Bedford said, hugging them.

"Great to see you, too. Dereka has been telling us how great her therapy sessions are going," Kenya said. Dr. Bedford looked confused.

"What do you mean? I haven't seen Dereka in over four months," Dr. Bedford replied. Kenya and Jasmine looked at each other in astonishment, each speechless for a moment.

"Wait a minute. Aren't you still seeing her twice a month?" Jasmine asked.

"No," Dr. Bedford affirmed. "She called my office back in March and said that you all had found another doctor through your church. Kenya, I left you several phone messages in regard to this because I wanted to at least speak with her new doctor and share records and notes. But I never heard back from you."

"I never got your messages. And there is no new doctor. We thought Dereka was still meeting with you. I can't believe this," Kenya exclaimed.

"Oh my God. Do you think Dereka deleted those messages because she didn't want us to find out she's not in therapy anymore?" Jasmine asked.

"At this point, I don't know what to think," Kenya replied, throwing her hands up in exasperation. Dr. Bedford looked from Kenya to Jasmine with a concerned expression on her face.

"Well, I don't want to alarm you all too much. But it's very important to get Dereka back into treatment as quickly as possible. Due to her genetic propensity to mental illness, coupled with the severe environmental trauma she suffered, therapy is crucial. Unfortunately, sometimes patients feel that they can make it on their own, especially after they've been in therapy for a few years. But often, without continued treatment patients can relapse, and not only negate any gains made, but mentally decline further. I'd like to see Dereka first thing Monday morning. I'll clear time on my schedule," Dr. Bedford said.

"Of course, Dr. Bedford. Thank God we ran into you. We had no idea," Kenya stated. She and Jasmine hurried to the parking garage, each still stupefied by what they'd just learned. It was a shocking revelation to say the least.

"What do you think is going on with Dereka? Why would she stop going to therapy?" Jasmine asked, her face etched with worry.

"I don't know," Kenya replied. "But I'm going to find out, that's for sure."

"Dr. Bedford said she hasn't seen Dereka in over four months? How could we have not known?" Jasmine inquired. Kenya was silent for a moment.

"Perhaps we've been too caught up in our relationships and our busy jobs to notice," she confessed, feeling somewhat guilty that she'd let Dereka down. And, not surprisingly, Jasmine felt the same way.

"But there's nothing we can do about that now," Kenya continued. "We just need to make sure she gets back into therapy ASAP."

"Amen to that," Jasmine concurred.

No Ifs, Ands, or Buts about It

Dereka was at home enjoying having the house to herself. Where once she would have jumped at the chance to go shopping with her favorite aunts, now she preferred being alone. Isolation was her friend—her salvation. Isolation allowed Dereka to just be herself. She made a cup of orange spice tea and relaxed on the sofa to enjoy it. Orange spice tea reminded her of her mama and Grandma Ruth. They had spent many lazy Saturday afternoons when she was young, sipping the fragrant tea. Dereka missed them so much and would give anything to have them back in her life. But they were gone except in her memories. Lost to her forever. *And it's all because of them*, she thought bitterly.

Dereka was surprised when she heard Kenya's car pulling swiftly into the driveway, burning rubber. *Aunt Kenya sure is in a hurry*, she thought curiously. Kenya and Jasmine burst through the door like ghostbusters.

"Dereka, guess who we saw at the mall today?" Kenya asked accusingly.

"Who?" Dereka replied.

"Dr. Bedford, that's who," Jasmine chimed in. "She told us that you haven't been in therapy for over four months." Dereka looked both surprised and guilty that her aunts had found her out.

"Dereka, why haven't you been going to therapy, and why did you lie to us about it?" Kenya asked.

"I'm sorry I lied, but I knew you all would just pressure me to go. And I don't need to see Dr. Bedford anymore. I'm fine," Dereka said earnestly. And, by this time, she erroneously believed that she was.

"You may be okay now," Kenya conceded, not knowing the reality of Dereka's declining mental health. "But Dr. Bedford said you could relapse without continued therapy."

That's because Dr. Bedford is probably working with them, Dereka thought. *She just wants to get into my head and find out what I'm planning to do. She wants to stop me. But I won't let her.*

"Dereka, remember when you talked to us about switching from weekly to biweekly sessions," Jasmine added. "At that time, you vowed to attend your sessions regularly."

"And I did for a while. But I don't need them anymore. I'm fine. I'm still going to my support group meetings, and I'm taking my medication. That's all I need," Dereka stressed, lying about the medication part. She was still discarding one Zyprexa pill a day into the trash just in case one or both of her aunts checked the bottle.

"Dereka, that may be all well and good, but you have to go back to therapy. No ifs, ands, or buts about it," Kenya stated emphatically.

"That's right, Dereka. This is not even open for discussion anymore. We know what's best for you," Jasmine stated.

Dereka felt cornered. *Who do they think they are? Talking to me like I'm a child*, she thought. But even at age twenty-four, she had too much respect for her aunts to say it out loud. But she began to wonder if her aunts were in cahoots with Dr. Bedford. Maybe they were all conspiring against her to stop her from her special task. *Can they be in on it too?* Dereka thought, looking suspiciously at her aunts. Then she quickly pushed that thought aside. Deep down she knew they were just concerned about her. To appease them she gave in to their demands.

"Okay, I'll go back to therapy if you all think I should. I'll call Dr. Bedford's office and make an appointment next week," Dereka said.

"No, I'll call Dr. Bedford tomorrow and make the appointment myself. She wants to see you first thing Monday morning. And I'll personally take you to her office," Kenya said.

"But, Aunt Kenya…"

"No buts, Dereka. Now that's the way it's going to be. I'm sorry, but I don't trust you to do it yourself. After all you've lied to us for months about going to therapy," Kenya said, not even trying to hide her disappointment. Dereka looked down at the floor feeling the full weight of her aunt's disapproval. Kenya was more like a mother to her than an aunt. She hated disappointing her and Auntie Jazz.

"I'm sorry, Aunt Kenya. Sorry, Auntie Jazz," Dereka stated sincerely.

"It's okay, honey," Kenya replied, softening her tone. "We just love you so much and want to make sure you stay on the right track."

"That's right, Boogie Boo," Jasmine teased, trying to lighten the mood by using the nickname her grandma gave Dereka when she was a little girl. Dereka laughed. She'd hated that name at the time, but now she'd give anything to hear her Grandma Ruth say it "just one mo'gin."

With the immediate crisis settled, the ladies changed into their pajamas, popped popcorn, and watched a hilarious comedy movie. They laughed nearly to tears. It was a wonderful evening. But it was just the calm before the storm.

Tit for Tat

Later that night, after Kenya and Jasmine had gone to bed, Dereka went to her room and immediately logged onto her computer. Her chats with Bat007 generally took place between midnight and one in the morning. This was a time, when unbeknownst to most parents, teens were fairly active on the Internet when they were supposed to be sleeping. Dereka had been keeping Scrappy updated on her chats with Bat007. They both figured that he was likely a married man with children, who did his Internet chatting with potential victims late at night when his family was asleep. Most nights, as soon as Dereka signed in, Bat007 would immediately send her an instant message. It was as if he was sitting at his computer waiting for the "signed-on" icon to appear next to her username. And over the six weeks since their first interaction, Bat007 had become more personal and sexually aggressive with Shybirdie. Tonight was no exception.

> *I've been waiting 4 u*, Bat007 posted.
> *U have?*
> *Yeah! TOY* (thinking of you) *all day.*
> *That's funny. TOY 2.*
> *Were your thoughts sexy like mine?*
> **G** (giggle)
> *R u blushing?*
> *Yeah!*
> *Want to see a funny picture?*
> *Sure?*

Dereka thought that he would likely send a picture of some young teen boy he was pretending to be. Last week, she'd sent him a picture of herself when she was a carefree young girl. Before them. A jpeg icon for a picture appeared on Dereka's computer. She clicked on it, and to her utter astonishment, it was a graphic picture of male genitals. Dereka's blood boiled when she saw the pornographic image. But she had to keep her composure and maintain her pretense of being a thirteen-year-old girl.

> *Uggggggggh! Gross!* she posted.
> *Ha, Ha! ROFL* (rolling on the floor laughing).
> *Not funny. I thought it was a pic of u.*
> *It may b me FAYK* (for all you know) *lol. I like your pic. You are SH* (so hot).
> *No, I'm not.*
> *You have nice lips. They look soft and juicy. I'd like to chew on them like juicy fruit,* ☺
> *Lol.*
> *So let's meet F2F* (face-to-face).
> *IDK* (I don't know)
> *Don't u like me?*
> *Yeah!*
> *So meet me just once. It will be fun. PLZ!*

Dereka hesitated for a while, making up excuse after excuse before agreeing to meet with him.

> *K. Just once. I'll let u know when 2morrow. GN.*
> *GN, luv. C u soon!*

This was it. The moment she and Scrappy had been waiting for. He had asked to meet with Shybirdie. Now they could go full speed ahead with their plan. Dereka called Scrappy.

"Hey, Scrappy, you still up?"

"Of course. You know us New Yorkers never sleep. What's up, girl? You got some good news about Bat007?"

Dereka told Scrappy about their chat and how she'd pretended to reluctantly agree to meet with him. For the next hour or so, the ladies planned the where, when, and how of the meeting. It would take place next Saturday night when Scrappy was in town. Dereka suggested they meet him at an abandoned baseball field in Hybla Valley that was once used by the Boys Club.

"I'll tell Bat007 it's where I go when I'm feeling sad and just want to be alone. I'll tell him that I can walk there or catch the bus since I'm only supposed to be thirteen. There's a small store on the corner where we can park our cars so he won't get suspicious. No one goes there anymore, especially at night. We'll have all the privacy we need," Dereka explained.

"That's good. We'll need our privacy 'cause it's about to go down, girlfriend," Scrappy said.

When Dereka hung up the phone, she sat at her desk thinking about what they were about to do. As Scrappy said, it was about to go down. Dereka felt her heart beating fast at just the thought of it actually happening. Was she ready for this? Could she really do it? She started getting nervous. Maybe this kind of thing wasn't for her.

That's when the voices started in Dereka's head. At first it scared her, and she looked around as if someone was in the room. But when she realized they were coming from inside her head, she listened intently to what they were saying. It was like nothing she'd ever experienced before—actual voices speaking to her. As far as she could tell there were three distinct voices. One male and two female. Dereka quickly picked up a pen and notepad, and began writing down the words she was hearing over and over in her head. It was a simple phrase—one that she'd not thought about or heard since she was a young child in grade school.

"Tit for tat, tit for tat, tit for tat," the voices chanted. Dereka scribbled the three words on paper over and over. She wrote the phrase in various sizes and shapes to capture the intensity, inflection, tone, and character of the voices she heard. She did this into the wee hours of the night.

Speaking of the Devil

On Sunday morning Dereka was feeling optimistic. She truly believed that God himself had spoken to her through the voices to reassure her that she and Scrappy were doing his will. Kenya and Jasmine had left around eight thirty to attend the early-morning church service. Dereka declined to go with them, preferring to watch the service via live streaming on her computer. She didn't like being in crowds of people anymore because she didn't know if any of "them" were around. She had an underlying fear of strangers, especially men.

Dereka's cell phone rang around nine o'clock, and she saw that Jia was Skyping her. She was somewhat surprised to hear from Jia that time of day because they usually talked late at night, and it was only 4:00 p.m. in Bordeaux. Dereka hit the phone icon and saw Jia's bright, smiling face.

"Hi, Jia. What's up?" Dereka asked.

"Hi, Dereka," Jia said, obviously excited about something. "I have a wonderful surprise to show you."

"You do?" Dereka asked, she too getting excited because Jia was so excited. Dereka knew it had to be something really special.

"Well, you recall a few weeks ago when I was talking about my mother. I said I was wondering if she was still out there somewhere looking for me. And if I'd ever see her again," Jia said, about to burst with the anticipation of revealing her surprise.

"Yes, I remember you saying that. Now what's this all about, Jia?" Dereka asked hesitantly, her excitement now turning to trepidation.

"Hold on just a minute. I have someone to show you."

Dereka watched as Jia motioned for her surprise person to join her on the bed where she was sitting. When she saw the person's face, Dereka's heart dropped, fear crept up her spine, and her mouth fell open in astonishment. *Speaking of the devil*, was the first thing that came to Dereka's mind. It was Sun-Yu and Jia's mother, Lihwa. The lady in the red dress that Dereka and Sun-Yu had seen at La Casa de Placer in Colombia. The lady that they had initially thought had come to rescue them and take them away from that chamber of horrors. The lady they'd discovered had not come to save them, but to solicit more money from the sex traffickers for the sale of her own daughters.

Dereka would never forget that face in a million years. Lihwa looked the same, only older and more mature. But she was still as beautiful as Dereka remembered, and she was wearing her trademark red dress and bright-red lipstick. But Dereka knew that Lihwa's outward beauty concealed the despicable ugliness that dwelled within.

"Dereka, this is my mother. She got here this morning. She's been looking for me and Sun-Yu for years. She found out where I was through the adoption agency in Colombia. It's a miracle that she found me," Jia exclaimed, hugging her mother.

"Hello, Dereka. Jia has told me so much about you. I feel like I know you already," Lihwa said, a sweet smile on her face.

Dereka was speechless. She simply stared at Lihwa's face. That face reminded her of how hurt and despondent Sun-Yu had been when she'd learned the truth about her mother.

"Dereka, honey, what's the matter?" Jia asked. "You look like you've seen a ghost."

"I think she's just surprised," Lihwa added.

Dereka was not only surprised, she was also afraid. It was as though she could feel the pure evil inside Jia's mother radiating through the phone. Lihwa was one of them. One of the people she despised most in the world. Dereka's hand trembled as she gripped the phone tightly to keep from dropping it.

"Yes, I'm just…surprised that's all," she stammered.

"Jia told me that you were Sun-Yu's best friend in that dreadful place. I was heartbroken to learn that my dear Sun-Yu died there. Such a terrible shame," Lihwa said, actually conjuring up two tears that rolled down her face.

The shame is that you left them there, Dereka thought. *The shame is that you betrayed them, like Judas betrayed Jesus for pieces of silver.*

"Sun-Yu was my best friend," Dereka confirmed, her own eyes earnestly misting with tears.

"And after Sun-Yu died Dereka took care of me," Jia pointed out.

"Well, that's my job now, darling," Lihwa said, looking lovingly at Jia. "Now that I've found you, I'm never going to leave you again. I'll always be here to protect and look after you," she pledged. *Oh my God*, Dereka thought. *She's actually planning to stay with Jia. I can't let her do that. I can't allow her to hurt Jia again.*

"Jia, I have to go now. Someone's at the door," Dereka lied, making up an excuse to get off the phone. She couldn't stand the sight of Lihwa's face any longer. "I'll call you later."

"Okay, hon."

When Dereka hung up the phone, she was frantic with fear and worry. Jia's mother was back in her life. Why had she come back? Why couldn't she just let sleeping dogs lie? Dereka had made a vow to Sun-Yu that she'd never tell Jia, or anyone, about the dastardly deed their mother had done. She didn't know what Lihwa had been doing or what she was planning to do. For all she knew, Lihwa could still be selling children to sex traffickers. She could be planning to abduct Jia and sell her as she'd done before. And that was one chance Dereka wasn't willing to take.

"I'm sorry, Sun-Yu," Dereka whispered, fighting back tears. "I'm sorry I have to break the promise I made to you. But I have no choice."

More Prone to Believe Than Not

Dereka waited on pins and needles for Kenya and Jasmine to come home from church. Around noon, she heard Jasmine's car pull into the driveway and rushed to the door to greet them.

"Aunt Kenya. Auntie Jazz," she said, motioning frantically to them. "Hurry up. I have something very important I need to tell you."

"What is it?" Kenya asked as soon as they got inside.

"Jia's mother is back. Her name is Lihwa Huang. She showed up at Jia's this morning."

"Wow! That's wonderful news," Kenya exclaimed. "I know Jia must be ecstatic to be reunited with her mother after all these years."

"That's amazing," Jasmine added. "Jia always wondered what happened to her mother. She thought she'd never see her again. I'm so happy for her."

"No, no, no. You don't understand," Dereka exclaimed. "Jia's mother is not a good person. She's not who she's pretending to be." Kenya and Jasmine looked at each other in confusion.

"But why would you say something like that, Dereka? You don't even know Jia's mother," Kenya said.

"Yes, I do," Dereka replied, taking a seat on the sofa. Kenya and Jasmine sat down beside her.

"I hadn't planned to tell anyone this until now," Dereka began. "One day, while Sun-Yu and I were cleaning that house in Colombia, I heard a lady's voice in the main room. I hid behind the staircase, looked down, and saw an Asian lady, dressed in red. I suspected right away it was Sun-Yu and Jia's mother. So I ran to get Su-Yu, so she could see if it was her mother. Her face glowed when she saw her. I'd never seen her so happy. But...but...," Dereka paused and swallowed hard as if the next words were almost impossible to utter.

"But what, honey," Kenya gently urged her.

"But she was asking for more money for them," Dereka spat out. "They hadn't been abducted at the airport as Sun-Yu thought. Her mother had sold them, and she was there asking for more money."

Jasmine and Kenya's jaws dropped. It took a moment for either of them to speak.

"Sold them!" Kenya exclaimed in disgust. "You mean the mother sold her own daughters into sex slavery?" Kenya asked incredulously. Dereka nodded her head.

"Sun-Yu made me promise never to tell Jia the truth. The next morning she hung herself. To this day Jia doesn't know how her sister died or that it was because of what their mother did."

"I can't believe it," Kenya said solemnly. "I just can't believe a mother could do something so wretched and vile." Kenya's head was spinning, not only from what Dereka had just divulged, but from what they had learned from Dr. Bedford on Friday. The doctor had said Dereka could relapse mentally. Could this mother have really sold her daughters or had Dereka just imagined it? Kenya didn't know what to believe.

"Dereka, are you sure about this? Are you sure you're remembering things right?" she asked.

"Of course I'm sure, Aunt Kenya. Why wouldn't I be?" Dereka asked.

"Well, because this is the first we've heard about this. And, we just found out you've been lying to us about attending therapy. It's just a bit confusing, that's all. Maybe this is something that you imagined. Like you imagined Ms. Vee," Kenya said skeptically.

"I didn't just imagine this," Dereka shouted indignantly. "This happened. I swear it did. And I'm scared for Jia. Suppose her mother is out to hurt her again. We can't let that happen," Dereka exclaimed, now near hysterics.

"Calm down, sweetie. You and I are going to visit Jia in a couple of weeks. We can look into it then," Jasmine offered.

"But you don't understand, Auntie Jazz. A couple of weeks may be too late. I don't trust that woman. Sun-Yu is dead because of her. You have to go now, Auntie Jazz," Dereka pleaded. Kenya and Jasmine looked at each other, not knowing what to make of Dereka's story.

"Okay, sweetie. I'll see what I can do. You go on upstairs and get some rest. You look exhausted," Jasmine stated.

"Yeah, I am a little tired. I'm going to lie down for a while," Dereka responded. Kenya waited until Dereka went upstairs, and she heard her bedroom door close before speaking.

"What do you make of this?" she asked Jasmine, rubbing her forehead in puzzlement.

"I guess I'm more prone to believe her than not," Jasmine replied. During her work with Operation Undercover, Jasmine had seen the most awful things done to children. Things that even brought some of the grown, strong men she worked with to tears. While doing undercover work in places like Cambodia, Haiti, and Thailand, Jasmine had sat across the table from mothers and fathers, and negotiated prices with them to sell or prostitute their own children, including girls and boys as young as three or four years old. But Jasmine did not have to think about faraway places to come up with horrific examples of sexual exploitation of children. All she had to do was remember her own troubled past. Her mother, Maddie, had pimped her out to grown men to get money to pay the house bills. So although she wasn't sure that Dereka's story was true, for Jia's sake she was determined to find out. She loved Jia too much to just wait and see what happened. That night she was on a red-eye flight to France.

Eyes Wide Open

Kenya was up early Monday morning getting ready to take Dereka to her appointment with Dr. Bedford. It had been a trying weekend to say the least. When Kenya dropped Jasmine off at the airport the previous night, they had taken a moment in the car to pray that God would be with her during the trip, bring hidden things to light, and help Jasmine deal with whatever she discovered. They'd also prayed that all would go well with Dereka's therapy session this morning. They needed God's wisdom and guidance to help them take care of their nieces. They both believed strongly in the scripture that says, *Be careful for nothing; but in everything by prayer and supplication with thanksgiving let your requests be made known unto God.*

After Kenya showered and dressed, she headed to the kitchen to make them a light breakfast before leaving. As she passed Dereka's room she knocked on the door.

"Dereka, honey, it's time to get up. We don't want to be late for your appointment," she yelled. After a short pause, she knocked again.

"Dereka, time to get up." When Dereka didn't answer, Kenya opened the door and poked her head into the room. But Dereka was not there. Kenya went downstairs and looked around, thinking that perhaps she was already up and waiting for her.

"Dereka," she called out as she walked from room to room. But it soon became apparent that Dereka had left the house to avoid going to therapy. And Kenya was peeved.

"Why in the world would she do something like this? She told me she was going, and I believed her," she said out loud. But her annoyance quickly turned to concern. *What is going on with Dereka?* she thought. Kenya decided to go into Dereka's room, and do some investigating.

When she entered her room, the first thing she noticed was that the room was in total disarray. The bed was unmade, balled up pieces of paper littered the floor and filled the trash can, and the desk was jumbled and messy. This was so unlike Dereka, who had always been the neat freak of the family. Kenya sat down at Dereka's desk and rummaged through the assortment of stuff piled on it. One thing that caught her eye was a yellow notepad with lots of writing on it. Kenya picked up the pad and saw the words, "tit for tat," scrawled all over the page. Some of the words were large and others were small. The words were written in all directions and practically filled every inch of space on the page.

"What in the world!" Kenya exclaimed as she flipped through the pages of the notepad and saw that each page was filled with the same erratic writing of the phrase, tit for tat. Kenya picked up one of the balled-up pieces of paper on the desk, and discovered it was also covered with the same writing.

"Lord Jesus," she murmured. She walked to the trash can and found more papers there just like the others. Kenya also noticed a small white pill on the floor beside the trash can. She picked it up and examined it carefully. The pill had a small number imprinted on it. Kenya knew right away it was one of Dereka's Zyprexa pills. Kenya dumped the remains of the trash can onto the floor and saw several pills fall out. She got on her knees, poked through the trash, and found fourteen pills.

"Oh my God," she said, sitting on the bed and staring at the pills in her hand. Not only was Dereka not in therapy, she was also not taking her medication. Kenya felt as though she'd been living the past months with blinders on—thinking that things were fine when they were evidently far from it. Anxiety gripped Kenya's heart for she now knew her niece was in real trouble.

♦ ♦ ♦

Kenya waited around the house all afternoon for Dereka to come home. Earlier she'd called Brandon to learn more about this special project they were supposedly working on, and found out there was no special project. Brandon said that he hadn't seen Dereka in weeks. So that was another lie in the web of deceit Dereka had spun. But Kenya knew she needed to be calm and supportive with Dereka, and not confrontational. She knew she could be bossy and overbearing at times, but that was only because she loved Dereka so much and wanted the best for her. And now she had to get through to Dereka and convince her to resume her therapy and medication. But how?

Dereka returned home at 2:00 p.m. When she opened the door, she was not surprised to see her aunt sitting on the sofa waiting for her.

"I'm sorry I left this morning, Aunt Kenya. But..."

"Dereka, it's okay. That's water under the bridge. But we do need to talk. Sit down, honey," Kenya replied. Dereka dutifully sat on the sofa beside Kenya. Kenya took a deep breath before continuing.

"I went into your room this morning, and I found these in your trash can," Kenya said, holding out her hand to show Dereka the pills. Dereka's entire demeanor changed from being apologetic to being downright agitated.

"Aunt Kenya, you had no right to go into my room," she shouted.

"I only went into your room out of concern for you. And it's a good thing I did because now I know you have not been taking your medication either."

"I knew it. I knew you and Auntie Jazz were spying on me."

"Spying on you. Honey, nobody's been spying on you."

"Then what were you doing in my room going through my trash can."

"But Dereka, you're missing the point, the point is..."

"No, Aunt Kenya," Dereka interjected, cutting her aunt off. "The point is that you invaded my privacy. How would you feel if I went into your room and dug through your trash? Huh? And how long have you all been spying on me?"

This conversation was not going as Kenya had intended, not at all. It was going to be much tougher to get through to Dereka than she had thought.

"Okay, Dereka. You're right. I invaded your privacy, and I'm sorry. But the point is you're not in therapy, and you're not taking your medication. Honey, don't you see how harmful that can be for you?" Kenya inquired. Dereka looked at her aunt and saw the concern and worry etched on her face. She knew her aunt loved her, so she tried to calm her worries.

"Aunt Kenya, I don't need those things anymore. I have something special that I'm working on that's given me purpose in my life. Just trust me. I'm fine. Really, I am," Dereka stressed.

"I don't think you are. That's why you need to take your meds and get back into therapy. Dr. Bedford believes you can have a relapse if you don't."

"Dr. Bedford doesn't know what she's talking about. She just wants to get into my brain to see what we're planning to do. She's working with them, you know?"

"Working with them? Do you actually think Dr. Bedford is working with sexual predators?" Kenya asked incredulously. "Dereka, listen to what you're saying. It doesn't make any sense."

"It makes perfect sense, Aunt Kenya. You just don't understand."

"Sweetie, please let me take you to see Dr. Bedford soon. You need help," Kenya pleaded.

"No, Aunt Kenya, I keep telling you I'm fine."

"But, honey, if you're so fine what is this all about?" Kenya asked, holding out one of the papers with "tit for tat" scrawled all over it. Dereka snatched the paper out of Kenya's hand.

"That's for me. Those voices were talking to me. What are you doing with this?" she said.

"I found it in your room. And what voices are you talking about? Are you hearing voices?"

"No," Dereka lied. But Kenya looked skeptical.

"Honey, I think all this proves my point that you have to get help. And I intend to take you to see Dr. Bedford ASAP. Now that's that."

"Aunt Kenya, I'm an adult and I can make my own decisions. And I'm not going back. Not ever. And please stay out of my room," Dereka said defiantly, getting up and going upstairs to her room.

"Honey, I'm just trying to help you," Kenya yelled. But her only response was the sound of Dereka's bedroom door slamming shut.

Kenya flopped down on the sofa, exhausted from their tense interaction. But although their conversation had gone terribly wrong, there was one thing it had done. It had opened Kenya's eyes to the fact that her niece was slipping away mentally.

Signs and Symptoms

The next morning Kenya met with Dr. Bedford to discuss Dereka's mental state.

"I was afraid this might happen," Dr. Bedford acknowledged after hearing Kenya's account of what she'd discovered. "That's why I really wanted to see Dereka yesterday. Generally, when patients stop attending therapy, they also discontinue using their medication, feeling both are no longer relevant. But that's absolutely the worst thing that patients can do."

"Dr. Bedford, I had no idea that this was going up. Dereka thinks that Jasmine and I have been spying on her. And she said something about hearing voices. And she even thinks that you're working with them. Them being sexual predators. I feel like…I've failed Dereka. I should have been more on top of things," Kenya professed.

"Please don't blame herself. It's not unusual for family members of a mentally ill person to miss or misinterpret signs that something is amiss. Often, it's because family members so desperately want the person to be well."

"But I didn't really see any signs until this past week when I found out about all this. Up until then she seemed fine."

"Hmmm," Dr. Bedford said, picking up a notepad to take notes. "You haven't noticed any changes whatsoever in her behavior over the past few months? Anything to show that she may be thinking irrationally?" Dr. Bedford asked. Kenya started to shake her head but then recalled the incident when she'd first introduced Dereka to Sean.

"Well, there was that one time when I introduced her to a close friend, and she asked him if he was one of them, meaning a sexual predator. It was kind of shocking, but she explained that she was just concerned about my well-being. So I didn't think much of it after that."

"I see," Dr. Bedford said, scribbling a few notes on her pad. "What about her social behavior? Have you noticed any changes in her relationships with family and friends?" she quizzed.

"Well, Dereka has been spending a lot of time alone working on her computer. She said she was helping a friend with a special project, but I found out from him yesterday there is no special project. He said he hadn't seen Dereka in weeks. And, she has been staying at home more. She won't go shopping or to dinner with us anymore. And she's been missing church a lot, too."

"Hmmm," Dr. Bedford said, scribbling more notes on her pad. "Now tell me about this writing you found in her room. Tit for tat. Have you ever heard Dereka use this term before?"

"No, I haven't. It's something my brother and I used a lot when we were kids playing around. She's heard me say it, but I've never heard Dereka use it before. And she had written it over and over again in such a disturbing way. There are literally pages and pages of it," Kenya stated, looking perplexed. Dr. Bedford put down her notepad and took off her reading glasses. She sat still for a moment, deep in thought.

"Kenya, I don't want to alarm you, but it's possible Dereka is exhibiting initial signs of paranoid schizophrenia," Dr. Bedford stated.

"Paranoid schizophrenia," Kenya repeated the word nervously as if just the mention of it was frightening.

"I'm afraid so. One of the common symptoms of the disease is delusions, which are false beliefs that contradict logical reasoning, for example that the government is spying of them, they have a personal relationship with a famous person, or they've been assigned a special mission. And these beliefs are so strong in the person's mind that he or she sometimes can't help but act on them. That's why their behavior may appear to others as irrational and bizarre, but to the paranoid schizophrenic, the behavior seems perfectly normal. Another common symptom is auditory hallucinations in which the person hears voices or sounds in his or her head. Visual hallucinations may also occur, but auditory hallucinations are much more common. These voices in the person's head may criticize the person's behavior, make crude comments about their appearance or self-worth, or command them to do things to themselves or others," Dr. Bedford explained. She could see the worry in Kenya's face deepening as she spoke.

"Do you really think Dereka has this disorder?" Kenya asked.

"I can't be sure until I talk to her and do a full diagnosis. But I want you to be aware of these symptoms so you'll know what to lookout for. And I can't stress the importance of getting Dereka in for treatment promptly," Dr. Bedford cautioned.

"But suppose she won't come?"

"Well, let's take it one day at a time," Dr. Bedford replied, feeling that she had laid enough on Kenya for now. "Do everything you can to persuade Dereka to see me within the next week or so. If she refuses, we can discuss other options then."

Kenya shook hands with Dr. Bedford and thanked her for the insightful information. Kenya's mind was racing a mile a minute on the drive home as she tried to think of how she could convince Dereka to get help. "Lord, show me what to do," she prayed.

Devil in a Red Dress

As soon as Jasmine disembarked the plane and entered the terminal, she saw Jia waving and smiling at her. They hugged each other tightly, simply delighted to see one another again.

"Jasmin de tante, bonjour. C'est génial de vous voir," Jia said. The translation was "Hello, Auntie Jasmine. It's great to see you." Jasmine had become fairly proficient in French. She took advanced classes, used software programs, listened to audio books in French while she drove, and watched French TV shows and movies. Since she visited Jia often, she at least wanted to be able to communicate with the French people and in particular with Nai Nai, who didn't speak much English.

"Bonjour, ma nièce chérie. C'est génial de vous voir ainsi," Jasmine replied proudly with her head held high. She'd said, "Hello, my darling niece. It's great to see you as well."

"You go, Auntie Jazz. I'm impressed," Jia said proudly, switching back to English.

"Thanks, sweetie. I'm not where I want to be, but I'm getting there," Jasmine replied. "Where's your mother?"

"She's waiting for us at home. I wanted to give her and Nai Nai some time alone to get to know each other."

On the ride home, it was evident to Jasmine just how excited Jia was to have her mother, whom she referred to as māma (the informal Chinese word for mother), back in her life. She talked practically nonstop about her māma during the hour-long ride home.

"I still can hardly believe she found me after all these years. She said she never stopped looking for us. Never stopped hoping that she'd see her girls again. It's just too bad that Sun-Yu's not here to witness this moment," Jia said.

"Yes, it is," Jasmine replied.

"And, Auntie Jazz, she's just as beautiful as I remember. The last time I saw her, I was only eight so I'd almost forgotten what she looked like. But when I opened the door and saw her standing there, I remembered her just like it was yesterday. She has the same beautiful eyes and skin, the same long, shiny hair, and she still always wears red," Jia exclaimed.

Jasmine smiled and pretended to be as excited as Jia was. For Jia's sake, she hoped that Dereka's tale of what her mother had done wasn't true. Hoped that somehow Dereka had misconstrued or misinterpreted the whole thing. Jasmine knew that if it was true, and Jia found out, it would be a crushing, devastating blow to her. Jasmine prayed internally, *Lord, please don't let it be true. Please let things be as wonderful as Jia thinks they are.* Dereka had asked Jasmine not to tell Jia the truth. She just wanted Jasmine to somehow get rid of Lihwa so she could never hurt Jia again. Jasmine had only promised Dereka that she'd try not to tell her. But if it turned out to be true that Lihwa had sold her own daughters, Jasmine didn't know if not telling Jia would even be an option. And Jasmine was sure, from her years of experience confronting sex traffickers, that she'd know the truth about Lihwa the minute she laid eyes on her. And she did.

When Jasmine entered Jia's home, she saw a beautiful, petite Asian lady, wearing a long red silk dress, sitting on the sofa beside Nai Nai looking at some photo albums. Jasmine's skin crawled when the woman got up and moved toward her with the sweetest smile on her face. *Devil in a red dress*, was the first thought that popped into Jasmine's mind.

"Auntie Jazz, this is my māma. Māma, this is my auntie Jazz," Jia said, beaming with pride at being able to introduce two of the dearest people in her life.

"Hello, my name is Lihwa. I am honored to meet you," Lihwa said, embracing Jasmine as if they were old friends. Out of politeness, Jasmine returned her embrace.

"Hello, Lihwa, I'm Jasmine. It's nice to meet you," Jasmine said politely, knowing she was lying through her teeth.

"Jasmine, you are just as beautiful as the fragrant flower your name represents," Lihwa said, her voice dripping with milk and honey.

"Thank you. You are beautiful also," Jasmine replied, and at least that was the truth. Jasmine turned her attention to Nai Nai, whom she was very fond of.

"Nai Nai, en quoi ma fille préférée? (How's my favorite girl?)" Jasmine said, greeting Nai Nai as she always did. Nai Nai laughed because she was always tickled when Jasmine referred to her as a girl.

"I am well. How are you, my dear?" Nai Nai responded slowly in English, trying to impress Jasmine.

"You've been practicing your English?" Jasmine said, laughing and hugging Nai Nai tightly.

"Yes, I have," Nai Nai replied with pride.

"Jasmine, dear, you must be hungry after your long flight," Lihwa chimed in. "Nai Nai and I have prepared a special meal just for you," she announced, leading the way into the kitchen.

"Yes, thank you. But I'd like to freshen up a bit first," Jasmine said.

"Of course," Lihwa replied, smiling sweetly. *She sure smiles a lot. I bet that smile has a lot to hide*, Jasmine thought cynically. Jia took Jasmine's hand and led her upstairs to the guest bedroom.

"Māma and I will share my room while you are here so you can have some privacy," Jia said, placing Jasmine's suitcase on a burgundy chaise lounge in the corner. Jasmine looked around at the beautiful, sunny room where she always stayed when visiting Jia. It had a wonderful French coziness about it that she loved.

"So, Auntie Jazz. What do you think of my māma?" Jia asked eagerly.

"Well, she's as lovely as you described her," Jasmine said.

"Did I tell you she's planning to stay with us?"

"Yes, you told me."

"In a few days she has to return to Taipei to take care of some things. But she'll be back in a month or so for good. This is a dream come true, Auntie Jazz."

Jasmine looked at Jia's beaming face. She couldn't recall a time when she'd ever seen her so happy. *Maybe I'm wrong about Lihwa*, Jasmine thought. *But what if I'm not. This could destroy Jia.* Two tears slid from the corners of Jasmine's eyes just at the thought of Jia being hurt. Jia mistook Jasmine's tears of sadness for tears of happiness that her mother was back in her life.

"Oh, Auntie Jazz," she said, hugging Jasmine and letting her own happy tears flow. They stayed that way for a moment, hugging each other and crying. But their tears were for two entirely different reasons.

She Must Not Know 'bout Me

During Jasmine's visit, Lihwa proved to be the perfect hostess. One would have thought she owned the place the way she controlled everything. She fluttered around the house like a beautiful butterfly, rearranging furniture and pictures to suit her taste. She cooked delicious authentic Chinese cuisine and brewed flavorful exotic teas. She waited on Jia, Jasmine, and Nai Nai hand and foot and would not allow Jasmine to so much as put a plate in the sink. Lihwa smothered Jia with plenty of love and affection, doting on her daughter at every turn. Jasmine hardly got to spend any alone time with Jia because Lihwa was always around, playing the loving mother role. Sometimes it made Jasmine sick to her stomach.

This afternoon Jia had gone to take Nai Nai to a doctor's appointment, so Lihwa and Jasmine were home alone. Jasmine was glad of the opportunity for some one-on-one time with Lihwa because she had some serious questions to ask her.

"Jia told me that you all were on your way to the United States when they were abducted from the airport in Colombia. She said you'd gone to get them a snack and had taken ill, is that right?" Jasmine inquired.

"Yes, that's correct. I remember feeling a sharp pain, and the next thing I remember is waking up in the hospital. They said I had been there for two days. And no one knew where my daughters were. It was just awful."

"Hmmm, what hospital in Colombia were you in?"

"Oh, I don't remember the name."

"When I found Dereka at the house where they were held captive, she was transported to the Centro Medico Imbanaco in Bogota. It's strange that you do not remember the name of the hospital that you were in."

"I was so worried about my girls. All I could think about was finding my daughters."

"How long were you in the hospital?"

"For a few days, I believe."

"Where did you go after you left the hospital?"

"I stayed in Colombia for a while?"

"Did you contact the police?"

"Of course, I contacted the police," Lihwa shot back rather impatiently.

"Which department did you contact?"

"I can't remember. Why do you ask?"

"Well, during my rescue work in Colombia we worked with several police departments. I was thinking I may have worked with the same department that you contacted to find Jia and Sun-Yu."

"Oh, I see. Well like I said, I don't remember."

"Where did you go after you left Colombia?"

"Back to Beijing."

"Where did you stay?"

"Why do you ask?"

"When the girls were rescued, our support team did its best to find all their relatives. I'm surprised they were not able to find you in Beijing. I believe they did look for you there."

"Well, I left Beijing after a year and went to live in Taipei. It was too painful being in Beijing without my daughters. Too many memories."

"I understand," Jasmine replied, trying to be sympathetic. "But did you keep looking for them?"

"Of course I did. I never stopped trying to find my precious girls," Lihwa stated. Jasmine could see that Lihwa was getting flustered by her line of questioning, so she decided to turn up the pressure to see if she would crack.

"That's strange, Lihwa. After Jia was rescued, her grandparents found her at the safe house in Colombia. It's a bit baffling that you were not able to locate Jia until now."

By now Lihwa was tired of Jasmine's questions. She went from being flustered to being upset.

"And what are you insinuating?" she asked indignantly, standing to her feet to intimidate Jasmine. *She must not know 'bout me,* Jasmine thought, rising to her full five-foot-seven-inch frame and towering over the smaller woman. Jasmine was from the tough streets of Baltimore, and she didn't back down from nobody. She was ready, willing, and able to go "old school" on Lihwa and jack that red dress up over her head and whoop her behind. Jasmine was a Christian and all, but right now she was tempted to beat Lihwa's butt and pray for forgiveness later.

But for Jia's sake, Jasmine decided to back off, at least for now. She couldn't imagine Jia coming home and finding her māma and auntie in a knock-down, drag-out fight.

"Lihwa, I meant no disrespect," Jasmine said, sitting back down. "And I'm not insinuating anything. I'm just the curious type. Always asking a lot of questions. Drives people crazy." Jasmine then decided to change the subject.

"Do you have any more of that delicious tea from this morning?" she asked. Lihwa looked relieved with the topic change.

"Yes, I do," she said, moving to the teapot on the stove. "I'm so glad you like this tea. It is my favorite. My māma used to make it for me when I was a little girl," Lihwa said. She talked on and on about the exotic flavors of Chinese tea. Jasmine and Lihwa made small talk the rest of the afternoon, each trying to be as cordial as possible. But it was clear that their earlier conversation and near confrontation had somewhat strained their relationship.

◆ ◆ ◆

When Nai Nai and Jia came home, Jia sensed tension in the air between the two ladies. She assumed that each was probably just a little jealous of the other. After all, her auntie Jazz had been the mother figure in her life for almost seven years. Perhaps she was afraid that her māma's return would impact their close mother-daughter relationship. And her māma was likely a bit envious of the strong bond that existed between her and Auntie Jazz. There was bound to be some tension between the two women.

Later that night, Jasmine was in her bedroom getting ready for bed when Jia knocked on the door.

"May I come in, Auntie Jazz?"

"Sure, honey." Jia came in and sat down on the chaise.

"I just want you to know that my māma's return is not going to affect our relationship one bit. You'll always have a special place in my heart that no one can replace. You know that, don't you?" she asked.

"You know I do. Just as you'll always have an irreplaceable place in my heart. Now is there a special reason for telling me that?" Jasmine inquired.

"Well, I sensed some tension between you and māma when I got home. I thought maybe her return was making you feel a bit…insecure," Jia admitted.

"Oh honey, don't worry about that. It was nothing. I just have to get used to the fact that you have a real mother now, that's all."

"But I've had a real mother for the past seven years. You."

"Thanks, sweetie," Jasmine said, sitting beside Jia and hugging her tight. "You just don't know how good that makes me feel. I love you so much."

"Love you too, Auntie Jazz. Goodnight."

When Jia left, Jasmine was both happy and sad. Happy that she had someone like Jia in her life, but sad because she truly believed that Jia's mother was a wolf in sheep's clothing. If what Dereka said was true, this woman was dangerous. In Jasmine's experience with sex traffickers, they rarely stopped unless they were caught and forced to. The sex business was just too lucrative. And if Lihwa sold her own daughters, it was highly likely she had sold many others. And it was also possible that she could harm Jia again. And there was no way this side of heaven Jasmine was going to let that happen. She had connections with Operation Undercover teams, government officials, and police departments in Asia, Colombia, and all over the world. And she planned to use those connections to find out exactly what had happened at that airport in Colombia when Jia and Sun-Yu were supposedly kidnapped. She would also discover where Lihwa had been for the twelve years since then, and what she was currently up to. If Lihwa was involved in sex trafficking, either now or then, Jasmine was going to take her down.

A Time to Snoop

Lihwa was traveling back to China today, and Jasmine could not have been happier. She had waited patiently for nearly a week for her to go, not wanting to leave Jia alone with her mother. Jasmine watched Lihwa floating around the kitchen like she was Betty Crocker, making sweet cakes for their breakfast. Sweet cakes were Chinese cakes, made from rice and sugar, that Lihwa said bring good luck.

Jasmine had already placed a call to an Operation Undercover team in Colombia to verify Lihwa's claim of having worked with a Colombian police department to find her missing girls, and having stayed there in a hospital for a few days. So far, the team had found no records of a Lihwa Huang being in any of the major hospitals during that time or contacting the police department. There was also no police record of two Asian girls being abducted from the airport. Jasmine was not the least bit surprised. She'd known Lihwa was lying.

Jasmine's ears perked up when she heard Lihwa asking Jia to visit her in China.

"Darling, you should come to visit me in Taipei. It's such a wonderful city. And there's so much I have to do to prepare to come and live with you and Nai Nai. I could really use your help."

"Māma, that's a wonderful idea. I would love to come," Jia exclaimed excitedly, jumping up to give her mother a hug.

"Well then, it's all settled. I will send for you in a few weeks. It's going to be so nice having you there. We'll have such fun," Lihwa assured her.

While Lihwa, Jia, and Nai Nai chatted happily about Jia's pending trip to China, Jasmine took advantage of their distraction to sneak away so she could do some snooping. With the talk about Jia visiting Lihwa, time was of the essence for Jasmine to find out exactly who this woman was and what she was up to. Jasmine went upstairs to look around in Lihwa's personal items to see what she could find out. She paused before entering their bedroom and listened to see if anyone else was coming up. But they were still chatting away, now in French mainly for Nai Nai's sake. Lihwa, like Jia, spoke several languages fluently.

After seeing that the coast was clear, Jasmine quietly opened Jia's bedroom door and went in. She saw Lihwa's luggage and red purse sitting on the bed. Jasmine picked up the purse and rummaged through it, hoping to find a driver's license or passport with Lihwa's personal information. She felt a little guilty about snooping through Lihwa's things, but she had to know the truth about her for Jia's sake. Jasmine took out her passport, opened it, and saw Lihwa's smiling passport photo. But the information was written in Chinese, which made sense, but Jasmine hadn't thought about that. She hurried across the hall to her room, retrieved her cell phone, and took a picture of the passport. She then located Lihwa's visa and driver's license and took pictures of them also. She'd have someone translate the information for her later. Satisfied that she had enough to go on for now, Jasmine carefully replaced the items and went back downstairs. And no one was none the wiser about what she'd been up to.

That afternoon Jia and Jasmine took Lihwa to the airport. There were tearful goodbyes between Jia and Lihwa, and Jasmine pretended like she too hated to see Lihwa go, more out of politeness than anything else. But she actually couldn't wait to get rid of her. There was something vile and malignant hiding behind her sweet smile. And Jasmine was determined to expose it. Her only regret was knowing it would be detrimental for Jia.

Later that evening, Jasmine e-mailed Lihwa's information to a friend who was also an Operation Undercover team member in Shanghai. She asked him to translate the information into English. While Jasmine waited she thought about how happy and content Jia had been with her mother. *I hope I'm wrong about her*, Jasmine thought. But the information she received from her friend only deepened Jasmine's suspicions.

It appeared that Lihwa had changed her identity. Now her name was Yanmei Chén. And, on top of that, she didn't live in Taipei as she'd said.

The address on Lihwa's, a.k.a. Yanmei's, driver's license was in Yunnan, one of China's top hubs for sex trafficking. Women and girls from poor villages in Yunnan were often kidnapped and sold to other areas there to balance out gender shortages. While the information was proof that Lihwa was a liar, it wasn't proof that she was a sex trafficker. To get solid evidence, Jasmine would have to do some more digging into her past, and set up a sting through Operation Undercover to catch her in the act.

The next day Jasmine took an early morning flight back to Virginia, anxious to get home and start coordinating the sting operation with her team in DC. She'd also spoken to Kenya a few times about Dereka and was a bit unnerved about what was going on with her. *Lord, help us*, she thought, anticipating the challenges ahead.

Crossroad

Elliott stretched out on the bed in the guest room of his home. This is what his life had come to. Being treated like a guest in his own home. Surprisingly, Nicole had not left him after she learned of his affair with Jia. One reason was because she really did love him. But the main reason was because of her ego. Nicole just couldn't fathom losing her husband to, as she put it, "some cheap whore." It would have been too humiliating for her, and she just couldn't summon the courage to face her family and friends in such a demeaning situation. After all, Nicole was beautiful, sexy, successful, smart, and of the upper crust of society. She'd told Brianna, "I don't understand how any man could choose another woman over me, no less choose a hooker, prostitute, working girl, lady of the night, or whatever the tramp calls herself."

But Nicole did ban Elliott from their bedroom. And she'd had herself thoroughly checked out medically to make sure Elliott had not passed on any unseemly disease to her. Elliott didn't blame Nicole one bit. He took full blame, knowing that the sad state of their marriage laid squarely on his shoulders.

Elliott glanced at the clock and saw that it was shortly after midnight. He sat on the guest room bed looking at the four walls, feeling lonely and blue. But he wasn't lonely for his wife. He was lonely for his mistress. He hadn't seen Jia since her mother and aunt came to visit her, and he felt he was having withdrawal symptoms. His friend Zack had teased him, saying that Jia had cast some kind of voodoo spell on him, or had seduced him with Love Potion No. 9. Elliott didn't know what she had put on him, but he surmised that if he could bottle and sell it, he'd be a wealthy man.

Jia had told him they would get together as soon as her family left town. So when she called Elliott around 1:30 a.m. asking him to meet her at the hotel, he was thrilled. He jumped off the bed and rushed around the room like a madman, tripping over himself as he fumbled to get dressed. He grabbed his car keys and hurried down the stairs in the dark, not daring to turn on any lights. For some reason, perhaps out of respect for Nicole, he still didn't want his wife to know when he was going to be with his mistress.

Elliott carefully treaded his way in the darkness, tipping around furniture in the living room, and headed for the door. He nearly jumped out of his skin when he heard Nicole's voice. She was sitting on the living room sofa in the dark.

"Are you going to be with her?" she asked.

"Nicole, you scared the daylights out of me. What are you doing sitting down here in the dark?"

"I couldn't sleep. Are you going to see her?" Nicole asked again, turning on the end-table lamp. She was sitting there, a vision of loveliness, in a white satin nightgown, looking lost and vulnerable. Elliott was tempted to lie about where he was going, but he owed her the truth. Besides, what did he have to hide at this point?

"Yes, I'm going to see Jia," he confessed.

"Why, Elliott? Why was I not enough for you?" she asked with a puzzled look on her face. But Elliott could think of no good reason because Nicole was everything that he'd once thought he wanted.

"I don't know, Nicole. I honestly can't answer that question," he stated. Nicole stood up and walked over to Elliott. She took a deep breath and exhaled slowly before speaking, as if to prepare herself for the speech she was about to give.

"Elliott, I've been doing a lot of thinking lately. I believe there's still a chance that we can save our marriage. I still love you, and I believe you still love me. I think this thing that you're going through with this prostitute is just a phase. Although you've hurt me to my core, I'm willing to forgive you and move on. I know it won't be easy, but I'm willing to try," Nicole said.

Elliott was somewhat taken aback by his wife's words. It was something he hadn't expected to hear from her. He knew that he should jump at her offer, but something, or better yet someone, was holding him back. And that someone was waiting for him.

"Can we talk about this when I get back?" Elliott asked. Nicole jumped as if she had been slapped in the face.

"Do you mean to tell me after all I just said that you're still going to walk out of that door?" she asked, bewildered.

"I have to go," Elliott replied, turning to leave.

"Elliott, I just poured out my heart to you. Don't you dare walk out of that door," Nicole said, her voice now as cold as ice. Elliott had one hand on the doorknob. He turned and looked into his wife's stern face. They stared at each other for a long moment, each knowing that they were at a crossroad in their marriage. An intersection where their marriage could go either way. Nicole's facial expression changed from hard to soft as she gazed at her husband.

"Please don't go," she whispered softly, her eyes pleading with him to choose her.

"I'm sorry, Nicole," Elliott said as he opened the door and left.

When Elliott returned home about six in the morning, Nicole was gone. And Elliott knew she was gone for good.

You against Yourself

Kenya realized that if what Dr. Bedford suspected about Dereka was true, she needed to better educate herself about mental illness in general, and paranoid schizophrenia in particular, so she'd be better prepared to help her niece cope with it. To be honest, up until the time Dereka was initially diagnosed with a mental disorder when she was first rescued, Kenya hadn't given it much thought one way or another. Mental illness was something her family just didn't talk about when she was growing up. It was as if the whole subject of mental illness was taboo in the Jones household.

Kenya remembered an Aunt Dana on her father's side of the family whom she'd rarely seen as a young child. Aunt Dana was always missing from family reunions and holiday gatherings. Kenya thought it was strange because her family was so close. She recalled asking her father why Aunt Dana was hardly ever around, but he'd just brushed her off at the time. And when she'd asked her mother, she was given a vague response. After a while, it became apparent to Kenya and her brother that something was wrong with Aunt Dana. They found out that she was often institutionalized at St. Elizabeth's Mental Institution in southeast DC.

Founded in 1855, St. Elizabeth's was the first federally operated psychiatric hospital in the United States. It was officially known as, "The Government Hospital for the Insane." As foolish children, they had sometimes joked about Aunt Dana being crazy and that she was in "the crazy house." That was the term kids used back then to refer to people in mental institutions. They'd even foolishly used insulting words to describe mentally ill people including nuts, loco, looney, basket case, not playing with a full deck, and so on. Now as an adult, Kenya knew that mental illness was no laughing matter. It was a serious illness that could be life crippling if not treated properly. According to the National Alliance on Mental Illness, nearly one in five adults in the United States suffers from mental illness during a given year.

Kenya spent an entire afternoon conducting Internet research on mental illness. She found loads of information, and downloaded and printed off several documents. Among other things, Kenya discovered, as Dr. Bedford had pointed out, that paranoid delusions could become so fixated in a person's mind that nothing, including clear evidence to the contrary, could convince the person that it's not true. These delusions often involved conspiracies, delusions of grandeur, or special missions from God. And it didn't matter how bizarre, unrealistic, outlandish, or even impossible the beliefs or thoughts were. The illness deluded the person into believing that they were real. And because these delusions were so entrenched and real to the person, he or she might act on these false beliefs, which could be dangerous and even deadly.

The information Kenya learned about auditory hallucinations was equally profound. These voices were as real to that person as when a so-called normal person hears the voice of someone actually talking. This may explain why sometimes we see people, particularly homeless people in which population there is a disproportionate number of people with severe mental illnesses, talking to themselves. In some instances, these sufferers may be responding to voices they hear in their heads.

These voices may threaten the person, give him or her commands, or even attack the person's appearance, behavior, personality, and such. For the sufferer, it has to be an extremely burdensome, challenging, and onerous thing to experience. The voices can be mean, brutal, demoralizing, and self-defeating. They may constantly ridicule and criticize the mentally ill person, and this type of constant assault can have detrimental consequences. Sometimes these voices told people to harm or kill themselves. Sadly, sometimes the sufferer succumbs to these commands and commits suicide.

Why are these voices so persuasive as to drive someone to commit suicide? Kenya wondered out loud as she continued to read. She discovered that hallucinatory voices are powerful because they are a part of the person's psyche, and thus, intimately know him or her. After all, other than God, who knows you better than you? The voices know about the person's strengths, weaknesses, fears, hopes, dreams, secrets, and faults. It appears as if the voices use this information to attack, prey on, defeat, humiliate, and break down the person mentally, emotionally, and psychologically. It seems that the voices, in an attempt to destroy the person, arm themselves with heavy artillery in the person's psyche and wage a well-coordinated, vicious war against the person.

"In a way, it's like you against yourself," Kenya contemplated out loud as a light bulb went on in her head. "No wonder this illness is so debilitating and devastating. Your own mind actually turns against you."

Kenya closed her computer and sat back, absorbing all the information. She recalled an episode of *Unsung* she'd watched a few weeks ago about Donny Hathaway. He was diagnosed with paranoid schizophrenia at the height of his career in the early seventies. Once during a recording session, he'd run out of the room screaming, and they found him huddled in a corner crying. When they asked him what was wrong, he said that white people wanted to kill him and that they had connected his brain to a machine to steal his music and sound. Later that same night, he was found dead outside of a hotel. It's believed he committed suicide by jumping from his hotel room window. He was only thirty-four years old.

What a shame, Kenya thought, shaking her head sadly. And now, with her newfound knowledge, she was more determined than ever to get her niece the treatment she needed.

God's Chosen Ones

It was Friday night—the night before Dereka and Scrappy's big showdown with Bat007. Dereka sat at her desk in her bedroom. She had stayed in her room most of the week, mainly to avoid another contentious interaction with Kenya about returning to therapy. Dereka had not even talked much to Auntie Jazz, who had tried desperately to reason with her after she returned from France. Dereka decided it was just best to keep to herself and remain mute. She also didn't want to say anything to them that could tip them off about what she and Scrappy were planning to do. *That's exactly what they want*, Dereka thought, referring to her aunts. *They just want to find out so they can stop us.*

So Dereka avoided them at every turn, only going out of her room to grab something to eat from the kitchen, and then hurrying back to her room. Once she had stood outside the kitchen door and eavesdropped on her aunts' conversation about her and Jia. She was glad to hear that Jasmine now fully believed her story about Lihwa and was planning an undercover operation to expose her. That was the good news. But Dereka got nervous when she heard them discussing Dr. Bedford's concerns about her mental state and what they should do about it. It seemed they were determined to coerce or force her into seeing that doctor again. From that day on, Dereka started locking her bedroom door at night and sometimes even during the day.

Dereka had spoken with Scrappy several times by phone over the past few days and everything was set for the big payback tomorrow night. Dereka had arranged to meet Bat007 at the abandoned baseball park in Hybla Valley at 9:00 p.m. Dereka informed him that she'd be sitting on the bleachers just behind the home plate and would flash a flashlight three times when he arrived to let him know where she was. He told her he'd be driving his parents blue Audi sedan and that he'd even bring a bottle of wine so they could loosen up and have fun. Imagine that, bringing a bottle of wine to meet with someone he thought was a thirteen-year-old girl. Bat007 was definitely expecting to have a good time—a real good time. But he was in for the surprise of his life. This pervert was going to be taught a lesson he'd never forget.

Scrappy and Dereka planned to meet at the ballpark an hour early just to get everything set up. Dereka had asked Scrappy what, if anything, she needed to bring.

"Nothing," Scrappy had replied. "Just bring yourself. I'll bring everything we need to make that low-down punk piss in his pants and cry for mercy." And, as a member of one of the toughest gangs in the Bronx, Scrappy knew a thing or two about inflicting pain. Scrappy told Dereka that she was even planning to use a few of the techniques the Tavaras brothers had used to torture them in the shed.

Dereka turned off the light and got into bed. She lay in the dark with her eyes open, contemplating what she was about to do. She was feeling anxious and began to wonder if she was doing the right thing. But the voices in her head started egging her on to do the vengeful act. Dereka cocked her head to one side and listened to the voices intently. This time there were two voices, one male and one female. Dereka got out of bed, retrieved her journal, and began writing down what the voices were saying to her.

> They deserve to be PUNISHED!
> You have to do this.
> They're SCUM! They must be stopped!
> It's God's will. Don't let God down.
> Suffer, Suffer, make them SUFFER!
> They have to be STOPPED!
> Don't worry. You can do this.

Dereka wrote as fast as she could. But it was impossible to write everything down because the words were coming so fast, and sometimes the voices overlapped. But she wrote and wrote until her hand got tired, filling up page after page in her journal. She wrote until the voices dissipated.

Unfortunately, Dereka mistook the voices to be the voices of God's angels that he'd sent to her to ease her fears, and validate that they were indeed doing the right thing by making sexual perverts suffer. *They are the scum of the earth, and they have to be stopped*, she thought. And Dereka felt privileged that she and Scrappy were the ones God chose to do it.

The Night of Reckoning

Dereka left her house around seven thirty Saturday evening and drove slowly toward the abandoned baseball park. It was a hot and sticky evening in late August. And it was judgment day for Bat007. If he turned out to be just some horny teenage boy, they'd give him a good scare and send him on his way. But if he really was one of them, as they thought, this would be a night he'd never forget.

While Dereka had always naturally looked young for her age, she'd attempted to make herself appear even younger. Her hair was pulled back in a ponytail. And she had on a T-shirt and some short-shorts, and was wearing no makeup whatsoever. In the dark, she could easily pass for a young adolescent girl.

She parked her car in the store parking lot just up the street from the ballpark, turned the car off, and rolled down the windows. She waited nervously for Scrappy to arrive, with only the loud sounds of crickets, cicadas, and grasshoppers to keep her company. Dereka was extremely jittery about what was about to happen. She could feel sweat beading on her forehead and rolling down her back. And her heart was racing a mile a minute. Dereka fanned herself with her hands and took deep breathes to try and calm her nerves. She was relieved when she saw Scrappy's car turn into the parking lot at exactly eight. Scrappy parked next to Dereka and hopped out of her car with an air of excited anticipation. She had a black duffel bag in one hand. Violence is what she lived for, what she thrived on. Scrappy wasn't a religious person, but she did take seriously the scripture that said,

Vengeance is mine; I will repay. Only in Scrappy's mind the "I" referred to herself, not the Lord.

"Hey, girl. It's good to see you," Dereka said, embracing Scrappy.

"It's good to see you too. You ready to do this thang?" Scrappy asked gleefully.

"I think so."

"You can't think so, Dereka. It doesn't work like that. You have to be all in. Now are you ready for this?" Scrappy asked again, her excitement mounting.

"I'm ready," Dereka assured her. Scrappy's excitement and confidence was rubbing off on her. They walked down the short gravel road to the ballpark and, as expected, it was completely deserted.

"Let's go sit on the bleachers. I want to show you what I have in my bag," Scrappy stated. They walked across the baseball field toward the bleachers. Once they were seated, Scrappy unzipped her duffel bag and began to lay the items out on the bench, doing a sort of show-and-tell for Dereka. She'd brought a short, thick crowbar, knife, duct tape, box cutters, a cigarette lighter, plastic zip ties, a wrench, a bottle of water, and some other devices Dereka didn't even recognize.

"What's the water for?" Dereka asked out of curiosity.

"That's in case he passes out. I'll pour the water on him to wake him up. I want him to be awake for the whole thing, so he can feel every pain like we felt in that shed," Scrappy replied. Dereka felt a cold chill creep down her spine.

"We're just going to hurt him bad, right? Not kill him?" she said.

"That's right. But we're going to make that m'fer wish he was dead," Scrappy assured her. Dereka started getting nervous again.

"But suppose he goes to the police afterward? Suppose they find out what we did and come looking for us," she inquired.

"He ain't going to no police. Because he'd have to explain what he was doing in an abandoned ballpark at night in the first place. And that pervert won't want to draw attention to himself. He can't take that chance. We got him by the balls."

"Yeah, you're right. He would have some explaining to do," Dereka concurred.

◆ ◆ ◆

Right around nine, Scrappy and Dereka saw a car traveling down the road toward the ballpark.

"That's probably him. I'm going to hide behind that tree over there. When he parks his car, flash this flashlight three times to lead him to you like we planned. I'll take it from there. You just follow my lead," Scrappy instructed.

"Okay," Dereka replied, her voice shaking a bit. Scrappy gave Dereka a quick hug.

"We got this," she said before moving away. Dereka's heart was beating so hard, she felt like it was going to explode in her chest. She watched as he parked the car and turned off the engine. It was now practically dark in the park with the only light coming from one dim light pole at the end of the ball field. Dereka flashed her flashlight three times in rapid succession. Bat007 flashed his flashlight three times in response. He kept his flashlight on as he walked toward her. Dereka felt her legs shaking as she sat on the bench, watching his flashlight move closer and closer. "Stay calm," she told herself, putting her arms around her trembling legs to keep them still.

But the closer he got, the more scared Dereka became. She wanted to get up and run away. When he got within about fifteen feet, Dereka shined her flashlight full in his face. He was a stocky white man with a mustache, blue eyes, and shoulder-length brown hair. He looked to be in his mid-thirties and was definitely not a high-school senior as he'd claimed. He shone his flashlight on Dereka and grinned when he saw her.

"You're a pretty little thing," he said with a slight southern accent.

Then Dereka heard a loud thump, and the man went crushing to the ground like a rag doll. Scrappy stood over him with the crowbar in her hand.

"Bat007," she said, "your night of reckoning has come." When Dereka saw the man lying motionless on the ground with blood coming from his head, she freaked out.

"No, no, no," she said, backing away. But Scrappy sprang into action. She grabbed the duffel bag, retrieved the zip ties, and tied the man's feet together.

"Dereka, tie his hands together," Scrappy instructed, but Dereka didn't move. Because she couldn't move. She was paralyzed by fear and literally exemplified the expression "scared stiff." She just stared at the man on the ground, her hands over her mouth, her eyes wide. Scrappy quickly realized she'd have to do everything herself. She moved with purpose as she zip-tied the man's legs and arms, and duct taped his mouth shut.

"There," she said, checking the strength of the ties. "That ought to hold him."

"Is he dead?" Dereka asked timidly.

"Nah, I just knocked him out," Scrappy assured her. She opened the bottle of water and poured about half of it on the man's face. But he didn't move.

"Are you sure he's not dead?" Dereka asked again.

"He shouldn't be," Scrappy said, pouring the rest of the water on him. But still he didn't move.

"Oh my God, Scrappy! I think you killed him," Dereka exclaimed. Scrappy kicked him with her foot a couple of times.

"Damn. I think he is dead," she stated, scratching her head in puzzlement that a big, burly man like him had been taken out by one blow. And she hadn't even put her full weight into it. Hell, she'd taken harder licks than that without losing consciousness, no less dying. *Punk ass, bitch*, she thought, looking down at him with disdain. He couldn't have survived one day in her world where death and dying were practically an everyday occurrence.

At this point, Dereka totally panicked and started crying and shaking uncontrollably. She was absolutely horrified that a dead man was lying there on the ground. And they were responsible.

"This was not supposed to happen. What are we going to do now?" she cried.

"Let's get out of here," Scrappy said, quickly stuffing the crowbar, duct tape, and other items into her duffel bag. Then she half dragged, half rolled the man's body behind the tree where she'd been hiding.

They both took off running across the field and down the gravel road with Scrappy leading the way with the flashlight. Dereka was crying so hard she could barely see where she was going.

"Do you think you can drive home?" Scrappy asked once they reached the parking lot. She was concerned about Dereka, who looked terrified.

"I think so," Dereka said, getting into her car.

"Everything's going to be okay, Dereka. Trust me. I'll be in touch in a few days. Just go home and wait for my call. And please don't tell anyone about this," Scrappy stressed.

Dereka nodded and started driving home. But she had to pull over to the side of the road shortly because her legs were shaking, and she could barely see the road through her tears. Dereka sat in her car for about forty-five minutes, crying and trembling with fear.

"We killed him," she cried. "Oh my God, we killed someone." Although she hadn't delivered the fatal blow, she felt that she was just as guilty as Scrappy. After all, they'd planned the whole thing together. Dereka had been the bait that lured Bat007 to the trap that resulted in his death. She started the car.

"I have to get home and tell Aunt Kenya and Auntie Jazz. They'll know what to do," she murmured.

Killed a Man?

Kenya was relaxing at home watching a romantic-comedy movie. Jasmine was out with her new fiancé, Percy, who was in town. During a commercial break, Kenya went into the kitchen, popped a bag of microwave popcorn, grabbed a diet Sprite, and went back to finish enjoying the movie. That's when Dereka burst through the door, looking like a frightened, wild woman. Her eyes were red and puffy from crying.

"Dereka, what's wrong?" Kenya shrieked, running to her niece. Dereka grabbed her aunt and held on to her, crying her heart out.

"Honey, what happened? Were you in an accident or something? Are you hurt?" Kenya asked, leading Dereka to the sofa and sitting her down.

"We killed somebody!" Dereka blurted. The words physically jolted Kenya. Her mouth fell open in astonishment, and she was speechless for a few seconds.

"You killed somebody?" Kenya exclaimed when she finally regained her voice.

"Yes. Scrappy and I killed a man!"

"Killed a man? Dereka, what are you talking about? What man?"

"I don't know. We met him online by pretending to be a young girl. It was part of our plan to make sexual predators suffer. We just wanted to give him a taste of his own medicine. We met him in that old ballpark in Hybla Valley. But we only intended to hurt him. We didn't mean to kill him. I swear, Aunt Kenya. We left his body in the ballpark behind a tree," Dereka said. Kenya could not believe what she was hearing.

"Dereka, are you sure you're not just imagining this?" she asked.

"No, me and Scrappy actually killed somebody!"

"But who's Scrappy?"

"The girl I met in Colombia. Remember I told you about her. Her name's Regine, but we call her Scrappy."

Kenya vaguely recalled Dereka mentioning a feisty young girl who had raised holy hell and fought back. But as far as Kenya knew, Dereka hadn't seen that girl since Colombia and had assumed that she'd died there. Now Dereka was saying that she and this Scrappy person had killed somebody. It was mind-boggling. But when Kenya looked at Dereka, crying and trembling with fear, it was obvious that something had deeply disturbed her. Kenya had no idea what. But she knew she had to find out. And there was only one way to know for sure.

"Dereka, let's go to the ballpark. I need to see what happened for myself."

"Aunt Kenya, I'm scared to go back there. Please don't make me," Dereka pleaded.

"But Dereka we have to go. I need to know what happened. I'll call Sean and have him meet us there. Everything's going to be all right." Kenya called Sean and asked him to meet them at the ballpark, and said she'd explain everything when they got there. Dereka continued to tremble and cry in the car as Kenya drove. Kenya silently prayed, "Lord, please let everything be all right. We need you, Lord. Please let everything be all right." When they got to the ballpark, Sean was already waiting for them in the parking lot.

"Wait here," Kenya said. She went to fill Sean in on what was happening. Dereka watched them talking and then saw Sean go into the truck of his car to get a flashlight. Kenya gestured for Dereka to join them.

"Hi, Dereka," Sean said. "Would you show us where it happened?"

"Over there," Dereka said, pointing to the bleachers behind home plate. She looked absolutely petrified. It broke Kenya's heart to see her niece so distressed.

"Dereka, honey. No matter what we find over there, you know that I love you, and I've got you. Right?" she said.

"I know," Dereka replied.

Sean led the way across the field. Kenya and Dereka held on to each other as they followed close behind him. Kenya could feel Dereka's body shaking more and more, the closer they got. Kenya was also afraid. Suppose Dereka was telling the truth, and they found a dead body.

"Lord, have mercy," she murmured under her breath. When they were almost at the bleachers, Dereka stopped.

"His body is over there behind that tree," she said.

"Stay here," Sean instructed. He walked ahead and looked around with the flashlight for a few moments.

"Come on over," he yelled.

Kenya and Dereka walked gingerly over to where Sean was standing beside the tree. They looked around, but nothing was there. No body, no blood, or no signs whatsoever that anything was amiss. Dereka's facial expression changed from fear to shock. She grabbed the flashlight from Sean's hand and started searching around the area frantically, looking for the man's body.

"It was here. We left him right here behind this tree," she proclaimed. Sean and Kenya exchanged knowing looks, and Kenya shook her head sadly.

"But, Dereka, as you can see there's nothing here. You just imagined the whole thing, honey," Kenya stated.

"No, no, no, no, no," Dereka said adamantly. "It happened. It really happened."

"Let's go home and talk about it," Kenya said, placing her arm around Dereka's waist and leading her away. Dereka walked as if she was in a stupor and kept looking back in puzzlement as if her mind wasn't deciphering what her eyes had just seen.

When they got back to the cars, Kenya thanked Sean for meeting them there and said she'd call him tomorrow.

"Are you all going to be all right?" Sean asked, worried about both of them.

"Yes, I think so," Kenya replied uncertainly, quite unnerved by the situation. Her niece had just told her that she and someone else had killed a man. And even though it had been proven untrue, it was still a lot for Kenya to absorb.

The Conspiracy Theory

While she drove, Kenya thought about what she was going to say to Dereka when they got home. She knew she'd have to choose her words carefully because Dereka was in a delicate state. Once they were home, Kenya went into the kitchen and made Dereka some orange spice tea, hoping it would calm her somewhat. Kenya watched Dereka sip her tea, waiting for the right time to speak to her, but Dereka spoke up first.

"It's a conspiracy," she blurted out.

"A conspiracy? What makes you think that?" Kenya asked.

"I know exactly what happened, Aunt Kenya. They must have been spying on us and knew what we were planning to do. After we left the ballpark, they took the man's body. That's why it wasn't there."

"They took it? You mean sexual predators took the body?"

"Yes, of course they did. Now it all makes sense."

"No, honey. No one took the body because you didn't kill anyone. It never happened. You're sick, honey. You need help. Your mind is playing tricks on you. Because you haven't been taking your medication, you're probably having delusions and hallucinations. Dr. Bedford said..."

"No!" Dereka shouted, cutting Kenya off. "Scrappy hit that man with a crowbar and killed him. But she didn't mean to. And they took the body."

"But if they knew you all killed a man, why would they take the body? Why wouldn't they just call the police?" Kenya asked, trying her best to reason with Dereka.

"I don't know. Maybe they're afraid to call the police. Or maybe the police are in on it too. Maybe they're helping them, like Dr. Bedford."

"Sweetie, don't you see how crazy this all sounds," Kenya stated, immediately regretting her use of the word "crazy."

"No, it's not crazy, Aunt Kenya. It's a conspiracy," Dereka said, sounding more convinced than ever. "Sexual predators are devious and evil. That's what Scrappy said. That's why we have to stop them. To keep them from hurting children."

"Dereka, there is no Scrappy. You just imagined her like you imagined Ms. Vee. Remember, she wasn't real either," Kenya said, getting a little exasperated that she wasn't getting through to her niece.

"No, Scrappy is real. Aunt Kenya, you have to believe me."

"Okay. Okay," Kenya said, deciding to try a different approach. "If Scrappy is real, why don't you call her and let me talk to her for myself."

"But she told me not to tell anybody. And I don't want to get her in trouble. She told me to just wait for her to call. She'll be mad at me if she found out I told you," Dereka said, sounding panicky. Kenya decided to call it quits for tonight, regroup, and continue their conversation tomorrow.

"Okay, honey. Go on to bed now. We can talk some more in the morning," she said.

"Okay, Aunt Kenya. Thanks for going out there with me. And tell Sean I said thanks. At least now I know what happened. It's a conspiracy," Dereka reiterated, kissing her aunt on the cheek before going upstairs.

When Dereka got to her room, she looked around trying to figure out just how they, the sexual predators, had spied on her and found out about their plan. *My computer,* she thought when her eyes landed on it. *They must have used my computer to watch me.* Dereka tiptoed to her computer which was off, but the lid was open. She peered into the blank screen and saw her reflection. *Perhaps they're looking at me right now,* she thought. Becoming frightened, she slammed down the computer lid, unplugged it, and placed it in the bottom dresser drawer underneath a pile of clothes. She sat on her bed, and thought about all that had happened. They had killed a man. She kept seeing his dead body lying on the ground. How could she have done something like that? Why had she let Scrappy talk her into it? A man was dead because of them. Because of her. She should have known better. She'd also let God down. They were only supposed to make him suffer. Dereka was horrified, disheartened, and disgusted with herself.

That's when the voices in her head started taunting her, using her fears and emotions to mock and attack her.

> Murderer!
> You killed him.
> You can't do nothing right. You're such a loser.
> Useless! Worthless!
> God's disappointed in you.

The voices were relentless in their attack, repeating the phrases over and over again. Their tone was harsh, cold, and daunting—like those of a gang of vicious bullies.

◆ ◆ ◆

Later that night when Jasmine got home, Kenya told her all that had happened.

"Jesus," Jasmine said as she listened to Kenya. She, like Kenya, was extremely worried about Dereka's mental stability and decided to check on her. Jasmine knocked on Dereka's door.

"Dereka, sweetie. Are you all right?" she asked. When Dereka didn't respond, she knocked again.

"Dereka, Kenya told me what happened. I just want to make sure you're okay." Still no answer. So Jasmine assumed that she was asleep. But Dereka wasn't asleep. She had not heard her aunt because she was in her bed, under the covers, with her hands over her ears. She was trying, unsuccessfully, to drown out the daunting voices in her head.

An Impossible Choice

For the next few days, Jasmine and Kenya tried desperately to reason with Dereka to convince her that she was sick and needed help. They used logic and rationale to show her that what she believed had happened could not have possibly happened, and that her conspiracy theory was all in her mind. They discussed the whys, ifs, hows, and buts about it. However, they didn't realize that trying to reason with someone who is indeed delusional is like trying to put out a blazing fire with a water pistol. It just doesn't work. For each of their logical arguments, Dereka had an equally, in her own mind, logical response. She was adamant in her belief that they had killed a man, and she dug her heels in on her conspiracy theory. Dereka even questioned why her aunts were so gung-ho about her going to see Dr. Bedford, whom Dereka was convinced was part of the conspiracy.

"Are you all in on it too," she'd asked her aunts. It hurt them that Dereka could even think that they could be part of a conspiracy against her. But they reminded themselves it was the illness thinking that way and not the niece they loved with all their hearts.

And when they finally convinced Dereka to call this Scrappy person, whom she had not heard from since it happened, the number was "out of service." Kenya and Jasmine thought for sure this would be definite proof to Dereka that Scrappy wasn't real. However, Dereka said that one of them had likely followed Scrappy from the ballpark, kidnapped her, and was holding her captive somewhere. And she was convinced they were coming after her next.

This morning Kenya and Jasmine were on their way to Dr. Bedford's office to discuss Dereka's increasing erratic behavior. They had an idea that they wanted to speak with the doctor about. When they arrived at the office, Dr. Bedford greeted them warmly. She listened intently to all they had to say, taking notes and asking questions throughout. She could tell from their worried faces they were extremely upset and concerned for Dereka. And her heart went out to them. Although she'd been in the mental-health field for many years, it was never easy to see the anguish on the faces of family members with loved ones who were mentally unstable.

Dr. Bedford knew what she was about to say to them would be difficult. But she was troubled by what they'd told her about Dereka. It concerned her that Dereka was convinced that she and another person had killed a man, and that Dereka believed it was her special mission from God to punish sexual predators to protect children. If Dereka was having delusions about hurting or killing sexual predators, Dr. Bedford was concerned that it could possibly escalate to her committing a harmful act in an attempt to fulfill what she considered her special mission from God. Over the past years, Dr. Bedford had come to know Dereka as a loving, kind, and compassionate person. In her right state of mind, Dereka wasn't capable of intentionally causing anyone harm or suffering. However, in her mentally impaired mind-set, she could possibly do harmful things to others, or even herself, for what she believed was the greater good of preventing another child from suffering as she had. That's why Dr. Bedford decided it was time for drastic measures.

"Ladies, what you've shared with me has strengthened my opinion that Dereka is suffering from paranoid schizophrenia and may no longer be capable of exercising sound judgment and controlling her behavior. Just the fact that she has thoughts of hurting others is quite troubling. The paranoia, delusions, and/or hallucinations she may be experiencing could cause her to think or do inconceivable things," Dr. Bedford stated. "And without the proper care of therapy and medication, her symptoms will only worsen. That's why if Dereka refuses to voluntarily seek treatment, as a last resort you all will need to consider involuntary psychiatric hospitalization. I know it's an impossible choice to make but…"

"You mean have Dereka committed?" Kenya asked, wide eyed.

"Well, I don't like to use the term 'committed.' It's involuntary mental hospitalization, and it's only used in situations where there is a high likelihood that a person may cause serious physical harm to self or others, or will suffer serious harm due to his or her inability to protect or care for themselves," Dr. Bedford stated.

"I don't really think Dereka is a danger to anyone. That whole thing about killing a man was all in her head. Dereka couldn't hurt a fly. She's always been one of the most kindhearted and loving persons I know," Jasmine pointed out.

"Yes, and under normal circumstances I couldn't agree more. But mental illness is such a powerful and controlling disease, it can totally alter a person's personality and behavior. And, unfortunately, it doesn't go away on its own. It has to be treated. And Dereka has been without therapy and medication for over five months. That's far too long for someone with her genetic propensity for mental illness. She could spiral out of control without immediate proper care."

"But having Dereka committed? I could never do anything like that. Jasmine and I have an idea we want to discuss with you. Since Dereka won't come to see you, perhaps you could come to the house to see her. Once you are there, I'm sure she'll talk to you. Will you come?" Kenya asked, her eyes pleading with Dr. Bedford to say yes.

"Kenya, you all are like family to me, and I'll do whatever is necessary to get Dereka the help she needs. But rather than coming myself, let me ask a close colleague of mine, Dr. Frieden, to come in my stead. You all mentioned that Dereka believes that I'm a part of the conspiracy. She may see me as a threat right now, and my coming to her home could possibly escalate her fears. Dr. Frieden is an outstanding psychiatrist, and I'm sure she'll be willing to help. Just let me know a good time for her to come by," Dr. Bedford replied. Although she didn't really believe that a house call was the answer, she was willing to do anything and everything she could to help them.

"I'll call you next week to set something up," Kenya said. She and Jasmine thanked Dr. Bedford for her time and counseling, and left the office.

"Dr. Bedford sure gave us a lot to think about," Jasmine said on the way home.

"Yes, she did. But I could never have Dereka committed to a mental institution. That's not a choice I'm willing to make," Kenya replied.

"But suppose we have no choice. Suppose the house call with Dr. Frieden doesn't work, and Dereka continues to get worse. What will we do then?" Jasmine asked.

"Pray for a miracle," Kenya replied without hesitation. "My mama believed in prayer, and so did my grandma Leona. And I promised my mama on her dying bed that I would take care of Dereka. And having her put away in some mental hospital is not my idea of taking care of her. So I'm just going to pray for a miracle." And that's what Kenya did.

So You're the One

Jia woke up in the luxurious bed in the penthouse suite and stretched her body, enjoying the feel of the soft silk sheets. The morning sun was just peeking through the panoramic windows. She looked over and saw Elliott sleeping soundly like a baby. They had enjoyed a hot, passionate night of lovemaking. Jia watched him for a while, a soft smile on her face. She never thought she'd have someone like him in her life. She straddled him and covered his face with soft, sensuous kisses. He opened his eyes, smiled, and encircled her with his arms. They stayed that way for a while—her small petite body atop his large, muscular one, just enjoying each other's aura.

"I wish you didn't have to go to Geneva today," Jia said, looking at him with big, adoring eyes. Elliott was flying to Geneva, Switzerland, that afternoon on business.

"Me too. If it was up to me, I would never leave this hotel room. I could live here with you forever. Just you and I against the world. What am I going to do without you when you go to visit your mother in China for two weeks?" Elliott replied, running his hands through her long, luxurious hair.

"It will be hard for both of us. But we'll survive," Jia said. She was happy about visiting her mother soon to help with her preparations to move to France. "Are you hungry?" she asked, already knowing the answer to that question. Elliott was always famished after one of their lovemaking marathons.

"You know I am," Elliott confirmed. Jia picked up the phone, dialed room service, and ordered a huge breakfast for two. While they waited for room service, they showered together, and put on the thick, soft hotel robes. Once the food arrived, they ate heartily, feeding one another and even licking the juices off each other's fingers. To Elliott, everything with Jia was an arousing experience. They spent the entire morning and afternoon together until Elliott had to leave for the airport around five o'clock.

"Are you working tonight?" he asked, pulling on his suit jacket and zipping up his leather garment bag.

"Yes, I have a job in Tresses. A longtime client is hosting a private party for some business associates. He wants me to dance and entertain a visiting dignitary." Elliott winced a bit inside. But by now he knew it was no use trying to talk Jia out of her chosen profession.

"Be careful out there, love," he said. He kissed her goodbye and hurried down to the limousine waiting to take him to the airport.

Jia spent a few hours relaxing before it was time to get ready for her job. After soaking in a scented bubble bath, she sprayed her body with fragrant perfume and draped a towel around her. She then blow-dried her hair and brushed it until it shimmered like diamonds. Next, she expertly applied her makeup, putting heavy black eyeliner around her eyes, attaching long curly false lashes, applying gold-shimmer eye shadow, rouge, and ruby red lipstick. Her skin was so translucent, she didn't need much foundation.

Once satisfied with her makeup, Jia put on a black-and-red lace bustier with attached garter belts, black G-string panties, a pair of thigh-high, lace-top stockings, and five-inch-high stilettos. The last component of her outfit was a long black silk dress that was held together by a single string over her left shoulder. While performing later, she would pull the string, allowing the dress to gradually cascade to the floor for the grand reveal. Jia had discovered over time that men preferred her to slowly remove separate pieces of clothing to prolong their excitement and anticipation. Jia enjoyed seeing and hearing grown men grovel like hungry dogs with the removal of each item of her clothing. She reveled in being the one in control.

Jia took the elevator to the lobby and handed her key to the valet parking attendant to retrieve her car. While she waited, she saw a tall beautiful woman walking toward her with long, purposeful strides. Jia had seen this woman before, but she couldn't quite place where. That is until she spoke. It was Elliott's wife.

"Alors vous êtes la prostituée qui a volé mon mari? (So you're the whore who stole my husband?)," Nicole said, eyes blazing with anger. Jia was completely caught off guard and just stared at Nicole. She could literally feel the malice radiating from the woman's body.

"You are Jia, right? The one who calls herself Lady Marmalade?" Nicole quizzed.

"I am Jia."

"I thought sluts like you were just in it for the money. But Elliott's money wasn't enough for you. You had to have him too," Nicole accused, glaring at Jia. Jia didn't respond.

"What's the matter with you, tramp? Cat got your tongue?" Nicole mocked, sensing she had the upper hand. Jia totally understood why Nicole was so angry. She'd be angry too if the tides were turned. Jia knew there wasn't much she could say to make her feel better, but she had to try.

"I'm so sorry. I didn't mean for it to happen," she said earnestly.

"You're sorry?" Nicole asked, rhetorically. "You know that's the same damn dim-witted thing Elliott said. That he was sorry. That he didn't mean for it to happen. But it happened just the same. And it hurts like hell," Nicole said, the anger now gone from her tone and replaced with pain.

By this time, the valet entered the lobby and handed Jia her key. Sensing tension between the two ladies he asked, "Is everything all right here?"

"Yes, everything's fine. Thank you," Jia said. The valet nodded and left them alone.

"I just had to see you," Nicole confessed. "I don't know why, but I had to see the woman who took Elliott from me. The infamous Lady Marmalade. I needed to see you face-to-face. But I don't really blame you. You're just a prostitute. I'm nothing to you, and you're nothing to me. But Elliot…he's my husband. He's still my husband, you know. Remember that the next time you f——k him."

Nicole exited the hotel, leaving Jia staring after her with a stunned expression on her face.

The Dealmaker

Lihwa was busy preparing for her transition to live with Jia in France. She'd already made travel arrangements for Jia to visit her in Yunnan next week, telling Jia that although she lived in Taipei, she was on a temporary teaching assignment in Yunnan. Lihwa was excited about relocating to France to live with Jia, but not because she loved and missed her daughter. It was because she needed a fresh start. Lihwa was beginning to feel the heat of the government crackdown on human trafficking in southwestern China. She'd been heavily involved in child sex trafficking since she moved to Yunnan four years ago. But due to the government's new anti-human trafficking efforts, her business was not nearly as prosperous as before. Her plans were to move to France and set up her human trafficking business under the guise of a legitimate adoption agency. She planned to use her connections in China to transport children from poor areas in Yunnan and Beijing to France.

Years ago, after selling her girls to the Tavaras brothers, Lihwa had traveled to the United States and married a rich white man she'd met online through a mail-order-Asian-brides website. When he'd dumped her two years later for a younger Asian mail-order bride, she'd traveled back to Colombia to negotiate more money for her girls. After her efforts were unsuccessful, she had moved to Shanghai for a few years and dabbled in child sex trafficking. Feeling that she was not making enough money, she had then relocated to Yunnan and got a job teaching English at a middle school. She also volunteered at an orphanage for children, where she conspired with the orphanage manager to abduct and sell children on the underground trafficking market. These unconscionable excuses for human beings preyed on helpless and forgotten children who had no relatives or loved ones to care for them.

Since Lihwa spoke multiple languages, her main job was to negotiate prices with their mainly foreign clients. She was quite good at her job and was known within the trafficking circles as the "dealmaker." Once the deal was struck, Lihwa would transport the children to an agreed-upon meeting place, hand them over, and collect the cash. No one missed the children because the manager was very good at covering his tracks with false adoption documents. It had been a very profitable business until the government crackdown about a year ago, and Lihwa's profits were cut. That's when she decided to relocate. She'd heard through the grapevine that Jia had been adopted by her paternal grandparents after she was rescued in Colombia, and that she still lived in Bordeaux. So Lihwa decided to use her daughter to relocate to France and continue her trafficking business there.

However, before moving to France she wanted to negotiate one last deal. Although she had saved enough money to last her for a while, Lihwa was greedy and always wanted more. For the past two weeks since she returned from visiting Jia, she'd been negotiating a deal with a wealthy oil mogul from Saudi Arabia. He wanted two children, a girl and a boy, between eight and ten years old. They were likely to be used for both sexual exploitation and forced labor. Lihwa had already met with him once to talk prices. She believed she could get top dollar from the filthy rich Arabian. He'd already given her a hefty cash deposit. And the man appeared to be in a hurry to get out of the country with the children, and he didn't seem to care about bartering. Lihwa decided to take advantage of the situation and inflate the prices. She'd negotiated 65,000 yuan (about $9,500) for the boy, and 25,000 yuan (about $3,600) for the girl. This was higher than China's market prices for trafficked children where boys averaged 45,000 yuan ($6,500), and girls averaged 10,000 yuan ($1,500).

On the day of the exchange, Lihwa drove to the orphanage to pick up the children and take them to the prearranged meeting place. When she arrived at the orphanage, she went directly to the manager's office where she found the children waiting for her. They were happy to see Lihwa. She had gained their trust through her many hours of volunteering at the orphanage. And the manager had told the children that they were being adopted, which was great news to them after spending nearly all of their lives at the orphanage. They were happy that somebody finally wanted them.

"Are you all excited about being adopted?" Lihwa asked them. They nodded eagerly with broad smiles on their faces. The manager handed Lihwa a folder that contained the phony adoption papers and travel documents she was to give to their client so he could easily transport the children out of the country. Lihwa chatted happily as she drove them to their destination. She told them how happy she was for them, what a better life they'd have, and so on. It didn't bother Lihwa one bit that she was destroying two precious, innocent lives. To her it was all about the money.

Lihwa pulled into the parking garage of a high-rise office building and drove to the top level where a long black limousine with dark tinted windows was waiting. This was where the exchange was to take place. The limousine driver got out and opened the back door for them. Lihwa ushered the children into the car and got in behind them. She turned around to face her client, but she got the surprise of her life. There in the back seat, staring at her with cold, hard eyes, was Jasmine.

"Got you, heifer," Jasmine said with a smirk on her face.

The Devil Exposed

Jasmine had dropped everything and flown to Yunnan to be part of the sting operation to snare Lihwa. Jasmine didn't have to be there—she just wanted to. The Operation Undercover team, working in conjunction with the Colombian and Yunnan authorities, had pieced together the ragged puzzle of Lihwa's life over the years. Based on their findings, they'd immediately placed her on their sex traffickers watch list. And it hadn't taken them long to catch her in the act.

If Jasmine lived a million and one years, she would never forget the look on Lihwa's face when she saw her in the back of the limousine. If the situation wasn't so sad and tragic, it would have been hilarious. But Jasmine knew the truth of the matter was that there were many other children who had slipped through the cracks. Innocent, faultless children that Lihwa, and others like her, had successfully relegated to a life of unspeakable pain and suffering. But now, thankfully, for Lihwa all that had come to a screeching halt.

"Jasmine! What are you doing here?" Lihwa asked, her face a picture of shock and awe. Jasmine didn't respond right away. First, she ensured that a team member removed the children from the car to be transported to a safe house. Then she turned to face Lihwa.

"You disgusting pig," Jasmine said, looking her straight in the eyes. Jasmine was so furious she wanted to cuss her up one side and down the other. But as part of a professional team, she knew she had to control her Baltimore homegrown street tongue.

"That you would prey on helpless children is wretched enough. But I now know that you sold your own sweet daughters into a life of sexual degradation. What kind of mother does that? How dark and empty your soul must be. But you'll pay dearly for the suffering you've caused. I'll see to that," Jasmine assured.

The police, who had been waiting nearby, opened the car door and motioned for Lihwa to get out. They handcuffed her, read Lihwa her rights, and escorted her to a waiting patrol car.

"You bitch!" Lihwa screamed at Jasmine as she was being taken away. "You set me up. How could you do this to me? I knew you were jealous of me. This is all your fault," she continued yelling, giving an Oscar-worthy performance of the victim's role. Jasmine watched as they took her away. Jasmine had to exercise every bit of her self-control to keep from running to Lihwa and beating her down. And she was elated that she'd exposed Lihwa for the devil that she was. Then she thought about Jia and was overcome with sadness. Now came the hardest part. Telling Jia who and what her mother really was.

♦ ♦ ♦

Later that night, Dereka received a frantic FaceTime call from Jia. She knew instantly, from the panic-stricken look on Jia's face, that something was terribly wrong.

"Dereka, I got a call from my māma. She's been arrested in Yunnan for child sex trafficking. She said Jasmine was there and set the whole thing up. My māma says she's innocent. That it's all Jasmine's fault. Why would Auntie Jazz do something like that? I sensed that she was jealous of my māma, but I never thought she'd do something like this. I thought she loved me," Jia cried.

Dereka knew she had to tell her friend the naked truth about her mother. She'd dreaded this moment for years, but the time had come.

"Auntie Jazz does love you, honey. That's why she did what she did," Dereka divulged.

"What are you saying?" Jia asked, a hint of trepidation in her voice.

"Jia, sweetie, your mother is one of them. Sun-Yu and I found out about her one day when we saw her at that house in Colombia."

"You mean my māma was there! She actually came to that place?"

"Yes, honey. But she didn't come to save you. She'd come to ask for more money. Jia, your mother sold you and Sun-Yu to that place," Dereka revealed, tears rolling down her face.

Jia looked dumbfounded for a moment as if her brain couldn't process the words. Dereka watched as a variety of raw emotions passed across Jia's face like clouds in the sky on a windy day. First there was disbelief, followed by confusion, horror, anger, astonishment, hurt, humiliation, sadness, and gloom until finally there was nothing. Just nothingness.

"I promised Sun-Yu that I'd never tell you or anyone else what she'd done. But when Lihwa showed up at your place, I had to tell. Auntie Jazz discovered that Lihwa was still involved in child sex trafficking. They caught her in China trying to sell two children she'd taken from an orphanage. That's why she was arrested. Honey, I'm so sorry," Dereka stated. Jia's face was still totally void of emotion.

"How did my sister die?" she asked soberly. Dereka swallowed the hard lump that suddenly appeared in her throat as she thought about the awful morning she'd found Sun-Yu dead.

"She hung herself," Dereka replied. "She just couldn't live with the truth about your mother." Jia stared at Dereka for a long moment, her face still emotionless.

"I have to go now. Bye, Dereka. I love you," she said, promptly ending the call. Dereka tried to call her back several times, but she wouldn't answer. Finally, Dereka gave up, deciding to give her friend time to process what she'd learned about her mother. Dereka shut off the lights, got into bed, and pulled the cover over her head.

What's Love Got to Do with It?

The house call that Kenya and Jasmine had arranged for Dereka did not go well. When Dr. Frieden had stopped by the house to see her last week, she'd locked herself in her room and refused to see the doctor. Kenya had even invited Pastor Bobby to the house to talk to Dereka, knowing how fond she was of him. But Dereka also refused to meet with her pastor, saying she preferred to wait and hear directly from God concerning his next mission for her. She'd failed God before and was determined not to fail him again.

Dereka's delusions were increasing in intensity as more time passed without treatment. Once Kenya and Jasmine had found her standing outside in the rain, looking up at the sky. When they'd asked her why, she'd told them that God told her to go outside and wait for him to speak to her through the raindrops. She was certain that God was about to give her a new mission to protect children.

Tonight, Kenya and Sean were watching a movie in the living room. All of a sudden, Dereka came running downstairs and started searching frantically through the closets.

"Sweetie, what are you looking for?" Kenya asked.

"Where is she?" Dereka replied, rummaging through the closets.

"Where is who?"

"The little girl you all are hiding. Where is she?"

"Dereka. We're not hiding any little girl. We wouldn't so something like that, honey."

"No, you're lying. There's a little girl here, and she needs my help," Dereka shouted. Kenya could see the desperation in Dereka's face as she tried to find this child who she thought needed her help. Kenya helped Dereka thoroughly search the closets until she was convinced no child was there. Then Kenya placed her arms around her niece and led her back upstairs to her bedroom. When Kenya returned downstairs, Sean was waiting for her, looking very worried.

"Kenya. Your niece is in bad shape. You really need to get her some help," he stated out of concern. Kenya was tired, frustrated, irritable, and at her wits end as to what to do about Dereka. It wasn't easy being a caregiver of a mentally ill person who refused to seek help, and Kenya sometimes felt as if she was losing it herself. So she took it out on Sean.

"Don't tell me what to do about my niece. I know what she needs," Kenya snapped.

"I didn't mean any harm. But Dereka seems to be getting worse. I just think…"

"Did I ask you what you think?" Kenya said, hands on her hips and neck rolling. "I think you need to mind your own business. You don't see me butting in your affairs telling you what your son needs. Even though I could," she insinuated. Sean could feel his anger rising. What did his son have to do with any of this?

"Sweetheart, I know you're tired and upset about Dereka. But please leave my son out of this. There's nothing wrong with my son, but your niece needs help."

"Don't you worry about my niece. I got this. When I want your advice, I'll ask for it," Kenya retorted.

Who does she think she's talking to? Sean thought. *I'm a man. I'm not some little boy she can talk to any kind of way.*

"I think I'd better leave before I say something I'll regret," Sean countered, picking up his jacket and heading toward the door.

"Bye!" Kenya yelled as he exited, slamming the door behind him. Kenya flopped down on the sofa and cried, knowing that she was dead wrong to take things out on Sean. He'd been nothing but caring and supportive. Later that night, she called and apologized, and he readily accepted. Sean realized that Dereka's illness had put a strain on his relationship with Kenya. But he loved her too much to desert her in her time of need.

The next morning as Kenya and Jasmine made breakfast, they barely said two words to each other. Ordinarily, their traditional Saturday morning breakfast routine was filled with chatter and laughter. But Kenya and Jasmine were at odds with each other when it came to Dereka's care. Jasmine wanted to meet again with Dr. Bedford and discuss involuntary hospitalization for Dereka, but Kenya wasn't having it. She was still praying, and waiting for a miracle. And in the meantime, she planned to take care of Dereka herself. Just as she promised her mama she would.

"I heard you and Sean arguing last night about Dereka," Jasmine said as she mixed pancake batter.

"So now you're eavesdropping on my conversations," Kenya challenged.

"No, I wasn't eavesdropping. But you all got pretty loud for a moment. And you know I've been telling you the same thing Sean said. Dereka needs help. And if she won't get it herself, we need to get it for her. I think we should seriously look into the involuntary hospitalization that Dr. Bedford mentioned."

"No!" Kenya shouted. "I'm not having Dereka committed to a mental institution. You just leave Dereka to me. She's my blood, not yours."

The wounded look on Jasmine's face revealed that Kenya had hit below the belt. Not once over all the years that they'd been friends had the fact that Jasmine was not a blood relative ever been an issue, especially when it came to Dereka. For Kenya to bring that up now was extremely hurtful. Jasmine blinked back tears as she threw the pancake spoon in the sink and left the kitchen. Kenya sat down at the table, placed her head in her hands, and sobbed.

"Jesus, Jesus, Jesus. Please help me, Lord," she said through her tears.

Although Kenya and Jasmine were conflicted regarding the best way to care for their niece, it was their strong love for Dereka that was the cause of their conflict. Their love for her had everything to do with what was happening between the two aunts. One of them loved Dereka too much to have her committed, and the other loved her too much not to.

Intervention

Ms. Ethel watched Dereka closely during the support group meeting. Dereka was fidgeting, shaking her head, and seemingly talking to herself. Ms. Ethel surmised that Dereka was likely hearing and reacting to voices in her head. Ms. Ethel had seen this type of thing before. Former sex trafficking victims who descended into the grips of mental illness. Ms. Ethel learned from Kenya that Dereka had stopped going to therapy and taking her meds. Thank God she was still attending the support group meetings. But the illness had changed her. Whereas once Dereka had been a pillar of support for the other members, now she mainly sat in chair, distracted and jittery. Dereka was there, but she wasn't all there. *Poor dear*, Ms. Ethel thought sadly, shaking her head.

Kenya had called Ms. Ethel about a week ago seeking her help. She'd asked Ms. Ethel to arrange an intervention for Dereka to try to persuade her to get treatment. Kenya knew that Ms. Ethel had successfully used intervention techniques for people with drug and alcohol addictions. She was hopeful that the same process would be useful in Dereka's case. Kenya had all the faith in the world but believed as the Bible teaches, *that faith without works is dead*. So while she prayed and believed God for a miracle, she kept trying different things to help Dereka. She still wasn't willing to have Dereka committed, but an intervention was definitely worth a shot.

Ms. Ethel eagerly agreed to help. She loved the Jones family dearly and was especially fond of Dereka. The intervention was set to take place at Ms. Ethel's after the support group meeting. Ms. Ethel asked Dereka to stay after the meeting for a counseling session. But unbeknownst to Dereka, her family and friends, including Kenya, Jasmine, Fatima, Brandon, and Trevon, would be waiting for her upstairs. These were the dearest people in Dereka's life. They were hopeful that together their strong love and faith would break down her resistance to seeking treatment.

The plan was for Ms. Ethel to bring Dereka upstairs after the meeting, explain to her why they were there, read scripture, and pray. Then each person would take turns telling Dereka how much they loved her, how important she was in their lives, and why they wanted her to get help. If all went well, after the intervention Kenya was prepared to take Dereka directly to see Dr. Bedford, who was on standby in case they needed her.

When Kenya and Jasmine arrived at Ms. Ethel's, Brandon, Fatima, and Trevon were already there. Kenya hugged them and thanked them for coming.

"Wouldn't have it any other way," Trevon assured her.

"I just hope Dereka will be all right. I really miss her," Brandon added. It was clear that he cared deeply for Dereka. Fatima informed them that the support group meeting should be ending in about ten minutes.

"I sure hope this works," Fatima said, her eyes watering. "Dereka's such a good person. It pains me to see her like this."

"I know. But we just have to have faith and believe that God has already worked everything out," Kenya replied.

They waited in silence for the meeting to end, lost in their own thoughts and prayers for Dereka. Soon the other support group members came upstairs. Aware of the intervention planned, they gave reassuring smiles and whispered encouragement as they quickly left. Kenya's heart began to race as she waited anxiously for Ms. Ethel to bring Dereka upstairs. What would Dereka do when she saw them? Would she be angry with them? Were they doing the right thing? Kenya was worried because she didn't know what to expect. But then she thought about the scripture, *Let not your heart be troubled; you believe in God, believe also in me.* It gave her some measure of peace. She had been praying steadily over the past few days, knowing that God is a hearer and answerer of prayer. *Giving it over to you, Lord,* she silently prayed. *Just believing that you've already worked everything out.*

When Dereka entered the room and saw her family and friends, she stopped in her tracks.

"What's going on?" she asked, looking around.

"Dereka, darling. We're here because we love you, and we're concerned about you. Please have a seat, precious," Ms. Ethel said, leading Dereka to a place on the sofa to sit between her aunts. Dereka looked skeptical but hesitantly obeyed. Ms. Ethel read Jeremiah 30:17, *For I will restore health unto thee, and I will heal thee of thy wounds, saith the Lord…*" She then prayed, "Lord you said in your Word, that *where two or three are gathered together in my name, there am I in the midst of them.* Well Lord, here we are gathered together in your name praying that you bless, lead, and guide us in helping our dear, sweet Dereka. Our hope is in the Lord, *the author and finisher of our faith*, the lily of the valley, our bright and morning star."

Next, Ms. Ethel asked each person to share their personal testimony of love and support for Dereka, and reveal why they wanted her to get help. Jasmine started by sharing a heartfelt profession of her love and concern for her niece, wiping away tears as she talked. After Jasmine, Fatima spoke, followed by Brandon and Trevon. Kenya held onto Dereka's hand throughout the testimonials. She could feel her niece trembling as if she was afraid.

"It's okay, honey. You don't have to be afraid," Kenya whispered. "We just love you so much and want what's best for you."

Dereka sat quietly and appeared to be listening intently. But, unfortunately, instead of hearing the stories of love and support, she was hearing the voices of threat and intimidation in her head. She placed her hands over her ears to try to block out the taunting voices so she could better hear what her friends and family were saying. But there was no blocking them. The voices, one male and one female, taunted her.

They're tired of you.
You're a burden!
You're to blame. It's all your fault.

Look at you. You're pathetic!
WORTHLESS!
Why don't you end it already?
They're better off without you!

Over and over the voices jeered until she could take it no longer.

"Stop it! Stop it! Just leave me alone. Go away," Dereka screamed. She jumped up and ran into the kitchen. The group followed and found her cowering in the corner, her hands covering her ears.

"Aunt Kenya, please make them stop. Make them go away," Dereka cried, reaching for her aunt. While Dereka was actually referring to the voices in her head, the group mistakenly thought she was talking about them. Kenya rushed to Dereka's side.

"I'm here, sweetie. It's okay. I've got you. Everything's going to be all right," she said soothingly as she sat on the floor beside Dereka. Kenya gently rocked Dereka in her arms and motioned for the others to leave. Ms. Ethel led them back into the living room.

"We've done all we can do today. It's in God's hands, which is the best place it can be," she affirmed. "Let's keep Dereka in our prayers. And pray for Kenya and Jasmine as well. In these situations, the caregivers need just as much prayer and support as their loved one."

"Thanks, Ms. Ethel," Jasmine replied. They all hugged each other and left, a bit discouraged but still hopeful.

Kenya stayed on the floor with Dereka for a while, comforting her until she seemed calm enough to go home. She helped Dereka up and led her outside to the car, where Jasmine was waiting for them. When they got home, the two aunts positioned Dereka between them, took her upstairs, and helped her into bed. Kenya remained with her niece until she fell asleep. Then, Kenya fell asleep in the bed beside her and stayed with her all night.

The Old Switcheroo

Breaking out of prison was much harder than Memphis had thought it would be, even for someone as savvy and cunning as he was. Escaping from jail wasn't at all like in the movies. Memphis couldn't exactly dig his way through his prison cell wall with spoons, and float to freedom on a raft constructed from raincoats like the actors in *Escape from Alcatraz.* Although the movie was based on a true story, Memphis had his doubts about whether it actually happened. Nor could he dig a tunnel and escape through the prison sewage pipes like Tim Robbins in *The Shawshank Redemption.* Sure the drug lord, El Chapo, had used a tunnel to escape from prison not once but twice. But he'd escaped through an existing tunnel underneath his prison cell. He hadn't dug the tunnel himself. Digging a tunnel big enough to escape through was damn near impossible as far as Memphis was concerned. Not that he hadn't tried. As a matter of fact, Memphis had even started to chip away at the wall under his prison bed with a sharp metal shank that he'd made. But he'd quickly discovered that chipping away at a solid concrete wall was for the birds, not him. He'd done it for about ten minutes before totally abandoning that idea. Escaping from prison was one thing that was definitely not as seen on TV.

But difficult as it may be, Memphis was determined to break out of jail against all odds. He had an itch to scratch and a score to settle with the Joneses. He'd tried to escape a couple of times already and failed. Once he'd hidden under a garbage truck and attempted to hold onto the underside of the truck as it exited the prison gates. But the truck had a damaged exhaust system which leaked hot noxious gas. The exhaust fumes had become so strong that Memphis had a coughing fit and was discovered by the guards.

Another time he coerced a prison doctor into helping him. The doctor was in charge of overseeing the transport of the bodies of prisoners who died while in jail. The game plan was to hide Memphis in a body bag and transport him to the coroner's office. The coroner, who was also in on the scheme, would then set Memphis free. On the night of the grand escape, two guards sneaked Memphis into the prison morgue to put him in the body bag. But when they unzipped the bag, to their surprise they found another prisoner already hiding there. He'd found out about the scheme and wanted to ride Memphis's coattail to freedom. How he'd sneaked into the body bag, nobody knew. Memphis had started to snatch his skinny behind out, but they had little time to waste. He'd gotten in the bag with the skinny dude, promising to handle him later.

All was going well as the two guards rolled the body bag through security—that is, until skinny dude farted. If the loud sound alone wasn't enough to alert security that something was wrong, the foul smell coming from the bag surely was. It just so happened that it had been Mexican food night in the prison cafeteria, and skinny dude had eaten a huge bean burrito. The security staff, suspecting that something was rotten in Denmark, unzipped the body bag and found Memphis and skinny dude inside. Needless to say, Memphis was furious that his elaborate, well-thought-out escape plan had been ruined by one loud, funky fart. And he saw to it that skinny dude paid dearly for that mistake. The story goes that after skinny dude's beatdown from Memphis, the poor fellow developed a strong aversion to bean burritos.

This afternoon Memphis sat in his office looking out the window at the prison yard, pondering his next move. Two of his minions, including No-tongue Louie, sat in the office with him, waiting for their next command. It still got Memphis's goat that he'd not been able to dispose of the Jones family. He'd taken care of Ryan in grand style, but the Jones women were a different story. It was as if they had some kind of impenetrable shield around them. It gnawed at him that they were still alive and well, and made him more irritable and mean than usual. His jaws clenched as he stared out the window, brooding and contemplating a new plan of escape and attack.

That's when a new prison guard crossing the yard caught his attention. For the most part, Memphis didn't pay new guards any heed. They came and went all the time. But this cat just happened to be the spitting image of Memphis. He was about the same height and weight, the same skin tone, and had similar facial features. The resemblance was so striking that the man could have been Memphis's brother from another mother. The only difference was that the guard was clean-shaven, and Memphis had a goatee, but that was fixable.

"Who's that new guard?" Memphis snapped.

"Oh, that's Andre. He just started working here yesterday," one minion responded.

"Get him in here," Memphis demanded. No-tongue Louie jumped up and ran out the door to get him. Memphis watched the guard as he walked toward the office. They even had a similar strut. The guard's eyes widened when he entered the room and saw Memphis sitting there. He'd heard that he resembled the notorious criminal, but even to him the resemblance was uncanny. Memphis didn't speak to the guard right away. He just stood and walked around the man, sizing him up. *Yeah, this just might work*, he thought. Memphis sat back down, took a cigarette from his shirt pocket, lit it, took a long drag, and deliberately blew the smoke in the guard's face.

"You ready to make some real money?" he asked.

"Hell, yeah," the guard responded without hesitation.

"Then take a seat, m'fer. Here's what I want you to do," Memphis instructed. They spent the next hour or so strategizing about a switcheroo between the two men that would allow Memphis to get out of prison, at least temporarily, to handle his business.

Dark Things Come to Light

Jasmine was on a plane back to Bordeaux to look for Jia whom they'd not heard from in weeks, ever since she'd learned the truth about her mother. Even Dereka hadn't spoken to her, which was highly unusual seeing how close they were. Dereka had only received a text from Jia, which came from an unknown number. The text simply stated "I'm okay. Please don't worry." However, they were all worried sick, especially Nai Nai. She'd called Jasmine in a panic, asking her to come right away. Jasmine hated to leave Dereka and Kenya at such a crucial time, but Kenya encouraged her to go.

"I'll take care of Dereka," she'd said. "You just go and find Jia. She needs our help too." Jasmine took a cab from the airport to Nai Nai's house. The kind, elderly lady greeted her with warmth and gratefulness.

"Thank you so much for coming. I'm so worried. It's just not like Jia to stay away from home so long. I called the police, but they don't seem to be doing much to find her. What if something awful has happened to her? I don't know what I'll do without Jia," Nai Nai confessed, wringing her hands nervously.

"It's okay, Nai Nai," Jasmine replied, embracing her. "I'm here now. And I'm going to do everything I can to find her."

"Thanks, dear. I knew you'd come." Nai Nai picked up an envelope and handed it to Jasmine. It was from the Banque Populaire, a major bank institution in France.

"I got this in the mail yesterday, dear. I just don't know what to make of it," Nai Nai said. Inside the envelope was a statement showing that Jia had transferred her entire savings account to Nai Nai, which was well over

$400,000. The huge sum of money puzzled Jasmine. Jia had told her she made good money working in a high-end restaurant, but even at that, Jasmine was surprised she'd been able to save so much.

"Why would Jia transfer all her savings to me? She's always taken good care of me. But what made her do something like this? I don't understand," Nai Nai said. But Jasmine had a good idea why Jia had done it. She wasn't planning on coming back, and she wanted to ensure her Nai Nai was taken care of.

"Did Jia say anything to you about Lihwa before she left?" Jasmine inquired.

"No, she didn't. And she was so looking forward to visiting her māma. That's why her disappearance is so troubling."

"Nai Nai, there's something I need to tell you about Lihwa. Something terrible that may explain Jia's leaving." Jasmine hated to be the bearer of bad news but she knew Nai Nai would find out eventually, so she told her about Lihwa. Nai Nai took the news extremely hard and felt terrible for Jia.

"Mon pauvre bébé (My poor baby)," she murmured over and over. Jasmine helped Nai Nai to her room so she could lie down and rest. Then Jasmine went into Jia's room to look around, hoping to find some clue as to where she went. The first thing Jasmine noticed was that Jia had left behind most of her personal items, including clothes, shoes, photos, jewelry, and so on. Jasmine spent hours going through every crack, corner, and crevice of Jia's room. But in her meticulous search, Jasmine discovered things about Jia that shocked her. Secret, dark things that Jia had managed to keep hidden for years.

Under the bathroom sink Jasmine discovered evidence of Jia's heroin use. There she found used syringes, burnt spoons, and trace elements of the drug. Jasmine knew heroin remnants because many of her mother's boyfriends from back in the day had been heroin addicts. In an antique oak chest, Jasmine found pictures of Jia dressed as Lady Marmalade. Sexy, erotic pictures of her in corsets, bustiers, garter belts, thongs, or nothing at all. And, as if those items weren't shocking enough, in the bottom of a dresser drawer Jasmine found a ledger outlining Jia's jobs. She had kept very detailed records of her services includes names, phone numbers, addresses, dates, times, and type of service provided, which included erotic dancing for groups, private dances, and all kinds of sexual acts. *Oh my God*, Jasmine thought as her eyes scanned through pages and pages of Jia's sexual services.

After Jasmine completed her search of the room, she sat on the bed exhausted, her head spinning from what she'd discovered. But the more she thought about it, the more she realized just how akin Jia's life and hers really were. Both had been betrayed and deeply wounded by their mothers, the one person who should have loved them unconditionally. Whereas Jasmine's mother had pimped Jasmine out, Jia's mother had sold her into child sex slavery. Each was an abomination beyond description. Jasmine too had turned to a promiscuous life as a working girl during her youth. And if it had not been for the Jones family, God only knows what Jasmine's life would have become. Jasmine knew then that God had redeemed her for a purpose. Part of that purpose was the role she'd play in finding Dereka when she was abducted. Now Jasmine felt compelled to find Jia.

"Lord, I need you to show me what to do. Please lead and guide me in the right direction. Help me to find Jia and bring her home," she prayed. Jasmine picked up the appointment book again and started to scan through it hoping something would stand out. After a while, she noticed a small asterisk beside the name, Elliott Tremblay. The name was only listed twice as far as she could tell, and each time it had the same symbol beside it. Jasmine quickly flipped through the pages, attempting to see if there were other names with the same symbol but found none. *Could this mean something?*" she thought. Jasmine decided to call the number, hoping that this Elliott Tremblay could help her find Jia. Jasmine waited anxiously as the phone rang. She knew that he may hang up on her, not wanting to discuss the fact that he was listed as one of Lady Marmalade's clients. After a few rings, a deep male voice answered the phone.

"Hello."

"Is this Elliott Tremblay?"

"Yes, it is," he replied. He sounded friendly enough.

"Elliott, this is Jasmine McKnight. I found your number in, uhh…Lady Marmalade's appointment book."

"Oh?"

"Lady Marmalade is my niece. Her name is Jia. I'm her aunt from the United States."

"You're her auntie Jazz?" Elliott replied, a hint of wonder in his voice.

"Yes, I am. You know about me?" Jasmine exclaimed, delighted that he evidently knew Jia well enough that she had mentioned her.

"Of course. Jia talks about you, Dereka, and her aunt Kenya all the time."

"She does? That's great. But we haven't heard from Jia in weeks. We're all worried about her. Do you know where she is?" Jasmine asked, her voice hopeful. Elliott was silent for a moment.

"Elliott, are you still there?"

"Yes, I'm here. Jia's in a bad place now. And she doesn't want anyone to know where she's at."

"Elliott, I have to find her. Please tell me where she is."

"I'm sorry, I can't. She made me promise not to tell anyone. I can't betray her trust," Elliott said, his voice filled with anguish. It was evident that keeping the promise he'd made to Jia was difficult for him.

"Do you love her?" Jasmine asked, already sensing the answer was yes.

"More than anything."

"Then tell me where she is. I love her too, and I have to find her. She needs my help. Please Elliott, please tell me where she is." A long silence followed.

"Elliott, are you still there? Elliott, pleeeease," Jasmine pleaded. Another long silence. And then finally, he responded.

"I'll take you to her."

Home Sweet Home

Jia woke up a little past noon. It had been a rough night. She gingerly touched her top lip, which was bruised and swollen. Traces of blood from her lip stained her fingertips. She wiped it on her nightgown. Jia looked over at Jérémy who was sound asleep beside her, snoring heavily. She gently picked up his arm that was draped over her and slid quietly away, careful not to wake him. He had been in such a foul mood last night when she got home. Which explained her bruised, bloody lip. She'd become the primary target of Jérémy's brutality. But Jia didn't mind. At least it kept him away from Tristin and Rochelle.

Jia embraced the physical and emotional abuse Jérémy dished out. It was as familiar and comforting as an old shoe. The two weeks of pure happiness she'd enjoyed after being reunited with her mother had been an illusion. A sick joke someone had played on her. She'd been a fool to believe that something good could actually happen to her. It seemed like happiness just wasn't in the cards for her. Jia knew that now. And she accepted it. And she'd never play the fool again.

Jia had left Bordeaux two days after learning the truth about her mother. She'd traveled to Pigalle, a notorious red-light district in Paris, and aimlessly roamed the streets for a few nights. Pigalle was nicknamed "Pig Alley" by World War II soldiers due to its raunchy sex shops, brothels, and adult movie theaters. It was the devil's playground. Jia had slept in alleys and doorways, hoping someone would come along and take her life. Just put her out of her misery. She didn't have the nerve, gumption, or whatever it took to take her own life like her sister had. Jia even admired the bravery of her sister to take matters into her own hands and end it all. But Jia couldn't do that, so she just resigned herself to a slow, painful death. That's what she felt she deserved. After all, her own mother had sold her to a sex-slave house. And Jia erroneously believed that something had to be wrong with her for her māma to do something so terrible. It was Jia's way of justifying, reconciling, and dealing with the immense betrayal and pain.

Jia had met Rochelle and Tristin, late one evening in a bar in the red-light district. She'd seen them walking the streets soliciting customers, so she knew they were working girls. Rochelle, twenty-two years old, and Tristin, twenty, were cousins. They'd left home shortly after Tristin graduated from high school and met their pimp, Jérémy, on the streets of Pigalle. He'd offered them a place to stay, all the drugs they desired, and protection, except from himself that is. Jérémy was a low-level drug dealer who used more drugs than he sold. He had a few working girls on the side to supplement his income. Most of the money Jérémy made was spent on drugs and alcohol.

Rochelle and Tristin bonded instantly with Jia and invited her to their place in Marseille to meet Jérémy, who was looking for another girl. Marseille, France's second largest city, housed some of France's poorest and violent neighborhoods that were permeated with poverty, drug dealing, and assault rifles. When Jia walked into their apartment, the smell of dope, piss, and rotten food assaulted her nostrils. Dirty clothes and trash littered the floors, and leftover food and booze bottles covered the tables and filled the sink. The place was a disgusting pigsty. But it was also a representation of the way Jia felt inside. And she knew she was home. Home sweet home.

Jia crawled over Jérémy and Rochelle, who was sleeping on the other side of him, and got out of bed. She heard Tristin moving around in the kitchen, no doubt trying to scrape together a meal for breakfast. Jia went into the bathroom and splashed water on her face. She watched as the dried blood on her face mixed with the water and swished away down the drain. She picked up a dirty towel and wiped her face. When Jia looked in the mirror she barely recognized herself. Which was fine by her. Because in Jia's mind she was no longer Jia, Lady Marmalade, or anyone else. She was nothing and nobody.

Jia finished washing up in the bathroom sink. The showerhead was broken and the tub leaked, so both were not useable. She retrieved a T-shirt and pair of sweat pants from a pile of dirty clothes on the floor, and put them on. Jia opened the medicine cabinet and took out a bottle of crystal meth. Although she still used heroin, meth was now her drug of choice. She poured a small amount of the crystal ice particles on the countertop and snorted it into her nose with a straw. She'd tried smoking and injecting meth but preferred snorting the drug because the comedown effect was less severe.

Jia knew Elliott was coming today because Jérémy had told her. Jia hadn't told Elliott where she was, but somehow he'd managed to find her. Jia wasn't permitted to directly communicate with Elliott or anyone else. And the only reason Jérémy even allowed Elliott to see Jia was because Elliott paid him good money for the five or ten minutes he spent with her. Elliott came once a week just to check on her, see if she needed anything, and mainly to try and convince her to leave with him. But Jia never asked for or took anything from Elliott unless Jérémy told her to. Jérémy demanded total control over his girls. And Jia willingly complied.

Unsavable

When Elliott and Jasmine pulled up in front of the run-down tenement building, Jasmine couldn't believe her eyes. It was even worse than she had imagined. They'd taken the high-speed train from Bordeaux to Marseille rather than make the seven-hour drive. During the train ride, Elliott had told Jasmine that Jia was now a streetwalker and lived with a pimp in deplorable surroundings. But even at that, Jasmine wasn't quite prepared for what she saw. In front of the tenement, people were openly selling and using drugs, and several men had their guns or assault rifles in plain view. And even in the early afternoon, scantily clad women were walking around soliciting customers for sex. The building was in total disrepair with several boarded-up, graffiti-covered windows, overflowing trash bins, a sagging roof, and more paint missing than not. There were several dirty mattresses and blankets in the front yard. Jasmine realized that Lihwa's betrayal must have affected Jia in the worse kind of way for her to move from her lovely home with Nai Nai to his god-awful place. She just hoped she'd be able to persuade Jia to leave with them.

When Jasmine and Elliott entered the lobby, a rotten, pungent smell filled Jasmine's nostrils causing her to gag. She wanted to pinch her nose with her fingers but decided against it. She didn't want to offend the few tenants loitering in the lobby and eyeing them suspiciously. Elliott led the way up three flights of stairs to Unit 3D. He hadn't told Jia that her aunt was coming with him, afraid she wouldn't see them if she knew. He knocked on the door, and a tall, ominous looking man opened it. He stared coldly at Jasmine.

"Who's that?" Jérémy asked.

"Just a friend," Elliott replied.

"It'll cost you fifty dollars extra," Jérémy barked. Elliott removed the money from his wallet and gave it to Jérémy. He quickly counted the money and closed the door.

"What's wrong?" Jasmine asked, afraid he'd changed his mind about allowing them to see Jia.

"Nothing's wrong. He's going to get Jia. I'm never allowed inside. We'll have to wait in the lobby."

They went to the lobby and sat on a wooden bench. After about ten minutes, Jia came down the stairs. For a moment, Jasmine didn't recognize her, thinking she was some other tenant who lived there. Her long beautiful black hair was cut short and looked as if someone had chopped it off with a butcher's knife. Her once clear porcelain skin was acne stained. Her top lip was bruised and swollen, and her eyes yellowish and dull. And her already small frame was much thinner. The dirty T-shirt and sweat pants hung loosely from her body.

"Jia?" Jasmine exclaimed, unable to disguise her shock. When Jia saw Jasmine, she stopped dead in her tracks, her eyes wide in surprise.

"Elliott, you promised me you wouldn't tell," she accused.

"I'm sorry, Jia. But I had to. I couldn't get through to you. I'm hoping your aunt can," Elliott responded. Jasmine ran to Jia and embraced her.

"Jia, I'm so glad I found you, sweetie," Jasmine said, kissing Jia's face and hair.

"Auntie Jazz, you shouldn't have come," Jia said, stepping away.

"How could I not come? I'm taking you away from here. We can leave right now. You don't have to go back upstairs. Just come with us now," Jasmine instructed.

"No. This is where I belong," Jia stated.

"No, Jia. You're wrong. You belong with us. People who love you," Jasmine said. She took Jia's hand and led her to the wooden bench to sit down.

"Listen to me, Jia. I know what your mother did hurt more than most people could ever realize. I know because my mother also betrayed me when I was a child. I never told you this, but my mother pimped me out.

She made me sleep with her boyfriends for money, and I was infected with HIV," Jasmine revealed, blinking back tears. "That's right, I'm HIV positive. And I've had to live with this daily reminder of my mother's betrayal for years, and I'll have to live with it until the day I die. But God brought me through it all, and he can do the same for you. All you have to do is trust in him," Jasmine stressed.

"Where was he?" Jia asked, looking at Jasmine quizzically. "Where was God when my māma sold me to perverts? Where was he when at eight years old I was raped over and over by grown men? Where was he when I screamed out in pain? Where was he when I cried myself to sleep at night? Wasn't he watching? Why didn't he stop it? And where was this God when my sister, the person I loved most in the world, hung herself. Where was he, Auntie Jazz?" Jia questioned, her eyes filled with pain. Jasmine understood Jia's questioning God. Her questions were the same kind of questions Jasmine had struggled with for years. Where was God when despicable things had happened to her? And how could a loving God allow those terrible things to happen, especially to helpless, innocent children.

"Honey, I believe God was right there by your side then, just as he is now because he said he'll *never leave us or forsake us*. And I know God hurts deeply each time one of his children is harmed. The Bible says that *God notices each time a sparrow falls to the ground*, so you know he grieves when one of us suffers. I don't pretend to understand why the most awful, horrific things happen to people. But Jesus said there will *be tribulations in this world,* and he said that *offenses must come*, at least for a time. And I believe with all my heart that God helps us to survive our tragedies and hardships, and catches those who don't survive," Jasmine said as passionately and sincerely as she could.

"Are you saying that he was there all along?" Jia asked, her brows furrowed deeply as she pondered all her aunt had just said.

"Yes, Jia. I believe God was right there beside you then just as he is now."

"Well…I'm sorry, but I just can't trust in a God who can stand idly by and let such horrible things happen to those he's supposed to love," Jia said, shrugging her shoulders and getting up to leave. She hugged Elliott and kissed his cheek before starting up the stairs.

"Jia, please don't go back up there," Jasmine pleaded, tears rolling down her face. "If you stay I'm afraid you're going to die here. Please, baby, please come with us."

"I love you, Auntie Jazz. But you can't save me. I'm…unsavable," Jia replied, with sadness as deep as the ocean in her eyes. She continued up the stairs, leaving Jasmine and Elliott alone, their hearts breaking for her.

The next day Jasmine went home, determined to return to France as soon as she could to see Jia again. Jia had said she was unsavable. But Jasmine knew better. She had once thought she was a lost cause too. Now Jasmine knew that no one was too far gone for God to reach. She was living proof.

Suffer the Little Children

Dereka sat beside Kenya in church on Sunday morning, feeling awkward and out of place. She hadn't been to church in months and was doubting whether she should have let her aunt talk her into coming. Whereas her church had once been a sanctuary of peace and joy, now the mental illness had stripped her of that. Her paranoia and delusions caused her to be suspicious and fearful of practically everyone, even those she once considered her spiritual family. Dereka looked around nervously wondering if "one of them" was sitting beside, behind, or in front of her. *They're everywhere, even in the church*, she thought, recalling the news stories of child molestation by priests in the Roman Catholic Church. *Why would the Baptist, Methodist, Episcopalian, or any other denomination be immune?* She scooted closer to Kenya to put more space between herself and the man sitting next to her.

Pastor Bobby stood up to deliver the sermon and instructed the congregation to turn to Matthew 19:14, *Suffer little children, and forbid them not, to come unto me: for of such is the kingdom of heaven.* The mention of "little children" caught Dereka's attention. She sat on the edge of her seat and listened intently to the sermon. Pastor Bobby preached about how people had brought little children to Jesus to be blessed and prayed for. And how the disciples, likely feeling that the children were insignificant and not worthy of Jesus's time, had attempted to stop them. But Jesus rebuked his disciples for having the audacity to try and block the children's blessings. Who were they to determine who was worthy and not worthy of his blessings? To Jesus, no one is too small, insignificant, weak, or unworthy of his love. He loves and accepts the little children just as he accepts all who come to him. And Jesus saw something extremely special in these little children that his disciples hadn't. He saw their childlike innocence, trust, simplicity, faith, and humility. Jesus said that, *Whosoever shall not receive the kingdom of God as a little child shall in no wise enter therein.*

After the sermon, Kenya looked at Dereka and saw her face aglow with joy.

"Thank you, Jesus," Kenya murmured, for she had not seen that look on Dereka's face in a long time. On the way home Kenya asked Dereka if she enjoyed the sermon.

"Yes," Dereka eagerly confirmed. "I felt like the pastor was speaking directly to me."

"That's great, honey. I'm so glad you decided to go to church with me. I knew you'd enjoy it," Kenya enthusiastically asserted. But what Kenya didn't know is that Dereka, in her weakened state of mind, had totally misconstrued the sermon.

As soon as they got home, Dereka went into her room, closed the door, and got her journal. She wrote the verse, *Suffer the little children to come unto me, for of such is the kingdom of heaven*, over and over in her journal. She not only truly believed that God had spoken directly to her through the sermon, but that he'd given her a new mission to protect children from sexual predators. Dereka thought that Jesus was telling her to bring the little children to him because he was the only one who could truly protect them and prevent them from suffering. People, no matter how well meaning, just couldn't protect them because they weren't capable of it. After all, she'd had the best Mama and Grandma in the world, but even they had not been able to protect her from being abducted and sold into sex slavery. Her mama, God rest her soul, had died trying to protect her. Yet even that hadn't been enough. And Dereka didn't want another child to suffer the barbarity that she, Jia, and countless others had suffered.

That's why Jesus wants me to bring the children to him. So that he can protect them and keep them safe, Dereka thought, her face filled with wonder. Finally, she had another mission, and she was determined not to disappoint God again.

"I won't let you down this time, Lord. I promise," Dereka professed. She sat down at her desk and grabbed her ink pen. *But how will I do it?* she pondered. *How will I get the children to Jesus?*

Dereka sat perfectly still for about ten minutes, her eyes darting around wildly as a plan of action began to form in her mind. Then she vigorously jotted down that plan in her journal. First, she'd gather together children in groups of twos and threes. Then God would show her a tunnel with a very bright light and she would take the children through the tunnel to Jesus, who would keep them safe. In the tunnel, they would die and leave their physical bodies behind. Their spirits would continue through the tunnel to heaven where there are no predators. The lighted tunnel would be her way of transporting little children from a wicked world to a glorious heaven where no evil existed. *That's where all the little children belong. In heaven*, Dereka thought. *And it's my mission to take them there.*

A "normal" person would have known this was unrealistic and irrational thinking. But at this point, Dereka was beyond rationality. And to make matters worse, the warped, distorted hallucinatory voices that had invaded Dereka's mind played upon her delusional thoughts and urged her on. Their goal was to trick her into harming the very ones she so desperately wanted to protect and save. It was a cruel, twisted attack by her psyche, and it was all part of the debilitating mental illness she suffered.

That night Dereka slept peacefully, believing that she was once again a part of God's plan.

Take Them to Jesus

Kenya sat at her desk in the office, feeling more optimistic than she had in weeks. She was glad that Dereka had gone to church with her yesterday and had enjoyed the sermon. Kenya had called Jasmine, who was in Los Angeles spending some much-needed time with her fiancé, and relayed the good news.

"God is up to something," Kenya had told her, recalling a phrase her mother used to say all the time. "I feel like my prayers are about to be answered."

"That's great news. I wish I could have been there with you all," Jasmine had replied.

At 11:00 a.m. Kenya was meeting with clients when Trevon poked his head into the conference room, a worried expression on his face.

"Sorry to interrupt," he said. He motioned for Kenya to join him outside, which she quickly did.

"What is it?" Kenya asked, sensing it was something important.

"There's a Ms. Hayes on the phone. Says she works at the day care center down the street from you."

"Yeah, Roberta Hayes. We went to college together."

"She needs to speak with you right away. Some kind of emergency concerning Dereka," Trevon said, looking very concerned.

"Emergency with Dereka?" Kenya exclaimed, her heart beating fast as she ran to the phone in her office.

"Hi, Roberta. What's going go?" she asked, slightly out of breath.

"Kenya, it's about Dereka. She came into the day-care center talking out of her head about taking some children to Jesus. My receptionist had let her in thinking she had questions about the center. But then Dereka tried to go into one of the children's playrooms. She was talking about taking the children through a lighted tunnel to Jesus to keep them safe. She wasn't making any sense, and she kept trying to get to the children. We had to restrain her and take her into our meeting room. I'm sorry, Kenya, but I had to call the police for safety reasons. I had no choice. They'll be here shortly. Honey, you need to get down here quick."

"Oh my God!" Kenya exclaimed. "I'm on my way." She grabbed her purse and rushed out of the door. Kenya was in a state of shock as she drove to the center. The notion that Dereka would try to abduct children from a day care was simply unimaginable to her. All kinds of questions raced through Kenya's mind as she sped toward the day care. Perhaps Jasmine had been right. Perhaps she should have looked into involuntary hospitalization before something like this happened. Had she allowed her love for Dereka to blind her to the seriousness of her mental illness?

When Kenya arrived at the day care, a police car was already parked out front and a few curious onlookers had gathered outside. Roberta met her at the door.

"How is she?" Kenya asked as Roberto led her to their meeting room.

"Not good," Roberta replied sympathetically. When Kenya entered the room her heart dropped. There was Dereka, looking flustered and agitated, sitting in a chair with two police officers around her. One of them was kneeling in front of her talking, but Dereka wasn't listening. She was babbling about taking children to Jesus, lighted tunnels, and such. When Dereka saw her aunt, she started to cry uncontrollably.

"Aunt Kenya. Please help me," she shouted. "They don't understand. God told me to do it. But they won't let me. I just want to protect the children, that's all. I have to take them to Jesus. You understand, don't you, Aunt Kenya?" she cried, tears streaming down her face. Her mental and emotional anguish was palpable in the room. It was clear that Dereka truly believed with all her heart that she was doing something to protect the children. It was also crystal clear that she was in a perilous mental state and needed immediate psychiatric care.

Kenya moved toward Dereka, but one of the officers blocked her. The other one, Officer Smith, who was certified in mental-health crisis intervention, signaled that it was okay to let Kenya pass. Officer Smith's primary focus was to keep Dereka calm, and she felt Kenya could help in that regard. Kenya knelt in front of Dereka and took her hands.

"Honey, we know you want to keep the children safe. That's what we all want. But you have to let us help you."

"You're going to help me take them to Jesus?" Dereka asked, hopeful expectation in her voice.

"Well...not today, sweetie," Kenya replied, not knowing what else to say. "But they'll be safe here. Ms. Roberta, her staff, and these wonderful police officers are going to do everything they can to keep the children safe. And God is always watching the little children. So they'll be safe, okay?" Kenya said. Dereka nodded.

"Now I'm going to talk to the police for a moment. I'll be right back. Okay, sweetie?" Kenya stated. Dereka nodded again. Kenya took the two officers aside and told them about Dereka's history as a former child sex trafficking victim and her subsequent mental struggles.

"She stopped taking her medication and going to therapy a few months ago. But I think now I can persuade her to get treatment. You're not going to arrest her or take her to jail, are you? Can I just take her home with me, please?" Kenya asked.

"Ms. Jones, we're not going to arrest your niece, but I'm afraid we can't let you take her home," Officer Smith replied. "Her actions today, no matter how well intended in her own mind, show that she poses a risk of serious harm to herself and others. In my opinion, Dereka needs emergency psychiatric care. We'll have to transport her to a hospital where she can be admitted for crisis intervention and evaluation. You mentioned that she was in therapy at one time. Is there a particular doctor you can contact?"

"Yes, Dr. Bedford. She's with Inova Fairfax Hospital."

"Great. We have a good working relationship with Inova Fairfax. Why don't you call the doctor and have her meet us there if possible?"

"Okay," Kenya replied, her eyes watering as the gravity of Dereka's situation sunk in. Officer Smith placed a comforting hand on her shoulder.

"I know this is tough. But the best thing we can do for your niece right now is get her the help she needs," she said.

Kenya called Dr. Bedford and explained the situation. The doctor dropped everything and agreed to meet them at the hospital. Then Kenya had the difficult task of telling Dereka that the police officers would be taking her to the hospital for urgent care.

"Nooooooo, Aunt Kenya. Please don't let them take me. I just want to go home," Dereka said, looking scared.

"I'm sorry, honey. But you have to go. You need help," Kenya said, trying her best to remain calm and not fall apart herself.

"Don't do this to me, Aunt Kenya. I was only trying to help the children. I won't do it again. I promise. Please just take me home with you," Dereka said, putting her arms around her aunt and holding on tight.

Fearing for Kenya's safety, the second officer moved in with handcuffs to restrain Dereka for transport to the hospital. When Dereka saw the handcuffs, she became even more frightened and held on tighter to Kenya.

"Do you have to handcuff her? Are those really necessary?" Kenya asked, her eyes pleading with the police.

"It's customary when transporting people with mental illness to handcuff them for their own safety and others. I've had a lot of experience with these types of transports. I'll make sure she's okay," Officer Smith responded. She and her partner separated Kenya and Dereka, and Officer Smith placed the handcuffs on Dereka, smiling and talking to her to calm her. Dereka stared at Kenya with a bewildered expression on her face.

"Can I at least ride in the car with her?" Kenya asked.

"I'm sorry, Ms. Jones. For safety reasons you're not allowed to ride with her. You'll have to follow in your car," Officer Smith informed her.

"I'll be right behind you, honey," Kenya told Dereka. "Don't worry. Everything's going to be all right."

Kenya watched in stunned disbelief as the two officers escorted Dereka out of the building and placed her into the back of the patrol car. Kenya got into her car and followed closely behind them to the hospital.

Kenya could see Dereka turning her head and peering through the rear window looking for her. Dereka looked so confused and frightened.

"I'm here, sweetie," Kenya said out loud, even though Dereka couldn't hear her. "I'm right behind you, baby." It devastated her to see her niece handcuffed in the back of a squad car, on the way to be admitted to a mental hospital.

"Lord, I don't know what you are up to. But I just got to believe that you are up to something. I'm just going to believe that *all things work together for good to them that love God.* And as my mama used to say, all means all."

Humpty Dumpty

The next several days were a flurry of activity regarding Dereka's care. Once she was admitted to the hospital, Dr. Bedford conducted an intensive evaluation and determined that Dereka was in the acute phase of paranoid schizophrenia, which was characterized by hallucinations and paranoid delusions. Dr. Bedford concurred with Officer Smith's assessment that she posed a risk of serious injury to herself and others. Kenya, now knowing she had no choice, filed for and was granted a Temporary Detention Order (TDO), which required Dereka to be held in a psychiatric hospital for one to five days until a commitment hearing was held. It was one of the hardest things she'd ever had to do.

The commitment hearing was held at 8:30 a.m. on the third Thursday in September. Kenya, Jasmine, and Dr. Bedford provided testimony during the hearing. Trevon, Ms. Ethel, Brandon, Fatima, and Sean attended for moral support. At the hearing Dereka sat and glared at her family and friends as if they were her worst enemies because she falsely believed they were. *How could they turn against me?* she thought. *They're stopping me from doing God's work. They're part of the conspiracy. I was right about them all along. Why are they punishing me for just wanting to protect little children? They're the ones who are crazy, not me.*

The voices in Dereka's head, aware that she was teetering on the brink, attempted to push her over the edge.

Told you so.
They're all against you.
They're tired of you. You're a BURDEN!
Such a disappointment!

> You can't do nothing right. YOU SUCK!
> They hate you too!

At the end of the hearing, the presiding special justice, having heard the testimony and reviewed the medical reports, ordered that Dereka be involuntarily hospitalized for psychiatric treatment for a maximum of thirty days. The deciding factor was the event at the day-care center, which the justice believed made her a risk to herself and children. It was paradoxical that her mental illness made her a threat to the very ones she wanted to protect.

Although Dereka's family and friends knew her commitment was absolutely necessary, it still was very painful for them, especially for Kenya. There was a deep raw ache in her heart. Sean and Jasmine tried to console her, but she was inconsolable. She blamed herself for not doing more to persuade Dereka to voluntarily get help earlier.

They all cried as they watched Dereka being led away by hospital security and medical staff. They professed their love and support to her as she passed by them.

"We love you, baby. We're praying for you. Coming to see you soon. God's with you, dear. God bless you," and such they professed to her. But Dereka just glowered at them with anger and disappointment in her eyes.

Later that night, Dereka lay in the bed all alone in the psychiatric ward, depressed and deflated. Earlier that afternoon in her mandatory therapy session with Dr. Bedford, she hadn't even looked at her doctor nor responded to any of her questions. She had also refused to voluntarily take her medication. The voices in her head convinced her that her doctor was trying to kill her and that the medicine was poison. She'd had to be restrained by attendants and injected with an antipsychotic medication. It was a totally demoralizing experience. Now as Dereka lay in the bed in her room, she thought about a nursery rhyme she used to recite when she was a little girl. She felt it so fittingly described her in her current situation.

> Humpty Dumpty sat on a wall,
> Humpty Dumpty had a great fall.
> All the king's horses and all the king's men,
> Couldn't put Humpty together again.

That's how Dereka felt that first night in the hospital. Like Humpty Dumpty, broken beyond repair.

Pass Interference, Foul on the Play

Kenya was on her way to the hospital to see Dereka. For the past week, either she and/or Jasmine had visited Dereka every day. So far, to Kenya's disappointment, she hadn't seen much improvement in Dereka's mental state. During their visits, Dereka seemed to be either unaware that Kenya was present or intentionally ignoring her. But Dr. Bedford had cautioned Kenya to be patient and not to expect too much too soon. She said that it may take at least two or three weeks for the medication and therapy to take effect, and even then signs of improvement may be slow in coming. Dr. Bedford was trying to prepare Kenya for the long haul.

For Kenya's own mental and spiritual well-being, she sought counseling from her pastor. She still struggled with the issue of having her niece committed and even questioned why God hadn't answered her prayers for Dereka's miraculous healing. Pastor Bobby had explained to her that all healing was from God.

"Sometimes he chooses to heal by miracle and other times by medicine," Pastor Bobby said. "But either way, it's God who does the healing because he created the medicine also. So, in my humble opinion, all healing is by divine intervention. And that makes it a miracle either way."

Amen to that, Kenya thought as she drove.

When Kenya arrived at the hospital at 6:00 p.m., she was greeted cheerfully by the hospital staff, whom she'd come to admire and respect. To Kenya's relief, her misconceptions about psychiatric hospitals had been quickly dispelled. It was not at all as pictured in the old horror movies that showed padded rooms, straitjackets, patients running and screaming, dingy hallways, and stern-faced nurses. Psychiatric wards had come a long way since early times when mental illness was thought to be caused by demonic possession, sorcery, and such. During these times, patients were subjected to brutal treatments including electric shock, lobotomy, and trepanation (drilling a hole in the skull to let the evil spirits escape). Now the psychiatric wards resembled college dorms, albeit with much tighter security. The patient's day typically started around seven o'clock, and included scheduled checks, personal hygiene time, meals, group and/or individual therapy, medication, free time, visitation hour, goal assessment, movie/TV time, and bedtime/lights out. To Kenya it appeared to be an efficient, well-structured system.

But what Kenya saw as structure, Dereka viewed as entrapment. She hated being told what to do and when to do it. She felt like a hamster in a cage, running on a spin wheel but going nowhere fast. Dereka despised having her freedom taken away and blamed her family and friends, mainly Aunt Kenya, for her imprisonment. During that first week, the voices in her head, though not as prevalent as before, were just as vicious. Once Dereka heard the voices even talking to each other about her.

> Look at her, she's pathetic.
> She's a danger to children. She can't be around them.
> Everybody knows about her.
> There's no God to save her.
> No one cares about her.
> She's going to die in here.

Dereka tried to resist the voices, but they were relentless. So she decided to just give herself over to the voices in her head that were hungry for her soul.

Dereka sat in the visiting room feeling as low as low can get. The voices were silent, at least for now, giving her some relief. When Kenya entered the visitor's room she saw Dereka in her usual place, sitting in a chair in the corner. Dereka's solemn expression and body language seemed in sharp contrast to the cheerful visiting room. The colorful chairs and furniture were grouped strategically around the room to provide a little privacy for the patients and their visitors. Kenya gave Dereka a hug and kiss and sat in a chair beside her.

"How are you, sweetie?" she asked.

How do you think I am? How would you be if you were cooped up in here? Dereka thought, but didn't respond.

"Dereka, I know you're mad at me for putting you here. But, honey, I had to do it. I know it's hard for you to understand right now. I did it because you need help. And I love you so much," Kenya expressed earnestly.

No, you don't. Nobody loves me. I know that now, Dereka thought.

"Please talk to me, baby. Tell me what you're thinking," Kenya implored.

You really don't want to know what I'm thinking. I'm thinking that you're a traitor. I never thought you would turn against me. Not you, Aunt Kenya. Not you of all people, Dereka thought.

Kenya could see that this visit was going to be like all the others this past week. Dereka would just sit there, look down at her feet, and refuse to talk. It hurt Kenya tremendously, but there was nothing she could do about it. Kenya resigned herself to sit quietly with Dereka, praying inwardly while she sat. When the visitation hour was nearly over, Kenya reached into her bag and retrieved a Bible.

"Honey, I brought you something. This is your grandma's Bible. I thought you'd like to have it with you," Kenya said, holding the Bible toward Dereka. Dereka glanced at the Bible, but didn't take it. Kenya opened it and flipped through the pages.

"Do you mind if I read to you the twenty-third Psalm? It was one of your grandma's favorites," Kenya stated. Dereka didn't reply. While Kenya read the Psalm, Dereka pretended that she wasn't listening, but she was. There was one verse that struck a chord within her. *He restores my soul.* Dereka pondered the words over and over in her mind. *He restores my soul. He restores my soul. He restores...my soul*, she thought, wondering what it really meant. *How can a soul be restored?* she reflected, feeling that her own could never be.

After Kenya finished reading, she closed the Bible and placed it on the table beside Dereka.

"I'll just leave it here for you," she said. About that time an announcement was made over the intercom signaling the end of visiting hours. Kenya, as she always did, got teary-eyed when it was time to leave. She kissed and hugged Dereka, letting her tears flow free.

"I'll be back to see you tomorrow," she promised before leaving.

When Kenya was gone, Dereka looked at her Grandma Ruth's old worn Bible. She reached for it, but the voices in her head, wanting no good thing for her, did a pass interference and committed a foul on the play.

DON'T TOUCH THAT!
You're dirty. FILTHY!
The Bible is for good people. Not you!
You're despicable.
UNGRATEFUL!
Don't touch it. Leave it alone!

Dereka hurried out of the room, leaving the Bible behind.

Captured by the Game

It had taken weeks of planning but the old switcheroo was happening tonight, and Memphis was pumped. Finally, he was going to take out the Joneses once and for all. Well at least two of them. He'd heard through the grapevine that Dereka was in the "looney bin," and for him that was punishment enough. He'd chuckled to himself when he found out, feeling that all his labor regarding her demise had not been in vain. Sure, she'd survived her abduction and time spent at the sex-slave houses. But she'd finally cracked under the pressure of it all. Now all Memphis had to do was eliminate her two darling aunts. Losing them would likely ensure that Dereka remained in the insane asylum for the rest of her born days.

    The game plan was for Memphis and the look-alike guard to switch clothes right before the guard was scheduled to go off duty. Memphis would change into the guard's uniform and the guard into Memphis's orange prison jumpsuit. Memphis would then use the guard's credentials to walk right out of the prison doors. The guard, pretending to be Memphis, would spend the night in his cell and serve as a proxy during the night checks. Memphis would return the next morning, still posing as the guard, and they'd switch back. And no one would be the wiser. Sure, Memphis had needed to call in some favors from other guards and security personnel to ensure his escape plan went off without a hitch. And they'd all eventually agreed to help, knowing good and well what would have happened to them if they hadn't. Besides, Memphis had made it worth their while with the promise of a huge payoff.

    Memphis had also arranged with his old friend, Hector, to have a car with a driver waiting from him in front of the prison. Hector helped him set up and kill Ryan, so Memphis had a lot of confidence in the man. The driver would take him to the Jones residence and provide him with a loaded Glock 26—Memphis's weapon of choice. Memphis would then break into their house and put a bullet right through Kenya and Jasmine's heads. He wasn't playing around; he meant business.

Memphis waited impatiently in the men's restroom for the guard to arrive. He looked at his watch and saw that the guard was already five minutes late. *That asshole better not back out now*, Memphis thought, pacing back and forth. A few minutes later the guard entered, out of breath and apologizing profusely for being late.

"Never mind," Memphis said, already starting to undress. "Let's hurry up and change so I can get out of here," he commanded.

It took about two minutes flat for Memphis and the guard to change clothes. Afterward, Memphis stared at his reflection in the mirror and was amazed by the transformation. He'd shaved his face so he was the spitting image of the guard. *Hell yeah, this is going to work*, he thought cockily. He placed the guard's belt, which contained a baton, pepper spray, cuffs, and a radio, around his waist.

"Man, you look just like me," the guard stated with a flabbergasted look on his face.

"I better get a move on it," Memphis said, looking at his watch. "My driver's probably waiting."

"Okay, brother. Good luck out there. See you in the morning," the guard stated.

"Sure thing," Memphis replied, walking out the door with a sly smile on his face.

What the guard didn't know was that Memphis wasn't planning on returning in the morning, or ever. He'd asked Hector to get him some new identification documents and a plane ticket to the Cayman Islands. He planned to live there incognito indefinitely. If the guard was dumb enough to think that once Memphis got out of prison he was going to willingly return—he was a damn fool. And, as far as Memphis was concerned, the guard deserved whatever punishment he got for his stupidity.

Memphis was as cool as a cucumber as he walked through the prison using the guard's badge and keys to open various doors. He didn't even break a sweat as he strutted out of the final door, and he even winked at the female security guard who was in on the plot. Once outside, Memphis deeply inhaled the night air and let it out slowly. It tasted and smelled like freedom. He spotted a white Mercedes as he had requested, parked at the curb. He quickly got into the back seat.

"Move," he instructed the driver.

"Yes, sir," the driver replied. Memphis relaxed into the soft leather seat as they rode. He had a smirk on his face. He'd actually pulled it off. He'd escaped from prison.

"You got the Glock?" Memphis asked, anxious to get his hands around the weapon.

"Yes, sir. Got it locked in the glove compartment," the driver said. He pulled the car over to the side, unlocked the latch, and retrieved the weapon.

The next thing Memphis knew, the gun was pointed directly at him. And Memphis got the shock of his life when he saw who was pointing the gun straight at his head. It was Ryan! Memphis's mouth fell open and his eyes bulged out as he stared into Ryan's face.

"What the f…" Memphis started to say.

"Looks like the hunter just got captured by the game," Ryan said, firing off two quick shots. He watched Memphis gasp and then slowly slump over in his seat. Ryan got out of the car, placed the gun in his holster, and disappeared into the night.

A Twisted Tale

Kenya arrived home around 9:30 p.m. and parked in the driveway. She'd stopped by Ms. Ethel's house after her visit with Dereka. She'd just needed some comfort and encouragement, which Ms. Ethel graciously provided.

"You just *wait on the Lord and be of good courage*," Ms. Ethel had wisely advised her. And that's just what Kenya intended to do. She got out of her car and walked toward the front door. Someone appeared out of the darkness, startling her.

"It's me, baby," a man said. Kenya recognized Ryan's voice instantly. For a moment, she was too stunned to speak. She hadn't seen or heard from him in years, ever since he betrayed her, leaving her humiliated and heartbroken. What was he doing here now? He had some nerve showing up at her house. Then she thought, *Maybe he's still working for Memphis. Maybe he's here to harm me.* Fear gripped her heart.

"You don't have to be afraid of me. I'm not here to hurt you," Ryan assured her.

For the past few months, Ryan had been hiding out in Mexico ever since he faked his own murder with the help of his Jamaican friends, Malique and Ashani. They'd told Ryan about the hit Memphis had put on him and decided to help him out. Even Memphis's so-called friend Hector had been in on it. Hector did it to right a wrong that Memphis had done to him years ago. So the four men had worked together to fake a very realistic looking murder. Knowing that Memphis had spies everywhere, they'd taken every precaution to make it appear to be a legitimate kill. They'd even provided the picture that showed body parts in a suitcase. It was an image they'd downloaded from the Internet when they searched for "suitcase full of body parts." It's amazing what one can find with just a simple Google search. They'd used photo-editing software to superimpose an image of Ryan's head on the picture. And it worked because it had fooled Memphis into believing that Ryan was really dead. Since then, Ryan had been relaxing on a white sandy beach in Cozumel drinking piña coladas.

It was Hector who'd told Ryan about Memphis's plan to escape from prison and murder two women. Ryan knew right away that Memphis was going after Kenya and likely her friend, Jasmine. Ryan had stopped him from killing Kenya before, and he was sure he could do it again. He'd asked Hector to let him be Memphis's driver. That's how he'd been able to execute his former boss. Ryan would never forget the dumbfounded look on Memphis's face when he saw him sitting there with the gun pointed at his head. It was priceless. If there ever was a national Hall of Fame for criminals, Ryan knew he'd be among the first inductees for having the guts, nerves, and balls to take out his ruthless rival. Many had tried, but he had succeeded.

Now there was one last thing that Ryan wanted to do before leaving the States permanently. He wanted to make amends to Kenya. Or at least try.

"Why are you here, Ryan? Did Memphis send you?" Kenya asked, crossing her arms over her chest.

"No, Memphis didn't send me. You don't have to worry about him anymore. Memphis is dead. I killed him."

"You killed Memphis!"

"Yeah. He escaped from prison tonight and was on his way to kill you and your friend. He never stopped seeking revenge. That carbon monoxide leak at your house was no accident. That was Memphis's doing. When a close contact told me what he was up to, I called 911. Memphis would have never left you alone. So I killed him, Kenya. I did what I had to do. He can never harm you or your family again."

Kenya shook her head in disbelief. Ryan's story was terrifying. Memphis had escaped from prison and was on his way to kill them! And Memphis was behind the carbon monoxide incident too. It was astonishing. But then again, why should she believe anything Ryan said. He was a pathological liar who had betrayed and wounded her like no other.

"I don't believe you, Ryan. I don't know what you're up to, and I don't care. You have some nerve coming here after what you did," Kenya said, trying to move past him. He reached out and took her arm.

"I'm sorry, baby. I know I hurt you, and if I could take it all back, I would. I don't regret many things in life, but I regret hurting you. You see, I wasn't supposed to fall in love with you, but I did. You got inside my heart. I didn't realize it until it was too late. But I'm not here to disrupt your life. I know you got a new man now," Ryan stated. That really caught Kenya's attention.

"What are you talking about?" she asked, wondering how he knew anything about her.

"His name is Sean Powell. He's from New Jersey. I had him checked out. He's one of the good guys. He's not like me."

"How do you know about Sean?" Kenya snapped.

"I had my niece keeping tabs on you for a while and reporting back to me. That is, until you approached her car one day. She got spooked after that and didn't come back."

"You mean the young lady with the braids."

"Yeah, that's LaShonda."

So that's who she was, Kenya thought. But she still wasn't buying the rest of Ryan's twisted tale.

"Kenya, I know you don't trust me. You have every reason not to. I just came to say I'm sorry for what I did." He took Kenya's hand and pressed it to his lips. Then he walked across the street, got into a black car, and drove away. And Kenya knew she'd never see him again.

The next morning Kenya heard on the news that the notorious criminal, Luther Curtis, known as Memphis, had escaped from prison last night by posing as a guard. He was discovered shot to death in the back seat of a car about four miles from the prison. Kenya knew then that Ryan's twisted tale was the truth.

Come Hell or High Water

Jasmine woke up in the middle of the night with Jia heavy on her mind. She felt that Jia was in dire trouble and was calling out to her. She wasn't Jia's mother, but she felt a mother's intuition toward her. It had been nearly three weeks since she'd last seen Jia. She'd tried to phone her, but Jia's number was disconnected. Jasmine had eventually contacted Elliott to see if he knew how she was. But he was in Canada for a family emergency and hadn't seen Jia in about two weeks. Suspecting that Jia urgently needed help, Jasmine decided to do what most mothers would do for their child. She was going to see about her baby and bring her home if possible. She booked her flight online early the next morning.

Jasmine's plane landed in Marseille on Saturday evening around six o'clock. It was mid-October, and the weather was dreary, chilly, and wet. She took a cab from the airport to a nearby hotel, showered, and ordered something to eat. Around eight o'clock, Jasmine took a cab to the place where she and Elliott had last seen Jia. She didn't know if Jia was still there or whether Jérémy would even allow her to see Jia if she was. Jasmine remembered his cruel, mean, ugly face as he'd stared at her. It was like looking at the devil himself.

As Jasmine rode in the back of the cab through the poverty-stricken areas of Marseille, she started to feel a bit nervous. Here she was, a lone female in a cab, riding through the dangerous streets of an unfamiliar, foreign city, and speaking a language she wasn't all that comfortable with. But then she thought about the scripture, *The Lord is my light and my salvation; whom shall I fear? The Lord is the strength of my life, of whom shall I be afraid?* Jasmine reached into her bag and got the small Bible she always traveled with. She held it tightly in her hand. Pastor Bobby had preached a while ago about how to win when you're boxing with the devil. Well, Jasmine had her weapon with her. The *sword of the spirit, which was the Word of God.*

When the cab stopped in front of the tenement, Jasmine paid the driver and asked him to wait for her. She entered the lobby and saw several scantily dressed women, likely working girls getting ready to hit the streets. They looked Jasmine up and down, one of them whispered something to the others, and they all burst out laughing. Jasmine didn't pay them no mind and hurried up the stairs to Unit 3D. She knocked on the door and a pretty young lady opened it.

"Yes," she said, looking at Jasmine suspiciously.

"Is Jia here?"

"No, she isn't," the young lady replied, starting to close the door.

"No, wait please. I'm Jia's aunt from the States. I'm really worried about her."

"Oh," the young lady said, opening the door wide. "You must be her Auntie Jazz or Aunt Kenya?"

"Auntie Jazz," Jasmine replied with a broad smile.

"Jia told us about you. I'm Rochelle. Come on in."

"Are you sure it's okay?" Jasmine asked, remembering what Elliott had said about not being allowed inside.

"Yes, I'm the only one home," Rochelle replied.

Jasmine walked inside and started coughing. The place smelled almost as bad as it looked, and that was saying a lot. Rochelle quickly cleared a space for them to sit on the sagging sofa. She started chattering away so fast that Jasmine had a hard time understanding her.

"Could you please slow down a bit?" Jasmine asked. "My French is okay, but I'm still learning."

"Oh, I'm sorry," Rochelle replied slowly and loudly as if Jasmine was deaf and dumb. "You just missed Jia. She and Tristin went down to Granges Street. That's where we work most nights. I'm going there shortly. You can go with me to look for Jia if you want."

"Yes, thank you."

Jasmine waited while Rochelle went into another room to finish dressing. About fifteen minutes later, Rochelle came out wearing a very short, tight black skirt, some thigh-high boots, a purple leather jacket, and bright red lipstick. She certainly looked the part.

"I'm ready," Rochelle said, grabbing her purse and sashaying out the door. When they out outside, Jasmine dismissed the cab, giving the driver a few extra dollars for waiting, and got into Rochelle's car.

"I'm glad you came to see Jia," Rochelle said as she drove. "I hope you can take her away from here. Jérémy beats her all the time now. I think he's going to kill her if she stays. Tristin and I fight him back so he doesn't bother us all that much. But Jia, she just takes it."

Jasmine groaned at the thought of that lowlife hitting Jia. Her instincts had been right. Jia needed her. And Jasmine was more determined than ever to take Jia home with her or at least convince her to move back in with Nai Nai. Come hell or high water.

In Harm's Way

Rochelle parked the car on a crowded, busy street cluttered with strip clubs, sex shops, fast-food joints, and adult movie theaters. The rain had stopped, and the street was bustling with working ladies, rowdy men, drunkards, homeless people, and a few tourists thrown in for good measure. Rochelle appeared to know everybody. She waved, talked, and yelled to people as they walked. One man called out to her and started making vulgar, gyrating movements. Rochelle shouted something back at him, and they both laughed. Jasmine didn't understand all they'd said, but what she grasped made her cringe. Jasmine was no prude, she'd been around the block a couple of times. But still.

Rochelle asked some people if they'd seen Jia around, but so far no one had. After about twenty minutes, Rochelle saw a young lady about to get into a car with a "John."

"Tristin!" she yelled.

"Hi, Rochelle. What's up?" Tristin asked.

"Have you seen Jia? This is her Auntie Jazz that she talks so much about."

"So you're her sassy Auntie Jazz. Nice to meet you," Tristin said.

"Hi, Tristin. Do you know where Jia is?" Jasmine asked, anxious to find her.

"I saw her about ten minutes ago. She said she was going to Po' Man's Row."

"What's Po' Man's Row?" Jasmine asked.

"I know where it is. I'll show you," Rochelle interjected. "See you later, Tris."

On the way, Rochelle explained that Po' Man's Row, as it was called, was just an alley off the main street where a lot of homeless people lived.

Some of the working girls went there between jobs to hang out, drink, smoke, or get high. Jasmine was so grateful to have Rochelle with her. It would have been much harder doing this alone. And Rochelle was kind and patient. She didn't seem to mind repeating or clarifying things when Jasmine had a hard time understanding the language.

"This is it," Rochelle said, stopping in front of a long, narrow, dimly lit alleyway between some buildings. There were rolls of tents, blankets, and makeshift cardboard shelters on both sides with barely enough room to walk down the middle. The alley reeked of piss and puke.

"Stay close to me," Rochelle instructed. "It can get crazy in here sometimes."

Jasmine stayed close to Rochelle as they carefully made their way down the alley, stepping over bottles, trash, and people. Jasmine looked at the faces of the homeless, and her heart went out to them. They were the lost and forgotten. Some were either asleep or passed out. Others were drinking. Several were fussing and cussing. And quite a few were smoking, snorting, or injecting drugs. *Lord help them*, Jasmine thought sadly.

When they got to the end of the alley, Jasmine spotted Jia slumped over in a corner. When she got closer, she noticed there was a cord tie around Jia's upper arm, and a needle was protruding from her arm.

"Jia, honey, it's Auntie Jazz," Jasmine said, kneeling in front of her. But Jia was unresponsive.

"Jia, can you hear me? Wake up, sweetie," Jasmine said, panic edging into her voice. Rochelle gently removed the needle from Jia's arm and applied pressure.

"Looks like she injected meth. There's a bad batch of that stuff on the street. A few people have died from it. I tried to get her to stop using meth, but...," Rochelle said, shrugging her shoulders.

"She's burning up," Jasmine said, feeling Jia's forehead and cheeks. "Call 112. Jia needs help," Jasmine implored.

"It won't do any good. If an ambulance comes at all, it will be a while. They see no need to rush down here to save degenerates, addicts, and whores," Rochelle stated bitterly. "Let's get her to my car, and we'll take her to the emergency room. There's a hospital not too far from here."

Rochelle and Jasmine gently lifted Jia between them. Jasmine was surprised at how light Jia was guessing she didn't even weigh eighty pounds. They hadn't gotten very far before Jérémy and another man blocked their path.

"Tris told me I'd find you hoes back here," Jérémy spat out.

"Jérémy, this is Jia's aunt…" Rochelle started to say.

"I know who the trick is," Jérémy shot back. "What the f——k are you all doing?"

"We're taking Jia to the emergency room. Now get out of our way," Jasmine demanded.

"Bitch, you're not taking Jia anywhere. And, your French sucks," Jérémy replied with a smirk on his face.

"Jérémy, Jia needs help," Rochelle said. "I think she got a hold of some of that bad meth. She may die if we don't get her to the hospital."

"Then let her die. It'll serve the stupid slut right," Jérémy countered, glancing at Jia who was dangling as lifeless as a rag doll between Jasmine and Rochelle.

"You piece of s——t," Jasmine blurted out without thinking and not sure if she had even used the right word.

"I think you just called me a piece of music, dumbass," Jérémy taunted, laughing and slapping hands with his friend. Jasmine ignored him.

"Let's go," she said to Rochelle, and they attempted to go around the men. Her main concern was getting Jia to the hospital.

"Give her to me. I'll take her myself," Jérémy said, reaching for Jia.

"No! Get out of our way!" Jasmine shouted. She was not about to hand Jia over to this scumbag. Jérémy slid his hand into his jacket pocket and pulled out a switchblade.

"Jérémy, nooooo," Rochelle pleaded. "Don't do this."

When Jasmine saw the knife, her heartbeat quickened. But she didn't back down. When it came to Jia, Jasmine was more than willing to put herself in harm's way.

"Let them pass," a deep male voice with a heavy African accent said. Then out of the shadows stepped a tall, muscular man with skin as dark as the night.

"Let the ladies pass," the man reiterated.

"This is not your business," Jérémy said, but with not as much bravado as he'd had when confronting the women.

"I'm making it my business. I said let them pass. Let them help their friend," the man said, moving closer to the two men. He towered over them and looked as if he could easily break them in two with this bare hands. Fear glued the men's mouths shut.

"Come, ladies," the man said, directing them to pass in front of him. This time, Jérémy did nothing to stop them. Jasmine and Rochelle moved quickly past them and started down the cluttered alley dragging Jia between them. The man, noticing they were struggling, offered his assistance.

"I will carry your friend for you if you wish," he said.

"Yes, please help us," Jasmine replied, relieved. The man easily scooped Jia into his arms and led the way back to the street.

"Our car is about two blocks this way," Rochelle said, pointing down the street.

The three of them half walked, half ran toward the car. The man cradled Jia protectively in his arms as he followed them. He told them his name was Adji Nzalankzi, and he'd come to France from the Republic of Congo three years ago to escape the civil war and government corruption there.

"I came here to work, save money, and send for my mother and three sisters. But things have not worked out so good for Africans here," Adji said. Jasmine knew exactly what he was referring to. Many Africans who immigrated to France seeking safe haven were subjected to blatant discrimination and disdain upon arrival to these "unfriendly shores." They risked their lives to flee danger, poverty, and government exploitation in their homeland only to encounter scorn, humiliation, and rejection in a foreign land. What Africans had hoped would be a land of opportunity turned out to be anything but. African immigrants in France were disproportionately unemployed and undereducated, and often faced overt discrimination including refusal of service and racial slurs, regularly being referred to as singes (monkeys). Many French citizens blamed immigrants for the rise in unemployment and crime.

When they arrived at the car, Jasmine got into the back seat and Adji carefully lay Jia across Jasmine's lap. She reached out and held one of his big, rough hands.

"Thank you so much," she said, her eyes glistening with tears of gratefulness.

"You are so welcome, pretty lady," Adji said, a huge smile on his face. "I hope your friend will be all right." Then he waved to them and walked away. Jasmine thanked God for Adji, the kind, gentle giant that he'd sent to help them.

While Rochelle drove to the hospital, Jasmine rubbed Jia's head softly, held her hand, and whispered encouraging words to her, not even knowing if Jia could hear her. Then she felt Jia squeeze her hand. It was barely perceptible, but there just the same.

"That's it, baby. You hang in there. We're going to get you some help. You're going to survive this," Jasmine reassured her.

When they got to the emergency room, Rochelle rushed inside to get help. She returned with two EMTs who quickly placed Jia on a gurney and wheeled her away. Once Jasmine completed all the necessary paperwork, she and Rochelle waited in the waiting room for word regarding Jia. Jasmine felt in her heart of hearts that Jia was going to survive. She believed by faith, without even having to hear the doctor's report. Because that's what faith is. *The substance of things hoped for, the evidence of things not seen.* It's believing something is done before it's done.

When the doctor came out three hours later and informed them that Jia, although in serious condition, was going to pull through, Jasmine just smiled. She'd had no doubt that she would.

Rock Bottom

By her third week in the mental hospital, the voices in Dereka's head had decreased considerably. But a deep depression had settled in. Dereka felt like she was falling into a dark, bottomless pit and no one was there to catch her. Kenya came to visit every day, but Dereka still wouldn't speak to her. Sometimes she even refused to go to the visitor's room to see Kenya. For the most part Dereka stayed in her room, doing only minimally what was required of her. And, unexplainably, she missed the voices. They had become her relatively constant companions, and she felt the voices validated her true worth. Now there was only silence and desolation.

Yet, at times, Dereka felt a voice calling out to her. Someone or something was trying to get her attention. And this voice was different from the other voices she'd heard. The others had been loud, intrusive, and brash. But this was a calm, gentle voice, tugging at her heart. Sometimes Dereka would sit perfectly still, trying to make out what it was saying. However, it always seemed just beyond her reach.

Dereka sat up in bed and turned on the lamp on her nightstand. She saw her Grandma Ruth's Bible lying there. Someone, likely one of the nurses, had found it in the visitor's room, seen her name recorded in the inside front, and brought it to her room. Dereka picked up the Bible and ran her hands over the cover. It felt good to just touch something her grandma had touched. Dereka truly believed if her grandma was still alive, she wouldn't be in a mental hospital. Grandma Ruth would have known what to do. She would have taken care of her. Not like Aunt Kenya, who she felt had discarded her. Dereka opened the well-worn Bible and flipped through it. Grandma Ruth had lots of yellow highlights and notes written in the margins, and some of the pages were torn and wrinkled from wear and tear. Tears welled in Dereka's eyes as she looked through the Bible, remembering all the times she'd seen her grandma reading it while sitting in her favorite blue chair.

Dereka closed the Bible, turned off the light, and lay down. She placed the Bible on her chest, right over her heart. It had been a while since she'd prayed because the voices had convinced her that she was too far gone for prayer. That God couldn't save her because he didn't want her. That he'd abandoned her. But then Dereka remembered how God had brought her through her horrendous ordeal as a sex slave. Even when she'd wanted to give up and just throw in the towel, he'd kept her going. She never would have made it without him. She'd prayed then. Perhaps she should pray now.

"Lord, you helped me before. Will you help me again? Pleeeease," Dereka whispered, tears streaming down her face.

And that's when an indescribable sensation started in her feet and radiated throughout her body. It was like nothing she'd ever felt before. It was a tingling feeling that sent chills through her body and filled her heart with joy. It was like light infusing her soul. And Dereka knew, without a doubt, it was the Spirit of God. She lifted her arms up to God, like a small child lifts his or her arms to a loving parent. And Dereka realized that God's voice was the still, small voice that had been calling to her, trying to break through. All she had to do was open her heart and let him in.

♦ ♦ ♦

The next day Kenya was at the office when she got a call from Dr. Bedford saying that Dereka was asking for her. Kenya dropped everything and rushed to the hospital. Dereka hadn't spoken to her in weeks, so wanting to see her now was definitely a good sign. When Kenya walked into the therapy room and saw Dereka sitting there, she immediately sensed a change in her. There was a peacefulness about her and a clarity in her eyes that had not been there for months. They ran to each other and hugged tightly, crying tears of joy, gratefulness, and relief. Dr. Bedford quietly left the room, giving them some much-needed time alone.

"I'm sorry I've been so mean to you, Aunt Kenya," Dereka said.

"You don't have to apologize to me, baby. Seeing you getting better is all I need," Kenya assured her.

"I was really hurt when you put me in here. But now I know you did it because I need help. And because you love me," Dereka divulged. Kenya was too choked up to respond. She just nodded her head in affirmation.

"And I'm going to get better, Aunt Kenya. You'll see. I'm going to do everything I can to get better and make you proud of me."

"Sweetie, you've always made me proud. I've been proud of you since the day you were born," Kenya professed. Dereka told her aunt how she'd prayed last night and felt God's presence.

"God's still with me," she exclaimed, her face radiant with awe and wonder. "Those voices said God didn't want me anymore. But he spoke to me last night, Aunt Kenya. And he said he's still with me. Always has been. And he'll never let me go."

"Thank you, Jesus!" Kenya said, knowing her prayers regarding Dereka's healing had been answered.

And Dereka, true to her word, began doing everything she could to get better mentally, emotionally, and spiritually. She readily took her medication and actively participated in the group and individual therapy sessions. She now talked openly about her pain, shame, hopes, and fears, no longer feeling a need for lies or pretense. Each night before going to bed, she read from her grandma's Bible and prayed. Things weren't always easy. There were good days and bad days. But she kept going as best she could and praised God through the highs and lows.

At the end of the thirty-day maximum period, Dereka voluntarily agreed to stay at the hospital for an additional two weeks. She felt she needed more time to mend. Her mental illness had wreaked havoc on her mind, spirit, and soul. She'd hit rock bottom, but she'd landed on a rock. Jesus Christ—the Rock of Ages, the Rock in a Weary Land, and the Rock of our Salvation.

The Real Deal

Kenya sat outside on the front porch on a Saturday afternoon enjoying the sunny, milder than usual weather in late October. She thought about all that had transpired over the past few weeks. Dereka had made tremendous progress and was due to come home in about a week. Then she would start her outpatient treatment. Dereka now realized that her mental illness was a serious disease that could have devastating consequences without proper care. She knew her treatment would be a lifelong commitment, and she was determined to do whatever was needed to stay well.

Jasmine was still in France with Jia. After spending four days in the hospital, Jia checked herself into a drug rehabilitation center near Bordeaux. Jasmine had researched and visited several centers before she located just the right place for Jia's recovery. Not only did the center provide medical detoxification and rehab, but they also focused on the total well-being of the body, mind, and spirit. Jia had never participated in therapy, even after she was first rescued from the sex-slave house years ago. Thus, she'd never dealt with the trauma of being a child sex slave beginning at the tender age of eight. For years Jia had carried the heavy burden of anger, guilt, pain, shame, and self-loathing. And learning of her mother's ultimate betrayal was the final straw that nearly broke her back. But now Jia was learning how to appropriately process and deal with her inner turmoil. She was finally learning her true worth. And Jasmine was there with her to help her do just that.

But Jasmine's dedication to Jia, with the long periods of travel back and forth to France, had placed a strain on her relationship with Percy. He wanted more from his fiancée, and she just didn't have any more to give. Jia had become her priority, plain and simple. They mutually decided to end the engagement and remain good friends.

Although one engagement had ended, another one had begun. Just the other night, Sean had popped the question to Kenya, and she had said yes. Kenya looked down at her engagement ring, sparkling as bright as the midday sun. After Ryan's betrayal, she never thought she'd be able to trust another man enough to get married. But here she was engaged. She smiled, thinking about a hymn her mama liked to sing, "It is No Secret What God Can Do."

Kenya heard a car coming down the street before she saw it. It had one of those loud, roaring engines that some young men loved so much. A beige hoopty, with peeling paint and rusty fenders, pulled up in front of the house, music blaring. A beautiful young lady got out of the car and walked up the path toward Kenya. She was wearing skin-tight blue jeans and a black sweater. Kenya knew she hadn't seen her before, but there was something familiar about her just the same. Kenya stood up to greet her.

"Are you Kenya Jones?" she asked.

"Yes, I am," Kenya replied.

"Hi. Dereka told me a lot about you. I'm..." she started to say. Kenya gasped, suddenly knowing right away who she was.

"The one called Scrappy!" Kenya exclaimed, her eyes wide in shock and her mouth agape. She could hardly believe that this person was real and was actually standing right in front of her.

"Yes, I'm Regine, but you can call me Scrappy. I see Dereka told you about me," Scrappy replied. Kenya was too stunned to speak. She just stared at Scrappy as if she was a ghost.

"Are you okay, Ms. Kenya?"

"You're real," Kenya stated, dumbfounded. "We thought you were one of Dereka's delusions. She told us about you, but we didn't believe her."

"I'm as real as real can get," Scrappy stated with a chuckle, finding humor in the fact that they'd thought she was a delusion. "Is Dereka home?"

"No, dear. Dereka's in the hospital right now," Kenya revealed. Then Kenya explained to her that Dereka had been diagnosed with paranoid schizophrenia and had to be hospitalized.

"I'm so sorry to hear that. Dereka's one of the nicest people I know. That's why we called her Angel Girl. But I suspected something was wrong when I came by once, and she was seeing some old lady she called Ms. Vee. But I proved to her that Ms. Vee wasn't really there. And I thought she'd be all right then. I wish I could have done something to help her," Scrappy said earnestly.

"Dereka had stopped going to therapy and taking her meds. And she started have delusions and hallucinations. But, thankfully, she's now getting the help she needs," Kenya stated. It was clear to Kenya that Scrappy cared deeply for Dereka.

Then Kenya's heart started racing, and dread crept up her spine. Since Scrappy was real did that mean that Dereka was telling the truth about what they did that night? *Oh my God*, Kenya thought. Her knees became weak, and she sat down suddenly.

"What's the matter, Ms. Kenya?" Scrappy asked, concerned.

"Dereka said that you all…she said that…that you all killed a man," Kenya spurted out the words as if they were poison in her mouth. Scrappy just chuckled.

"Well, we thought we had. But that mother f…excuse me, I mean that man wasn't dead. That night I called my uncle, told him what happened, and he went with me back to the ballpark. When we got there the man had come to and was struggling to free himself from the ties around his arms and legs. I guess I knocked that fool out cold with that hit on the head. I must have really laid it on him," Scrappy said, a slight smirk on her face. Kenya could see why they called this one Scrappy.

"Anyway," Scrappy continued. "My uncle and I put him in the back seat of his car. We looked in his wallet and got his address from his driver's license. I drove his car, and my uncle followed me to his house in Clinton, Maryland. We parked his car out front, blew the horn until someone came to the door, and then we left. I'm sure that he had some explaining to do when they found him, bloody and tied up, in the back seat of his car. And there was no way he could tell them what really happened or call the police because the pervert thought he was meeting a thirteen-year-old girl to have sex that night."

"So that's why we didn't find anything when we went to the park with Dereka," Kenya said in amazement.

"Yeah, that's it."

"But when we tried to call you a few days later, your number was out of service."

"Well, that's probably because I use prepaid phones. You can't trace them," Scrappy said, no explanation provided. "I likely just got a new one. People like me change phones a lot."

"Oh, I see," Kenya replied, nodding that she understood. Although she was incredibly relieved that they had not killed the man, she was disappointed that they'd actually harmed him. Disappointed that Dereka had participated in something of this nature. Scrappy sensed her feelings.

"I regret getting Dereka involved. And honestly, we just wanted to teach him a lesson. Give him a taste of his own medicine. I kept his driver's license and did some Internet searches on him. That...that..." Scrappy said, searching for the right non-cuss word. She decided on "sucker" since it was only one letter away from what she really wanted to say. "That sucker was a registered sex offender in Virginia and Arizona."

"But still...," Kenya replied.

"I know. I stopped contacting Dereka after it happened. She was so scared that night, and I felt bad that I had talked her into doing it. After that I figured she'd be better off without me around. She has a good heart. She's not like me," Scrappy acknowledged.

And for a fleeting moment, Kenya saw a vulnerability in Scrappy's eyes that was in sharp contrast to the harsh outward appearance she projected. It was like she longed to be different but just accepted who she was. Kenya recalled Dereka saying that Scrappy was part of a street gang in the Bronx, where turf wars, torture, drugs, and murder were commonplace. It was survival of the fittest. Kenya's heart went out to her for having to struggle to survive in such a grim environment.

The young man driving the hoopty blew the horn, signaling that it was time to go.

"It was nice meeting you, Ms. Kenya. Would you tell Dereka I came by to check on her? Tell her that I love her and hope she gets better," Scrappy requested.

"Of course I will," Kenya assured her. Scrappy turned and walked toward the car.

"Scrappy!" Kenya yelled. She hurried down the walkway to Scrappy and hugged her tight. "You take care of yourself," Kenya whispered in her ear.

"Thanks, Ms. Kenya. You're just as beautiful and kind as Dereka said you were," Scrappy whispered back, her eyes tearing. She hastily got into the car and they sped off, engine revving and music blasting. Kenya watched until the car disappeared. Of all of Dereka's delusions, she was glad that "the one called Scrappy" turned out to be the real deal.

Let's Twist Again
(One Year Later)

Kenya stood in the vestibule of Mt. Lebanon Baptist Church, holding onto Uncle Isaac's arm. It was her wedding day. She was dressed in a gorgeous off-white wedding gown that fit her to perfection. She looked absolutely stunning. As Kenya stood in the foyer of the church waiting to walk down the aisle, a ton of memories flooded her mind. This was the same church where she and her brother, Derek, had attended Sunday school together, participated in Easter egg hunts, and rushed to the store across the street after service to buy candy with the money they were supposed to put in church. This was where her mama, BabyRuth, had served as an usher and sang in the choir. And where her father, DJ, sat at the end of the second pew every Sunday morning, bleary and red-eyed from hanging out late on Saturday night. Kenya had grown up in this church—attending revivals, church meetings, picnics, choir rehearsals, weddings, funerals, bake sales, and baptisms. It was a place of joy, comfort, and refuge for her family. Her mama, daddy, and brother were all gone now. Kenya missed them greatly and wished that they could be with her on her wedding day. But Kenya had learned over the years to not dwell on what she didn't have, but to be grateful for what she did have. And she had so much to be grateful for.

When the wedding march song began to play, Uncle Isaac looked at Kenya, his face full of love and pride. He was so honored that she'd asked him to stand in for her father and walk her down the aisle.

"Your parents would be so proud of you," he said, looking handsome and distinguished in a black tuxedo. "You ready, sweetheart?"

"Yes, I'm ready, Uncle Isaac," Kenya replied.

Kenya and Sean had chosen "Unforgettable," Natalie Cole's duet with her father Nat King Cole, as their wedding march song. When Kenya stepped into the aisle with her uncle, the whole church gasped at the lovely vision she made. When Sean saw her, his eyes bugged out and his mouth fell open, causing a few folks in the audience to snicker. As Kenya moved down the aisle, she looked at all the beaming faces of her family and friends. And even from a distance, she could see that Sean was genuinely moved, his face gleaming with pride and love. Percy, his best man, and Sean's two brothers, the groomsmen, stood proudly by his side. *Don't cry*, Kenya told herself. *Keep it together. Don't mess up your makeup.*

But when Kenya saw her maid of honor, Jasmine, and her two bridesmaids, Dereka and Jia, standing at the altar in elegant purple gowns, smiling and crying tears of joy, she lost it. Kenya let the floodgates open and wept her own tears of joy and thankfulness, no longer caring if her mascara ran or her makeup smeared. She knew the struggles and heartaches the four of them had endured, and how the Lord had brought them through it all. Jasmine, Dereka, and Jia surrounded Kenya, and the four women stood in a circle, holding hands and crying together. After shedding so many tears of sorrow, it was wonderful to cry tears of pure happiness.

"We've got to stop this," Kenya uttered through her tears. "I'm about to get married."

"Well, I'll stop if you all stop," Dereka stated. Someone handed Jasmine a box of tissues and she passed them around the circle. They all dabbed at their eyes and gathered themselves so that the wedding could proceed.

Pastor Bobby performed the wedding ceremony, and Kenya and Sean recited their own personal vows. Sean's mother cried throughout the ceremony, and Ms. Ethel, who Kenya had asked to sit in for her mother, also cried. After saying their vows, Kenya and Sean knelt at the altar for prayer, and a soloist performed a heartfelt rendition of the gospel hymn, "He Touched Me." Kenya chose the song as a fitting tribute to all that Dereka and Jia had overcome. After the solo, Pastor Bobby turned to the congregation and announced, "It is my distinct honor, privilege, and pleasure to present to you Mr. and Mrs. Sean Powell." The audience exploded with cheers as Sean and Kenya walked down the aisle as husband and wife.

The wedding reception was held at a beautiful, historic building in Old Town Alexandria. The place was exquisitely decorated in the wedding theme colors of purple, lavender, and gold. After the formalities of announcing the wedding party, it was time for the first dance. Many people were expecting the happy couple to dance cheek to cheek to a romantic love song. But Sean and Kenya had other plans. They chose Chubby Checker's "Let's Twist Again" because it was reminiscent of their first date when they'd twisted the night away at the Roof Terrace atop the Kennedy Center. As they'd done then, they now twisted with wild abandon, laughing and singing along with the Chubby Checker tune.

> Come on let's twist again like we did last summer.
> Yea, let's twist again like we did last year.
> Do you remember when things were really hummin'.
> Yea, let's twist again, twistin' time is here.
> Round 'n' around 'n' up 'n' down we go again.
> Oh, baby make me know you love me so again.

After a while Kenya signaled for others to join them, and Jasmine and Percy were the first to hit the dance floor, followed by Dereka, Jia, Trevon, Fatima, and Brandon. The fun they were having was contagious, and others flocked to the dance floor to join in. Even Pastor Bobby and his wife got into the act. Those who couldn't make it onto the dance floor, twisted in the aisles or in their seats. But the one who really took the cake was Ms. Ethel. She twisted all three hundred plus pounds back and forth, up and down, and round and around. It was a sight for sore eyes, and one for the record books. The wedding party and everybody there had themselves a ball, twisting the night away.

Going Back to Move Forward
(Five Years Later)

Dereka and Jia kissed and hugged each of the young girls who had insisted on coming to the airport to see them off. Two years ago, Dereka, using funds she'd inherited from her grandparents' estate, and Jia, using money from her vast savings account that Nai Nai hadn't touched, pooled their resources together and established a safe house in DC for child sex trafficking survivors. They named it "Sun-Yu's Place," honoring their dear sister and friend's memory. Currently, seven girls lived there—young survivors who had been rescued from dreadful conditions but had no family or guardians willing to take them in. At Sun-Yu's Place, the girls received shelter, food, counseling, tutoring, life-skills training, and spiritual guidance. But mostly they received unconditional love. Dereka and Jia managed the place with the help of a small staff and volunteers, including Kenya and Jasmine who generously donated as much time as they could.

"Let's take a selfie together," one of the girls said. They all gathered around Dereka, Jia, and Ms. Connors, a staff member, and took a group selfie. Some of them made funny faces, and Tiffany, the prankster of the group, did the "bunny ears" gesture behind her girlfriend's head. When Dereka and Jia looked at the picture of the girls smiling, laughing, and just being goofy, it warmed their hearts.

"Do you remember a while back when I said that perhaps we were saved for a reason?" Jia whispered to Dereka.

"I remember."

"Well, they're the reason," Jia acknowledged, looking lovingly at her girls.

"Yes, they are," Dereka concurred wholeheartedly. And it all made sense to Dereka now. Her purpose from God was helping children, and she was grateful to have discovered God's true path to do so.

At the departure gate, Dereka and Jia said their goodbyes to the girls, and advised them to behave and mind Ms. Connors and the other staff. Then they boarded their flight to Colombia. They were going back to visit the building that once housed La Casa de Placer, a place where a huge part of their childhood had been stolen. A place where rape, abuse, degradation, and humiliation were daily occurrences with no reprieve. Going back was part of their healing and recovery process. It was their way of reclaiming and redeeming a part of themselves they felt they'd left behind.

Jasmine had used her extensive contacts with Operation Undercover and the Colombian authorities to arrange for Dereka and Jia to visit the house. The Colombian government had seized the building years ago after the girls' rescue, and it was now just a vacant structure. Kenya and Jasmine had wanted to join them on this journey, but this was something they felt they had to do alone. By going back, they hoped to conquer any remaining remnants of doubt and fear that still haunted them.

During the flight they sat next to one another, each lost in her own thoughts and memories. Dereka thought about the other girls she'd met there. They'd called her "Angel Girl," but they'd really been her angels in a demonic place. With some research, Dereka had been able to locate Crystal's family, the blonde-haired girl from Charlotte, North Carolina, who had died there after being tortured in the shed. Dereka gave them Crystal's comb as a memento of one of the last things their daughter had touched on this earth. It wasn't much, but Crystal's mother wept tears of gratitude when she'd received it. It brought the family some closure.

Dereka never heard back from Scrappy, but she and Kenya had located her uncle in DC. They were greatly saddened to learn that Scrappy had been killed in gang-related violence in the Bronx. It had happened shortly after her visit with Kenya. Dereka knew as long as she lived she would never forget her fierce, fiery, fearless friend.

Dereka was now in a flourishing relationship with Brandon, having learned to trust men in a way she'd not thought possible. All men weren't bona fide devils from hell like the Tavaras brothers or their customers who patronized the House of Pleasure. Most men in the world were good, kind, and loving. And Brandon was certainly one of those men. He'd stuck by her through thick and thin.

Dereka thought about all she'd been through in her life, from her captivity as a sex slave at thirteen, through her subsequent battle with mental illness. She likened her journey to that of the woman in the Bible who had an affliction of her blood for twelve long years. But when the woman heard that Jesus was near, she'd pressed through the crowd to touch the hem of his garment, and she was healed. Dereka felt as though she had pressed through all her struggles and infirmities—the rapes, abuse, heartache, self-loathing, guilt, shame, delusions, voices, depression, and more. She'd pressed and fought her way through the muck and the mire until, finally, she'd reached out and touched the hem of his garment and was made whole.

Jia's life journey was equally compelling for she too had overcome much. After spending months in a rehab center, she was now clean and sober. She finally knew that she was worthy of love and was not just a commodity to be lusted after. And where once she'd used drugs and prostitution as tools for survival, she now used as her tools love, friendship, hope, prayer, and compassion for others. Her mother's betrayal was the hardest pill Jia had to swallow. Lihwa had been convicted of several crimes against children, including child abandonment, abuse, neglect, and sex trafficking. She was currently serving consecutive life sentences in a Beijing women's prison. But Lihwa never once showed remorse or apologized for any of her wrongdoings, swearing that she was an innocent victim and had been forced to do what she'd done. Jia finally just had to accept who and what her mother was and move on. And, surprisingly, Jia still loved her māma. There's something innate about a child's love for a mother that just cannot be explained.

Nai Nai passed away about three years ago, dying peacefully in her sleep. After her death, Jia moved to Virginia to be close to Dereka and her aunts. She remained close friends with Elliott, although she had no interest in anything further at this point. She just needed time to focus on herself and her work helping young girls. Elliott eventually divorced Nicole, realizing that their core values about life and people were just too different. Jia also remained close friends with Rochelle and Tristin. Rochelle had finally broken free of Jérémy, but Tristin was still under his control. Jia kept her in prayer.

Dereka and Jia were returning to that house in Colombia, but this time it was on their own terms. They were going back to move forward. They'd been enslaved there as young frightened girls—disheartened, distressed, and discouraged. Yet they were returning as strong, healthy, productive, spirit-filled women.

He Restores My Soul

Once Dereka and Jia arrived at the airport, a driver took them to a hotel in Cartagena. Early the next morning, the same driver picked them up for the two-hour ride to the former La Casa de Placer. Dereka and Jia sat in the back seat and held hands. It was a bit eerie going back to a place where incomprehensible atrocities had taken place. As the car slowly moved up the steep, narrow dirt road that led to the house, Dereka remembered how frightened she had been when she and three other girls had been driven up that same precarious, bumpy road in the cab of a pickup truck. She looked at the dense jungle, knowing that her friends, Sun-Yu and Crystal, were buried out there somewhere. She knew, but for the grace of God, she could have been buried there too.

When they arrived at the house, the custodian met them at the gate. He told them his name was Juan and that he took care of the building. He was a friendly man who spoke fluent English. He also knew the history of the building and had been advised that Dereka and Jia were once held captive there. He briefly shared a few facts about what had happened to the place after the raid. And he verified a story that Dereka had heard about Mario, the evil Tavaras brother who had escaped. Mario had been tracked down and cornered at a house in Buenos Aires, Argentina. He was severely wounded in a shoot-out with the police and ended up in a wheelchair. Mario would spend the rest of his life in prison as a cripple. Dereka was elated that Mario was captured and couldn't harm others, but she found no glee in his physical impairment. Dereka had finally come to forgive her captors, knowing that without forgiveness she'd never truly be whole.

"You ladies are very brave to come back to such a place," Juan stated. "I hope you find the peace you seek. The door is open. You can go in when you're ready. Take as much time as you need. I'll be right over there," he said, pointing to a gatehouse that had once been used by the Tavaras brothers' guards.

"Thank you," Dereka replied. She and Jia stood outside for a moment, just looking at the daunting gray stone building.

"You ready to go in?" Dereka asked. But Jia just stared at the building, fear in her eyes.

"I can't go in there. I'm sorry, Dereka, but I just can't do it," Jia replied. Dereka could sense the emotional turmoil that Jia was experiencing. Of course this was harder for her. She had been only eight years old when she was brought to this hell on earth. And as difficult as it had been for Dereka at thirteen, she couldn't imagine what it had been like for Jia at eight.

"It's okay, Jia. You stay here. I'll do it for both of us," Dereka stated.

"Thanks," Jia said gratefully. Dereka had always looked out for her, especially during her darkest days in that house. And here she was, still taking care of her.

Dereka retrieved a box from the back seat of the car, climbed the steps, and entered the house. The place was dank and stuffy, and it smelled of mold and mildew. According to Juan, all the Tavaras brothers' lavish furnishings had been auctioned off, and the money was distributed to local anti-human-trafficking organizations. Dereka recalled how the brothers had lived like kings upstairs while the girls lived in squalor beneath their feet in the basement.

Dereka went upstairs and looked in some of the barren rooms. These were the rooms where they had been forced to "pleasure" the men. Where she'd lain on her back, night after night, and stared at the ceilings while her body was brutalized. Chills went down Dereka's spine as horrific memories flashed across her mind. "Lord, help me," she prayed.

Dereka then went downstairs and stood in front of the basement door, taking a moment to mentally prepare herself to enter. She saw that the same lock, now rusted a bit, was still on the door. She thought about all the times she'd seen the guards lock and unlock that door. Behind that door was the place she'd felt was the dungeon of doom. Dereka opened the door and slowly made her way down the steep steps. A lamp, no doubt placed there by Juan, illuminated the dark space. Dereka sat the box she was carrying on the floor.

It was surreal being back there. She remembered exactly where each girl's cot had been, including her own, which was right next to Sun-Yu's. Painful memories flooded her mind, but Dereka pushed them aside, choosing to focus on the positive ones, like the kindness Sun-Yu and the others had shown her when she first arrived. Like the angel, carved from soap, they'd given her on her thirteenth birthday. And Esmeralda, the brothers' elderly aunt, who'd treated them with affection and tenderness when she served their meals. And even Ms. Vee, the kind, elderly lady she'd created in her mind to help her endure the unbearable.

A noise at the top of the steps caught Dereka's attention. She looked up and saw Jia standing in the doorway. Jia had summoned the courage to join Dereka inside the house, believing she'd come too far to let fear stop her now.

"I'm coming down," she said.

"Are you sure?"

"Yes. I have to do this," Jia confirmed. Dereka went up, took Jia's hand, and helped her down the steps.

"I had to come down here," Jia admitted. "This is the last place I saw my sister." Then Jia began to sob uncontrollably. She wept for the sister she'd lost there, and she wept for the mother who'd placed them there. Dereka held Jia until she stopped crying, and she helped wipe the tears from her face.

"I think it's time," Dereka said. Jia nodded.

Dereka opened the box they'd brought along with them and gently took out twelve long-stemmed red roses. These symbols of love represented each of the twelve girls, including themselves, that had been there when Dereka first arrived. They took the roses and placed them in a circle in the middle of the basement floor, calling out each girl's name as they did so. Sophia, Camila, Gabriela, Milena, Emma, Catarina, Lydia, Selena,

Crystal, Sun-Yu, Dereka, and Jia. Lastly, Dereka retrieved a beautiful wild orchid from the box and placed it in the middle of the circle.

"For the one called Scrappy," she whispered.

Then Dereka and Jia walked up the basement steps with their heads held high. Dereka turned around and took one last look at the place that had been like a tomb to her for five horrifying years. There was a time that she'd felt she lost her soul. That she'd left it there, floating around in the darkness. But now she realized she never lost her soul. It had just been fractured, marred, mangled, and wounded. Shattered in a million pieces. But God, the master builder, had taken her broken, fragmented pieces, and put them back together again. Because that's who he is. And that's what he does. He repairs. He rebuilds. He restores my soul.

Author's Note

I hope you enjoyed *Restored*, the final book in my Faith Under Fire Trilogy about the Jones family. It has been my absolute joy and honor to create these compelling characters and share the twists and turns of their tumultuous, yet inspiring, life's journey. It's been quite a ride.

I must admit that, in a way, it's bittersweet for me to end this trilogy because over the years I've come to relate to, love, loathe, cry for, cheer for, criticize and empathize with the characters, whether heroine or villain. I hope my readers have had the same or similar reactions to the intriguing characters within the pages of this trilogy (*All Means All, If You Believe, Endurance,* and *Restored*).

I am pleased that God placed it on my heart to explore mental illness in *Restored*. I personally know how destructive mental illness can be for the sufferer, as well as his or her family. My mother committed suicide when I was ten years old, and I believe mental illness played a crucial role in her decision. Although the majority of people with mental illness do not commit suicide, more than 90 percent of those who do, have a diagnosable mental illness. That's why it's important to be aware of the symptoms of this serious disorder and ensure that proper treatment is provided.

If you have feedback, questions, or comments about *Restored* or my other books, please contact me at:

Website: www.lifthimupproductions.org
E-mail: lifthimup3@verizon.net

Also, please review this book on Amazon.com or other book retailers' websites.

Peace and blessings to all.

Gwen Sutton

Biblical Quotes
(King James and New King James Versions)

And the Lord will make you the head and not the tail; you shall be above only and not beneath, if you heed the commandments of the Lord your God. (Deuteronomy 28:13)

Nay, in all these things we are more than conquerors through him that loved us. (Romans 8:37)

But without faith it is impossible to please him: for he that cometh to God must believe that he is, and that he is a rewarder of them that diligently seek him. (Hebrews 11:6)

O taste and see that the Lord is good: blessed is the man that trusteth in him. (Psalm 34:8)

Yet in all these things we are more than conquerors through Him who loved us. (Romans 8:37)

The devil walks about like a roaring lion, seeking whom he may devour. (1 Peter 5:8)

Put on the whole armour of God, that ye may be able to stand against the wiles of the devil. (Ephesians 6:11)

When he [the devil] speaks a lie, he speaks from his own resources, for he is a liar and the father of it. (John 8:44)

For we walk by faith, not by sight. (2 Corinthians 5:7)

The effectual fervent prayer of a righteous man availeth much. (James 5:16)

Love your enemies, bless them that curse you, do good to them that hate you, and pray for them which despitefully use you. (Matthew 5:44)

For he shall give his angels charge over thee, to keep thee in all thy ways. (Psalm 91:11)

Be careful for nothing; but in every thing by prayer and supplication with thanksgiving let your requests be made known unto God. (Philippians 4:6)

Vengeance is mine; I will repay, saith the Lord. (Romans 12:19)

But do you want to know, O foolish man, that faith without works is dead? (James 2:21)

Let not your heart be troubled; you believe in God, believe also in me. (John 14:1)

For I will restore health unto thee, and I will heal thee of thy wounds, saith the Lord. (Jeremiah 30:17)

Where two or three are gathered together in my name, there am I in the midst of them. (Matthew 18:20)

Looking unto Jesus, the author and finisher of our faith. (Hebrews 12:2)

Are not two sparrows sold for a copper coin? And not one of them falls to the ground apart from your Father's will. Do not fear therefore; you are of more value than many sparrows. (Matthew 10:29-31)

I will never leave thee, nor forsake thee. (Hebrews 13:5)

In the world you will have tribulation; but be of good cheer, I have overcome the world. (John 16:33)

For it must needs be that offences come; but woe to that man by whom the offence cometh! (Matthew 18:7)

But Jesus said, Suffer little children, and forbid them not, to come unto me: for of such is the kingdom of heaven. (Matthew 19:14)

Verily I say unto you, Whosoever shall not receive the kingdom of God as a little child shall in no wise enter therein. (Luke 18:17)

Wait on the Lord: be of good courage, and he shall strengthen thine heart: wait, I say, on the Lord. (Psalm 27:14)

The Lord is my light and my salvation; whom shall I fear? The Lord is the strength of my life; of whom shall I be afraid? (Psalm 27:1)

And take the helmet of salvation, and the sword of the Spirit, which is the word of God. (Ephesians 6:17)

Now faith is the substance of things hoped for, the evidence of things not seen. (Hebrews 11:1)

He restores my soul. (Psalm 23:3)

Further Reading

ABC News. "Online with a Sexual Predator." Deborah Amos. Last modified August 14, 2016. http://abcnews.go.com/WNT/story?id=130735&page=1.

Fairfax-Falls Church Community Services Board. "Involuntary Psychiatric Hospitalization of Adults." Last modified July 2015. http://www.fairfaxcounty.gov/csb/services/involuntary-psychiatric-hospitalization.htm.

Living with Schizophrenia (LWS). "Understanding Voices." Accessed January 2017. www.livingwithschizophreniauk.org/advice-sheets/understanding-voice-hearing/.

National Alliance on Mental Illness (NAMI). "Mental Health by the Numbers." Accessed October 2016. http://www.nami.org/Learn-More/Mental-Health-By-the-Numbers.

National Institute of Mental Health (NHI). "Schizophrenia." Accessed September 2016. www.nimh.nih.gov/health/topics/schizophrenia/index.shtml.

"Paranoid Schizophrenia: Causes, Symptoms and Treatments." Christian Nordqvist. Last modified May 27, 2015. www.medicalnewstoday.com/articles/192621.php.

Pulitzer Center. "Unfriendly Shores: African Immigrants in France (Part 1)." Rodrigue Ossebi. Last modified October 21, 2015. http://pulitzercenter.org/reporting/unfriendly-shores-african-immigrants-france-part-1.

PureSight Online Child Safety. "How Do Online Predators Operate?" Accessed November 2016. http://www.puresight.com/Pedophiles/Online-Predators/how-do-online-predators-operate.html.

University of Washington, Mental Health Reporting. "Facts About Mental Illness and Suicide." Accessed March 2017 http://depts.washington.edu/mhreport/facts_suicide.php.

Wikipedia. "Paranoid Schizophrenia." Last modified January 20, 2017. https://en.wikipedia.org/wiki/Paranoid_schizophrenia.

Quora. "What Is the Experience of Being in a Psychiatric Hospital Like?" Ariel Williams. Last modified July 17, 2015. https://www.quora.com/What-is-the-experience-of-being-in-a-psychiatric-hospital-like.

COMING NEXT FROM GWEN SUTTON

THE PREACHER AND THE PIMP
(Saint or Sinner Trilogy, Book 1)

A NEW SAGA BEGINS.

Made in the USA
Columbia, SC
03 December 2018